TWICE
CURSED

A Universe of Wishes: A We Need Diverse Books Anthology

Cursed: An Anthology

Dark Cities: All-New Masterpieces of Urban Terror

Dark Detectives: An Anthology of Supernatural Mysteries

Dead Letters: An Anthology of the Undelivered, the Missing, the Returned…

Dead Man's Hand: An Anthology of the Weird West

Escape Pod: The Science Fiction Anthology

Exit Wounds

Hex Life

Infinite Stars

Infinite Stars: Dark Frontiers

Invisible Blood

Daggers Drawn

New Fears: New Horror Stories by Masters of the Genre

New Fears 2: Brand New Horror Stories by Masters of the Macabre

Out of the Ruins: The Apocalyptic Anthology

Phantoms: Haunting Tales from the Masters of the Genre

Rogues

Vampires Never Get Old

Wastelands: Stories of the Apocalypse

Wastelands 2: More Stories of the Apocalypse

Wastelands: The New Apocalypse

Wonderland: An Anthology

When Things Get Dark

Isolation: The Horror Anthology

Multiverses: An Anthology of Alternate Realities

TWICE CURSED

EDITED BY
MARIE O'REGAN
AND PAUL KANE

TITAN BOOKS

TWICE CURSED
Paperback edition ISBN: 9781803361215
Electronic edition ISBN: 9781803361222

Published by Titan Books
A division of Titan Publishing Group Ltd
144 Southwark Street, London SE1 0UP

First edition: April 2023
10 9 8 7 6 5 4 3 2 1

Introduction © Marie O'Regan & Paul Kane 2023.
The Bell © Frogspawn Ltd 2023.
Snow, Glass, Apples © Neil Gaiman 1994. Originally released by
Dreamhaven Press as a benefit book for the Comic Book Legal Defense Fund.
Reprinted by permission of the author.
The Tissot Family Circus © Angela Slatter 2023.
Mr Thirteen © M. R. Carey 2023.
The Confessor's Tale © Sarah Pinborough 2009. Originally published in
Hellbound Hearts, edited by Paul Kane & Marie O'Regan (Pocket Books, 2009).
Reprinted by permission of the author. Clive Barker is the owner of the copyright of the
Hellbound Heart and Cenobite mythology, and Sarah Pinborough gratefully acknowledges
Mr Barker's permission to draw on this mythology for "The Confessor's Tale".
The Old Stories Hide Secrets Deep Inside Them © Mark Chadbourn 2023.
Awake © Laura Purcell 2023.
Pretty Maids All In A Row © Tina Raffaele 2023.
The Viral Voyage Of Bird Man © Katherine Arden 2023.
The Angels Of London © Adam L. G. Nevill 2013. Originally published in
Terror Tales of London, edited by Paul Finch (P&C Finch Ltd, 2013).
Reprinted by permission of the author.
A Curse Is A Curse © Helen Grant 2023.
Dark Carousel © Joe Hill 2018. Originally published as a vinyl original
(HarperAudio 2018). Reprinted by permission of the author.
Shoes As Red As Blood © A. C. Wise 2023.
Just Your Standard Haunted Doll Drama © Kelley Armstrong 2023.
St Diablo's Travelling Music Hall © A. K. Benedict 2023.
The Music Box © L. L. McKinney 2023.

A CIP catalogue record for this title is available from the British Library.

Printed and bound by CPI (UK) Ltd in Great Britain.

TWICE CURSED

TABLE OF CONTENTS

INTRODUCTION

BY MARIE O'REGAN & PAUL KANE

*C*ursed...

We were certainly beginning to think things were, when our first anthology with that name came out. In fact, the signing for that book at Forbidden Planet in London, back in March 2020, was the last live event we attended for more than two years because of the pandemic. Very shortly after that, the UK went into its first lockdown. The huge convention we'd been working on for three years by that point had to be postponed with only a few weeks to go (StokerConUK™, which subsequently became the highly successful ChillerCon UK), we were all in lockdown and the world suddenly seemed a very strange, often frightening place. At the time of writing it still does to some extent. It's definitely a different world to the one we knew when we penned our introduction to the original *Cursed*.

Nevertheless, here we are again with *Twice Cursed*. Some might say we're tempting fate, especially given other recent events globally. However, as we all found during these unprecedented and trying times, fiction – films, TV and books especially – proved a welcome distraction from real life. It's kept us going ourselves, honestly – has kept most people going, as indeed it did in other challenging periods of history. Fiction in whatever form serves an important function, and reading about curses, of one sort or another, is definitely preferable to being traumatised in your everyday life. Cursed, but in a good way – there's safety in keeping these curses contained within a book's pages. The reader, at least, can get out.

Therefore, we're proud to present another batch of excellent fables from a group of superb writers at the top of their game. Each one of them with a different variation on what curses are, and what they mean to us as individuals or as a collective.

Joanne Harris reminds us of the true nature of curses, while Neil Gaiman and Laura Purcell tackle *Snow White* from very different perspectives. A. C. Wise introduces us to some cursed footwear, Mark Chadbourn is in archaeological territory and Sarah Pinborough's Hellish Faustian Pact shows us the power of keeping secrets. And while Kelley Armstrong gives us her own unique twist on the old favourite of cursed dolls, Christina Henry takes a look at the subject from the opposite perspective, and Katherine Arden uses a well-known bad luck legend as her inspiration. Angela Slatter, Joe Hill, and A. K. Benedict all deal with curses connected to entertainment – at a circus, on a pier and in music hall – and Adam L. G. Nevill's tale is also rooted in a sense of place, this time a strange lodging house. M. R. Carey focuses on the people you should turn to if you need support when you have a curse, L. L. McKinney presents us with a very unique music box, and Helen Grant's story is a cautionary piece that resonates in our present day.

All very different, all excellent. All a thoroughly enjoyable break from the realities around us. So settle back, with a glass or mug of your favourite tipple, and enter a world of magic. Of trickery and despair.

Curses again… *Twice Cursed*, but in a good way.

MARIE O'REGAN & PAUL KANE
Derbyshire, July 2022

THE BELL

BY JOANNE HARRIS

In a village by the edge of a forest, there lived a woodcutter's family. They were poor; they lived from the land, and the land was far from generous. They ate black bread, and roots, and seeds, and small fish from the river. But they were free, and happy – except perhaps for the woodcutter's son, who longed for something different.

In all his life, the woodcutter's son had never drunk wine, or eaten bread that was not black and unleavened. In all his life he had never worn clothes that had not been first worn by someone else. And he was always listening to tales of ancient Kings and Queens – their wealth, their adventures, their glamour – and longing for the old days, when things were very different.

He often asked his father where those ancient Kings and Queens had gone, and how their kingdoms had fallen.

But his father would always tell him: "That was long before my time. No-one remembers the old days now."

The boy was disappointed, but he did not forget the tales of knights and ladies, Kings and Queens. He would often roam the forest alone, searching for signs of the old days.

Sometimes he even found them – pieces of masonry sunk in the ground, scattered fragments of coloured glass. A gilded comb, a strand of hair still caught between its ivory teeth.

Then one day, in the heart of the woods, he came across a city, ruined and abandoned in the scrambling undergrowth. Great pillars of marble and arches of stone were draped in morning glories. And under an intricate vaulted dome, through which a curtain of ivy fell, he found a great gathering of stone, a feasting-hall of statues.

The boy walked through the hall of stone. On either side, lords and ladies, some holding goblets to their lips, some laughing, some dancing; some hiding their smiles behind their painted ivory fans. On the tables between them, platters of fruit and cakes were spread out, all in stone, and perfect, even to the water-droplets on the bunches of grapes. Above them, a minstrels' gallery, its music silenced, except for the drip of water from the ceiling. At either side of the room, stone guards in their helmets and armour. And at the head of the great hall, the King and Queen of the city sat on thrones of polished marble; and to the boy they looked both wise, and very, very beautiful.

"What happened here?" he said aloud.

A voice spoke up behind him. It was that of a ragged old crone, hiding among the statues.

"I remember all this," she said. "I was a servant in this place. Oh, it was beautiful in its time, a place of joy and music. But it fell under a spell – a curse – and its people were all turned into stone."

The boy's eyes widened. He could already imagine himself a member of that gilded throng. He saw himself dancing with beautiful girls, and eating all kinds of sweetmeats. His father would wear furs, he thought: his sisters, gowns of silken brocade.

"If only the curse could be broken," he said.

"Oh, but it can," the old crone replied, her dark eyes gleaming like gemstones. "All it needs is for one brave boy to ring that big old bell up there."

And she pointed to a great brass bell, hanging from the ceiling in a mass of vines and spiders' webs.

"And that will bring them back?" said the boy.

The old crone nodded. "A single note would be enough to awaken them."

The boy looked up, and started to climb. It was a difficult, dangerous task. But finally, he reached the bell, and pulled its clapper free, and it rang. The brass note shimmered in the air like a cloud of fireflies.

And slowly, below him, the courtiers of stone began to awaken; began to move. The beautiful ladies shifted and yawned; the guards stood to attention. Laughter rang once more through the hall that had been silent for hundreds of years.

But somehow, the joyful scene was not quite the way the boy had imagined it. There was something about the laughter that came from the throats of the courtiers: a cruel and acquisitive look in the eyes of the ladies.

The boy clambered down from the ceiling and waited for someone to notice him.

Surely, my reward will come, he thought, looking at the magnificent feast, and imagining all the things he would buy with the gold they would give him.

But instead of showing their gratitude, the beautiful King and Queen just spread their wings and watched the boy with hungry eyes. The courtiers and their ladies, too, crowded round the frightened boy, licking their lips and smiling. The music from the gallery began to play – an evil tune, that made his head spin and sent his pulses racing.

The boy grew pale and turned to run. But there was nowhere to run to. And the Queen put her thin white hand on his neck and drew him closer, smiling.

When they had finished with the boy, the King and Queen and their courtiers and guards took wing and flew over the land like locusts. They enslaved the people, slaughtered their flocks, burnt down their homes and their settlements. For centuries, the enchantment had kept them tame and helpless. Now, at last, they were awake, and they had no mercy.

Back in the deserted hall, the old crone shrugged her shoulders and smiled. "Before you ring the bell," she said, "be sure to know what tune it plays."

And at that she turned and went into the woods, leaving the stone hall empty.

SNOW, GLASS, APPLES

BY NEIL GAIMAN

I do not know what manner of thing she is. None of us do. She killed her mother in the birthing, but that's never enough to account for it.

They call me wise, but I am far from wise, for all that I foresaw fragments of it, frozen moments caught in pools of water or in the cold glass of my mirror. If I were wise I would not have tried to change what I saw. If I were wise I would have killed myself before ever I encountered her, before ever I caught him.

Wise, and a witch, or so they said, and I'd seen his face in my dreams and in reflections for all my life: sixteen years of dreaming of him before he reined his horse by the bridge that morning and asked my name. He helped me onto his high horse and we rode together to my little cottage, my face buried in the gold of his hair. He asked for the best of what I had; a king's right, it was.

His beard was red-bronze in the morning light, and I knew him, not as a king, for I knew nothing of kings then, but as my love. He took all he wanted from me, the right of kings, but he returned to me on the following day and on the night after

9

that: his beard so red, his hair so gold, his eyes the blue of a summer sky, his skin tanned the gentle brown of ripe wheat.

His daughter was only a child: no more than five years of age when I came to the palace. A portrait of her dead mother hung in the princess's tower room: a tall woman, hair the color of dark wood, eyes nut-brown. She was of a different blood to her pale daughter.

The girl would not eat with us.

I do not know where in the palace she ate.

I had my own chambers. My husband the king, he had his own rooms also. When he wanted me he would send for me, and I would go to him, and pleasure him, and take my pleasure with him.

One night, several months after I was brought to the palace, she came to my rooms. She was six. I was embroidering by lamplight, squinting my eyes against the lamp's smoke and fitful illumination. When I looked up, she was there.

"Princess?"

She said nothing. Her eyes were black as coal, black as her hair; her lips were redder than blood. She looked up at me and smiled. Her teeth seemed sharp, even then, in the lamplight.

"What are you doing away from your room?"

"I'm hungry," she said, like any child.

It was winter, when fresh food is a dream of warmth and sunlight; but I had strings of whole apples, cored and dried, hanging from the beams of my chamber, and I pulled an apple down for her.

"Here."

Autumn is the time of drying, of preserving, a time of picking apples, of rendering the goose fat. Winter is the time of hunger, of snow, and of death; and it is the time of the midwinter feast, when we rub the goose fat into the skin of a whole pig, stuffed with that autumn's apples; then we roast it or spit it, and we prepare to feast upon the crackling.

She took the dried apple from me and began to chew it with her sharp yellow teeth.

"Is it good?"

She nodded. I had always been scared of the little princess, but at that moment I warmed to her and, with my fingers, gently, I stroked her cheek. She looked at me and smiled – she smiled but rarely – then she sank her teeth into the base of my thumb, the Mound of Venus, and she drew blood.

I began to shriek, from pain and from surprise, but she looked at me and I fell silent.

The little princess fastened her mouth to my hand and licked and sucked and drank. When she was finished, she left my chamber. Beneath my gaze the cut that she had made began to close, to scab, and to heal. The next day it was an old scar: I might have cut my hand with a pocketknife in my childhood.

I had been frozen by her, owned and dominated. That scared me, more than the blood she had fed on. After that night I locked my chamber door at dusk, barring it with an oaken pole, and I had the smith forge iron bars, which he placed across my windows.

My husband, my love, my king, sent for me less and less, and when I came to him he was dizzy, listless, confused. He could no longer make love as a man makes love, and he would not permit me to pleasure him with my mouth: the one time I tried, he started violently, and began to weep. I pulled my mouth away and held him tightly until the sobbing had stopped, and he slept, like a child.

I ran my fingers across his skin as he slept. It was covered in a multitude of ancient scars. But I could recall no scars from the days of our courtship, save one, on his side, where a boar had gored him when he was a youth.

Soon he was a shadow of the man I had met and loved by the bridge. His bones showed, blue and white, beneath his skin. I was with him at the last: his hands were cold as stone, his eyes milky blue, his hair and beard faded and lustreless and limp. He died unshriven, his skin nipped and pocked from head to toe with tiny, old scars.

He weighed near to nothing. The ground was frozen hard, and we could dig no grave for him, so we made a cairn of rocks and stones above his body, as a memorial only, for there was little enough of him left to protect from the hunger of the beasts and the birds.

So I was queen.

And I was foolish, and young – eighteen summers had come and gone since first I saw daylight – and I did not do what I would do, now.

If it were today, I would have her heart cut out, true. But

then I would have her head and arms and legs cut off. I would have them disembowel her. And then I would watch in the town square as the hangman heated the fire to white-heat with bellows, watch unblinking as he consigned each part of her to the fire. I would have archers around the square, who would shoot any bird or animal that came close to the flames, any raven or dog or hawk or rat. And I would not close my eyes until the princess was ash, and a gentle wind could scatter her like snow.

I did not do this thing, and we pay for our mistakes.

They say I was fooled; that it was not her heart. That it was the heart of an animal – a stag, perhaps, or a boar. They say that, and they are wrong.

And some say (but it is *her* lie, not mine) that I was given the heart, and that I ate it. Lies and half-truths fall like snow, covering the things that I remember, the things I saw. A landscape, unrecognizable after a snowfall; that is what she has made of my life.

There were scars on my love, her father's thighs, and on his ballock-pouch, and on his male member, when he died.

I did not go with them. They took her in the day, while she slept, and was at her weakest. They took her to the heart of the forest, and there they opened her blouse, and they cut out her heart, and they left her dead, in a gully, for the forest to swallow.

The forest is a dark place, the border to many kingdoms; no one would be foolish enough to claim jurisdiction over it. Outlaws live in the forest. Robbers live in the forest, and so do wolves. You can ride through the forest for a dozen days and never see a soul; but there are eyes upon you the entire time.

They brought me her heart. I know it was hers – no sow's heart or doe's would have continued to beat and pulse after it had been cut out, as that one did.

I took it to my chamber.

I did not eat it: I hung it from the beams above my bed, placed it on a length of twine that I strung with rowan berries, orange-red as a robin's breast, and with bulbs of garlic.

Outside the snow fell, covering the footprints of my huntsmen, covering her tiny body in the forest where it lay.

I had the smith remove the iron bars from my windows, and I would spend some time in my room each afternoon through the short winter days, gazing out over the forest, until darkness fell.

There were, as I have already stated, people in the forest. They would come out, some of them, for the Spring Fair: a greedy, feral, dangerous people; some were stunted – dwarfs and midgets and hunchbacks; others had the huge teeth and vacant gazes of idiots; some had fingers like flippers or crab claws. They would creep out of the forest each year for the Spring Fair, held when the snows had melted.

As a young lass I had worked at the fair, and they had scared me then, the forest folk. I told fortunes for the fairgoers, scrying in a pool of still water; and later, when I was older, in a disk of polished glass, its back all silvered – a gift from a merchant whose straying horse I had seen in a pool of ink.

The stallholders at the fair were afraid of the forest folk; they would nail their wares to the bare boards of their stalls – slabs of gingerbread or leather belts were nailed with great iron nails to the wood. If their wares were not nailed, they said, the forest folk would take them and run away, chewing on the stolen gingerbread, flailing about them with the belts.

The forest folk had money, though: a coin here, another there, sometimes stained green by time or the earth, the face on the coin unknown to even the oldest of us. Also they had things to trade, and thus the fair continued, serving the outcasts and the dwarfs, serving the robbers (if they were circumspect) who preyed on the rare travelers from lands beyond the forest, or on gypsies, or on the deer. (This was robbery in the eyes of the law. The deer were the queen's.)

The years passed by slowly, and my people claimed that I ruled them with wisdom. The heart still hung above my bed, pulsing gently in the night. If there were any who mourned the child, I saw no evidence: she was a thing of terror, back then, and they believed themselves well rid of her.

Spring Fair followed Spring Fair: five of them, each sadder, poorer, shoddier than the one before. Fewer of the forest folk came out of the forest to buy. Those who did seemed subdued and listless. The stallholders stopped nailing their wares to the boards of their stalls. And by the fifth year but a handful of folk came from the forest – a fearful huddle of little hairy men, and no one else.

The Lord of the Fair, and his page, came to me when the

fair was done. I had known him slightly, before I was queen.

"I do not come to you as my queen," he said.

I said nothing. I listened.

"I come to you because you are wise," he continued. "When you were a child you found a strayed foal by staring into a pool of ink; when you were a maiden you found a lost infant who had wandered far from her mother, by staring into that mirror of yours. You know secrets and you can seek out things hidden. My queen," he asked, "what is taking the forest folk? Next year there will be no Spring Fair. The travelers from other kingdoms have grown scarce and few, the folk of the forest are almost gone. Another year like the last, and we shall all starve."

I commanded my maidservant to bring me my looking glass. It was a simple thing, a silver-backed glass disk, which I kept wrapped in a doeskin, in a chest, in my chamber.

They brought it to me then, and I gazed into it:

She was twelve and she was no longer a little child. Her skin was still pale, her eyes and hair coal-black, her lips blood-red. She wore the clothes she had worn when she left the castle for the last time – the blouse, the skirt – although they were much let-out, much mended. Over them she wore a leather cloak, and instead of boots she had leather bags, tied with thongs, over her tiny feet.

She was standing in the forest, beside a tree.

As I watched, in the eye of my mind, I saw her edge and step and flitter and pad from tree to tree, like an animal: a bat or a wolf. She was following someone.

He was a monk. He wore sackcloth, and his feet were bare and scabbed and hard. His beard and tonsure were of a length, overgrown, unshaven.

She watched him from behind the trees. Eventually he paused for the night and began to make a fire, laying twigs down, breaking up a robin's nest as kindling. He had a tinderbox in his robe, and he knocked the flint against the steel until the sparks caught the tinder and the fire flamed. There had been two eggs in the nest he had found, and these he ate raw. They cannot have been much of a meal for so big a man.

He sat there in the firelight, and she came out from her hiding place. She crouched down on the other side of the fire, and stared at him. He grinned, as if it were a long time since he had seen another human, and beckoned her over to him.

She stood up and walked around the fire, and waited, an arm's length away. He pulled in his robe until he found a coin – a tiny copper penny – and tossed it to her. She caught it, and nodded, and went to him. He pulled at the rope around his waist, and his robe swung open. His body was as hairy as a bear's. She pushed him back onto the moss. One hand crept, spiderlike, through the tangle of hair, until it closed on his manhood; the other hand traced a circle on his left nipple. He closed his eyes and fumbled one huge hand under her skirt. She lowered her mouth to the nipple she had been teasing, her smooth skin white on the furry brown body of him.

She sank her teeth deep into his breast. His eyes opened, then they closed again, and she drank.

She straddled him, and she fed. As she did so, a thin blackish liquid began to dribble from between her legs…

"Do you know what is keeping the travelers from our town? What is happening to the forest people?" asked the Lord of the Fair.

I covered the mirror in doeskin, and told him that I would personally take it upon myself to make the forest safe once more.

I had to, although she terrified me. I was the queen.

A foolish woman would have gone then into the forest and tried to capture the creature; but I had been foolish once and had no wish to be so a second time.

I spent time with old books. I spent time with the gypsy women (who passed through our country across the mountains to the south, rather than cross the forest to the north and the west).

I prepared myself and obtained those things I would need, and when the first snows began to fall, I was ready.

Naked, I was, and alone in the highest tower of the palace, a place open to the sky. The winds chilled my body; goose pimples crept across my arms and thighs and breasts. I carried a silver basin, and a basket in which I had placed a silver knife, a silver pin, some tongs, a gray robe, and three green apples.

I put them on and stood there, unclothed, on the tower, humble before the night sky and the wind. Had any man seen me standing there, I would have had his eyes; but there was no one to spy. Clouds scudded across the sky, hiding and uncovering the waning moon.

I took the silver knife and slashed my left arm – once, twice, three times. The blood dripped into the basin, scarlet seeming black in the moonlight.

I added the powder from the vial that hung around my neck. It was a brown dust, made of dried herbs and the skin of a particular toad, and from certain other things. It thickened the blood, while preventing it from clotting.

I took the three apples, one by one, and pricked their skins gently with my silver pin. Then I placed the apples in the silver bowl and let them sit there while the first tiny flakes of snow of the year fell slowly onto my skin, and onto the apples, and onto the blood.

When dawn began to brighten the sky I covered myself with the gray cloak, and took the red apples from the silver bowl, one by one, lifting each into my basket with silver tongs, taking care not to touch it. There was nothing left of my blood or of the brown powder in the silver bowl, nothing save a black residue, like a verdigris, on the inside.

I buried the bowl in the earth. Then I cast a glamour on the apples (as once, years before, by a bridge, I had cast a glamour on myself), that they were, beyond any doubt, the most wonderful apples in the world, and the crimson blush of their skins was the warm color of fresh blood.

I pulled the hood of my cloak low over my face, and I took ribbons and pretty hair ornaments with me, placed them above the apples in the reed basket, and I walked alone into the forest until I came to her dwelling: a high sandstone cliff, laced with deep caves going back a way into the rock wall.

There were trees and boulders around the cliff face, and I walked quietly and gently from tree to tree without disturbing a twig or a fallen leaf. Eventually I found my place to hide, and I waited, and I watched.

After some hours, a clutch of dwarfs crawled out of the hole in the cave front – ugly, misshapen, hairy little men, the old inhabitants of this country. You saw them seldom now.

They vanished into the wood, and none of them espied me, though one of them stopped to piss against the rock I hid behind.

I waited. No more came out.

I went to the cave entrance and hallooed into it, in a cracked old voice.

The scar on my Mound of Venus throbbed and pulsed as she came toward me, out of the darkness, naked and alone.

She was thirteen years of age, my stepdaughter, and nothing marred the perfect whiteness of her skin, save for the livid scar on her left breast, where her heart had been cut from her long since.

The insides of her thighs were stained with wet black filth.

She peered at me, hidden, as I was, in my cloak. She looked at me hungrily. "Ribbons, goodwife," I croaked. "Pretty ribbons for your hair…"

She smiled and beckoned to me. A tug; the scar on my hand was pulling me toward her. I did what I had planned to do, but I did it more readily than I had planned: I dropped my basket and screeched like the bloodless old peddler woman I was pretending to be, and I ran.

My gray cloak was the color of the forest, and I was fast; she did not catch me.

I made my way back to the palace.

I did not see it. Let us imagine, though, the girl returning, frustrated and hungry, to her cave, and finding my fallen basket on the ground.

What did she do?

I like to think she played first with the ribbons, twined them into her raven hair, looped them around her pale neck or her tiny waist.

And then, curious, she moved the cloth to see what else was in the basket, and she saw the red, red apples.

They smelled like fresh apples, of course; and they also smelled of blood. And she was hungry. I imagine her picking up an apple, pressing it against her cheek, feeling the cold smoothness of it against her skin.

And she opened her mouth and bit deep into it…

By the time I reached my chambers, the heart that hung from the roof beam, with the apples and hams and the dried sausages, had ceased to beat. It hung there, quietly, without motion or life, and I felt safe once more.

That winter the snows were high and deep, and were late melting. We were all hungry come the spring.

The Spring Fair was slightly improved that year. The forest folk were few, but they were there, and there were travelers from the lands beyond the forest.

I saw the little hairy men of the forest cave buying and

bargaining for pieces of glass, and lumps of crystal and of quartz rock. They paid for the glass with silver coins – the spoils of my stepdaughter's depredations, I had no doubt. When it got about what they were buying, townsfolk rushed back to their homes and came back with their lucky crystals, and, in a few cases, with whole sheets of glass.

I thought briefly about having the little men killed, but I did not. As long as the heart hung, silent and immobile and cold, from the beam of my chamber, I was safe, and so were the folk of the forest, and, thus, eventually, the folk of the town.

My twenty-fifth year came, and my stepdaughter had eaten the poisoned fruit two winters back, when the prince came to my palace. He was tall, very tall, with cold green eyes and the swarthy skin of those from beyond the mountains.

He rode with a small retinue: large enough to defend him, small enough that another monarch – myself, for instance – would not view him as a potential threat.

I was practical: I thought of the alliance of our lands, thought of the kingdom running from the forests all the way south to the sea; I thought of my golden-haired bearded love, dead these eight years; and, in the night, I went to the prince's room.

I am no innocent, although my late husband, who was once my king, was truly my first lover, no matter what they say.

At first the prince seemed excited. He bade me remove my shift, and made me stand in front of the opened window, far from the fire, until my skin was chilled stone-cold. Then he asked me to lie upon my back, with my hands folded across my breasts, my eyes wide open – but staring only at the beams above. He told me not to move, and to breathe as little as possible. He implored me to say nothing. He spread my legs apart.

It was then that he entered me.

As he began to thrust inside me, I felt my hips raise, felt myself begin to match him, grind for grind, push for push. I moaned. I could not help myself.

His manhood slid out of me. I reached out and touched it, a tiny, slippery thing.

"Please," he said softly. "You must neither move nor speak. Just lie there on the stones, so cold and so fair."

I tried, but he had lost whatever force it was that had made him virile; and, some short while later, I left the prince's room, his curses and tears still resounding in my ears.

He left early the next morning, with all his men, and they rode off into the forest.

I imagine his loins, now, as he rode, a knot of frustration at the base of his manhood. I imagine his pale lips pressed so tightly together. Then I imagine his little troupe riding through the forest, finally coming upon the glass-and-crystal cairn of my stepdaughter. So pale. So cold. Naked beneath the glass, and little more than a girl, and dead.

In my fancy, I can almost feel the sudden hardness of his manhood inside his britches, envision the lust that took him then, the prayers he muttered beneath his breath in thanks for his good fortune. I imagine him negotiating with the little hairy men – offering them gold and spices for the lovely corpse under the crystal mound.

Did they take his gold willingly? Or did they look up to see his men on their horses, with their sharp swords and their spears, and realize they had no alternative?

I do not know. I was not there; I was not scrying. I can only imagine…

Hands, pulling off the lumps of glass and quartz from her cold body. Hands, gently caressing her cold cheek, moving her cold arm, rejoicing to find the corpse still fresh and pliable.

Did he take her there, in front of them all? Or did he have her carried to a secluded nook before he mounted her?

I cannot say.

Did he shake the apple from her throat? Or did her eyes slowly open as he pounded into her cold body; did her mouth open, those red lips part, those sharp yellow teeth close on his swarthy neck, as the blood, which is the life, trickled down her throat, washing down and away the lump of apple, my own, my poison?

I imagine; I do not know.

This I do know: I was woken in the night by her heart pulsing and beating once more. Salt blood dripped onto my face from above. I sat up. My hand burned and pounded as if I had hit the base of my thumb with a rock.

There was a hammering on the door. I felt afraid, but I am a queen, and I would not show fear. I opened the door.

First his men walked into my chamber and stood around me, with their sharp swords, and their long spears.

Then he came in; and he spat in my face.

Finally, she walked into my chamber, as she had when I was first a queen and she was a child of six. She had not changed. Not really.

She pulled down the twine on which her heart was hanging. She pulled off the rowan berries, one by one; pulled off the garlic bulb – now a dried thing, after all these years; then she took up her own, her pumping heart – a small thing, no larger than that of a nanny goat or a she-bear – as it brimmed and pumped its blood into her hand.

Her fingernails must have been as sharp as glass: she opened her breast with them, running them over the purple scar. Her chest gaped, suddenly, open and bloodless. She licked her heart, once, as the blood ran over her hands, and she pushed the heart deep into her breast.

I saw her do it. I saw her close the flesh of her breast once more. I saw the purple scar begin to fade.

Her prince looked briefly concerned, but he put his arm around her nonetheless, and they stood, side by side, and they waited.

And she stayed cold, and the bloom of death remained on her lips, and his lust was not diminished in any way.

They told me they would marry, and the kingdoms would indeed be joined. They told me that I would be with them on their wedding day.

It is starting to get hot in here.

They have told the people bad things about me; a little truth to add savor to the dish, but mixed with many lies.

I was bound and kept in a tiny stone cell beneath the palace, and I remained there through the autumn. Today they fetched me out of the cell; they stripped the rags from me, and washed the filth from me, and then they shaved my head and my loins, and they rubbed my skin with goose-grease.

The snow was falling as they carried me – two men at each hand, two men at each leg – utterly exposed, and spread-eagled and cold, through the midwinter crowds, and brought me to this kiln.

My stepdaughter stood there with her prince. She watched me, in my indignity, but she said nothing.

As they thrust me inside, jeering and chaffing as they did so, I saw one snowflake land upon her white cheek, and remain there without melting.

They closed the kiln door behind me. It is getting hotter in here, and outside they are singing and cheering and banging on the sides of the kiln.

She was not laughing, or jeering, or talking. She did not sneer at me or turn away. She looked at me, though; and for a moment I saw myself reflected in her eyes.

I will not scream. I will not give them that satisfaction. They will have my body, but my soul and my story are my own, and will die with me.

The goose-grease begins to melt and glisten upon my skin. I shall make no sound at all. I shall think no more on this.

I shall think instead of the snowflake on her cheek.

I think of her hair as black as coal, her lips, redder than blood, her skin, snow-white.

THE TISSOT FAMILY CIRCUS

BY ANGELA SLATTER

The road into Pleasance does it no favours.

The big old welcome sign telling you where you are and how many souls are living there looks as if it's not been maintained for some time – peeling paint, colours bleached by sun and wind and rain. The grass is high along the verge, the treeline thick and dark, and the scent of rotting vegetation carries on the breeze.

I've never been here before, but I've been lots of places like it. They all smell the same: desperation turned in on itself. Needless to say I wouldn't be here if I didn't have to be; doesn't mean I'm not a little resentful, but I try to keep that to a minimum. Resentment just leads to worse things.

"Ichabod?" I say and receive absolutely no reaction whatsoever. So I clear my throat and yell, which has a spectacular effect on the bat-faced man snoozing beside me on the bench. Hurts his ears no doubt. He jerks awake, pulls at the reins and the two old roan mares, who've been doing perfectly well without his attention, protest the violence. They stop, look around and glare; stomp their feet in a delicate *don't fuck with us* jig. "Ichabod, the next left, I think. Looks to be a field there."

"Do you think I can't see that?" he grumbles, even though his eyes have been closed for quite some while. "When exactly do you think I got demented, missy?"

If I were of a differing temperament – like my mother (and likely her mother before her and so on and so forth) – I might slap him up the side of the head. But he's ancient, is Ichabod, and even given to impromptu naps as he is he still knows the old ways and the things we're bound to do. He's been at this longer than me, after all. So, I just pretend anticipation isn't making my skin dance, clear my throat like that might pass for an apology, and he gees up the horses.

A ways ahead, the trees taper back and the road dips, widens, spears into what passes for the built-up area, darting off left and right to form streets on a neat grid. Very tidy but a tidiness from another era when some city planner with a penchant for sharp corners and straight lines held sway. That individual is long gone, I'm willing to bet. From the tiny knoll we've surmounted, I can see houses and shops, a brickworks chimney and a sawmill even further on; how much employment might they offer? Pleasance has the air of a spot that could be dying but doesn't know it yet. Towards the outskirts on the other side are farms and pastures, cutting into the woods; from above it'll look like jigsaw puzzle pieces.

Then up on the left a dirt track runs along beside the three-strand barbed wire fence. Ichabod takes it without comment and we follow until there's a sagging ingress. Nothing else around, no houses, no barns. The pasture's close enough to town for kids to find us; far enough there're no witnesses. I climb down, feel the buzz pressing up through my boots, tell it to *hush*, and examine the gate. It's rickety, and I'm trying to find where to put my fingers without getting splinters.

I fail. "Son of a bitch."

"Tsk. Language," admonishes Ichabod and I raise a middle finger in his direction without turning around. The wooden barrier protests but I'm gentle, lifting and carrying it like an aged aunt who has trouble getting out of her chair; the hinges squeak.

After the wagon rolls through, I close the gate again, amble as if there's nothing fluttering inside me like *want*, and survey the area. Over by that stand of trees there's a creek, I can hear it trickling in the early afternoon's silence. No sign of cattle or sheep, no grazing animals. No one around.

In roughly the middle of the field I take the knife from the worn leather sheath at my belt. I hold my breath like I always do, and whisper the words he taught me but once. I don't know their meaning because my lessons were brief and time was short; I only know what they do. The blade's weirdly hot-cold on my palm as it slices. It heals fast, never leaves a scar. Anything that's done to me now just slides right off – doesn't mean nothing hurts.

Blood wells dark and red-blue, and I make a fist, release it, make a fist, release it, watch the little waterfall hit the grass, get soaked up like the earth's greedy. I do this until

I'm starting to feel dizzy, then wrap my pocket handkerchief around the hand.

I retrace my steps quickly, carefully, and climb up beside Ichabod once more. He's alert, watching avidly. Leaning over, he says, "There's just something a little bit spectacular when you do it. The old man? He was very workmanlike, but you, Evangeline? You're an artist."

Which makes me proud, though maybe it shouldn't. But it does, and I watch too as if it's the first time I've seen it. *Deep breath, Evangeline*, I think as the little circus begins to grow up from the ground and that tiny red sacrifice I give whenever we arrive at the place we need to be. It curls like a mist, all blues and purples and pinks, shading into vibrant oranges and reds, then yellows and greens, and back again and again. Swirling until things become solid and settled.

First come the little concession stands: Samuel's Sweet Shop for all your sugary needs; Pearl's Popcorn; Cora's Candy Cotton; Harry's Hushpuppies and Corndogs; Fidel's Libations for the thickest malts or a jar of the best moonshine this side of any river you care to mention. Next, the games: the shooting gallery; the dime pitch; the milk bottle knockdown; test your strength and ring the bell. Each and every one rigged in some way, shape or form. On occasion the luck runs in the other direction, and we hand over a goldfish in a bag, a giant teddy bear, a fairy doll on a beribboned cane. The prizes look shiny and new, but anything you win from the Tissot Family Circus won't exist in the morning; that's just how it is. Doesn't matter – we're never around the next day, are we?

Now the carousel, brightly coloured and lit up like a small city, all those carved horses with golden bridles, hollowed-out swans, swirling teacups for folk to sit in. It remains my favourite – always was even before. It was the very first thing my eyes lit upon all those years ago – well, the second after the Impresario – but it was my first view of the circus *per se*. There's something magical about it, the music and the movement, the speed, the sense that you're no longer in the world, and that's got a lot to recommend it to a lot of kids. Adults too. But kids especially.

Next, the cages and pens: a zebra and a giraffe; two big cats; three bears; and a small pool and slide set up with an ill-mannered troupe of otters and seals. There's a petting farm with lambs, goats, calves, a donkey, a sleepy opossum with the good deal of personal charm required to overcome his looks. And a camel that thinks it's a dog and acts accordingly – which is fortunate because Lord knows a camel has not really got the temperament for being petted.

Then at last the Big Top, pushing up like a big old pointy mushroom. Here, the clowns will carouse; the acrobats will tumble and do handstands and contort themselves like they're made of rubber; Tilda will run her prancing ponies around the ring; the lion and tiger will sit on stools and pretend to be vicious; the fliers will take to the wires and tightropes high above the audience and the sawdust on the ground – no net because it's not like it matters if any of them fall.

Finally, everything's in place, looking as if it's all made of something more than blood and magic. A small circus, certainly, but a perfect distraction for somewhere like this. I release my breath only when the little ones begin to appear, stepping from air as if through a door, their costumes bright and shiny, covered in spangles so they catch every beam of light. Faces turn towards us, smiling, waving, not a one over seventeen, but oh, they do love to put on a show. Love to be seen no matter that no one understands their true nature, or maybe because of it. Maybe because only the wrong person saw them in life.

All waiting for their time to be done, but knowing it might never be.

I wave back – there's always the same sense of relief that things *worked* – then climb down. The pulse shoots up through me as soon as my feet touch the ground. I can't help but think that this might be the night. Might be the one. That I might find the one I need.

"You off, then?" Ichabod asks casually.

I nod. "Just a quick recon. Get the lay of the land. Drum up some business."

"Watch yourself, Evangeline."

I shrug. "Make sure they don't roam."

* * *

I walk in the middle of the main street – no traffic at this point in the day, which is fortunate – so I can get a good view of what's on either side of me. Not too close to the mouths of alleyways; once bitten, twice shy. And it's easier to feel the buzz beneath the soles of my boots – something about the centre line makes it more certain. Still quite weak, but definitely there, a thud and a thump to tell me I'm on the right path. Whenever we're on those long straight highways, I'm fine to ride up with Ichabod if there's no choices of left or right, but when we come into cities? Places with twisty avenues and thoroughfares? Then I spend a lot of time walking, building blisters on my heels, thighs chafing rosy.

There's a corner store with a notice board outside. Lots of tinted sheets of paper there, affixed with thumbtacks. I veer from my comfort zone and head over, examine them to find the oldest ones, the ones no one needs anymore. Sure enough: four out-of-date bake sales, three trucks for sale so faded they're barely readable, and too many church groups holding dances to count.

I leave all the ones about lost pets. None about missing children, no milk carton faces staring out at me. This is the sort of place where kids either don't get found, or their bodies turn up but their murderers never do. I think about how desperate you must be in a town so small that everyone knows everybody else at least to nod to, to put up flyers to remind your neighbours that your child is gone. Pondering, as I remove leaflets and tacks, if my parents bothered with any such thing, or if my father would have considered it advertising the shame I'd caused him by getting "misplaced". I wonder now, as I occasionally do when I've got too much time on my hands, if he ever suspected his own brother.

I think about the lives these sorts of kids – like me – won't have.

Sometimes we get to choose our paths, but families have a lot of influence. Your father's a doctor or a lawyer or a mechanic, so you become a doctor, a lawyer, a mechanic, or your mother's Suzy Homemaker and you think you can't do any better than cooking and breeding and cleaning. Sometimes it's easier to go into the shrink-wrapping someone prepared earlier – you don't have to think of a different shape to take on. Or your family is forceful as a Jell-O mould and presses you the way they want. You might not feel able to resist. You might spend your life living out a cookie-cutter version of your parents' existence, and that's what you pass on to your own kids. Or maybe you wanted something different and even though you didn't get the chance to reach for it, you encourage your children to find their own way; do your best to give them wings. Sometimes you get a few years to yourself, then it's time to become "responsible", follow in someone's footsteps and the family business just eats you up.

Sometimes all your choices are just taken away.

Shaking my head to clear the thoughts for a while, I imagine the brightest pinky-purple I can and pull a flyer from the deep pocket of my green hippie skirt. Exactly the colour I'd imagined. Not too purple, though, because even black can be hard to read on a dark background – just purple enough, this, to make the lettering *pop*.

The Tissot Family Circus!
Ride the Carousel of Light.
Games of chance, skill and strength!
Prizes to win!
See the lions and Tigers and bears!
Watch the death-defying Adelita!
Tilda and her Prancing ponies!
Laugh at the Zany antics of our Clowns!
Come one, come all!
In Pleasance for One Night Only!
TONIGHT!
Follow the lights…

Random capitalisations and so many exclamation marks – who could resist?

I make a few more and pin them in a row. Eye-catching. Carefully pocketing the remaining thumbtacks, I head back to the centre line and continue on my way. Every so often I find another store of some description, produce another poster, pin it up, do that until I'm out of tacks. By then I've found the schoolyard, and just in time, kids are pouring out the main door. Small school, but large enough – people in places like this never stop breeding, it's about the only thing left to do.

I stand outside the fence – I know better than to go in – try to sense the thud beneath my feet, but it feels weaker. *Harrumph.* The first line of kids sees me, slows down, remembering to be wary of strangers, no doubt. I smile. Hand in my pocket, I pull out one of those pinky-purple sheets, hold it up, turn it around and around so they can see: No strings attached. Then I fold it and fold it and fold it until it's a tiny square. I make a fist and stuff that neat square into the hole at the top, into the cage of my fingers and palm. I shake it, one, two, three, then put the hand up to my lips, tilt my head, and *blow*.

A flight of pinky-purple cranes flows into the air, floating over the fence to hover above the gathered crowd – all staring upwards, mouths open, sighs of wonder issuing forth. The cranes flap for a few seconds, then unfurl and drift gradually down to grabby hands. After the first small finger touches the first piece of paper, I turn and walk away – no need to talk to anyone, and best if I don't, it makes me harder to remember. We'll have a full house tonight, with all these kids running home to show their parents the flyers that will be gone by tomorrow morning, turned into dust.

Marching away, I pout: the rhythm of the road is weaker and weaker. I'd fully expected to see a pale face amongst the healthy pink ones; a small form that gave off nothing but cold. A space around them no child would step into though they didn't know why. Couldn't see anything, except maybe a fog, a lack of focus on certain angles. I can't help but feel that little drop of disappointment. No one, not proper dead or otherwise. No use to me.

Yes, the pulse is weak, but the circus lights will draw them, like moths to a flame. It's the way they're designed after all. Even if you're not aware of it, somehow, the lights bring you home. And I think about the man who came for me when I wasn't quite dead. How I still kicked when he tried to pick me up from the suitcase my uncle had packed me in. How happy he seemed to see me, to realise what I was. How greedy he appeared as he said, "Ah little one, look at you. Wanting to live, so badly."

And here's me now, living so badly. I wonder if I look just like him?

* * *

By the time I get back to the field, Ichabod's changed into his Ringmaster's uniform: black trousers and shiny boots, a red jacket with tails trimmed with gold braid and buttons over a crisp shirt, and a top hat as dark as ebony. White gloves that he somehow manages to keep pristine no matter what – of all the magic I've seen, that's the bit that amazes me the most. He nods at me, tips his hat as he sets off to walk through the avenues of our ephemeral little city, and I take my position on the bench seat again, breathing in the moments of quiet before it all kicks off. Night's falling and headlights are coming down the road, engines rumbling. There's the scuff of shoes, the murmur of voices of those who've decided to walk, finding the evening air was too good to waste.

A family with four teenaged boys and two small girls arrives first. The parents look quite young, must have started early; school sweethearts. They're holding hands and I smile without meaning to, though my heart hurts at the sight. Things denied to me often make me ache. The woman catches my eye and smiles back. The man calls, "Who's Tissot?" without using the French pronunciation, so it comes out a hard "sot".

"My great-great-great grandmother," I lie, then gesture for them to move along – not bossy-like, but the same way a wave carries you to the shore, or out to sea. The teenage boys give me a glance, nudging each other and blushing as they follow their parents.

I don't know who the original Tissot was – by the time I caught the Impresario's eye all that remained was the name on the wagon (which Ichabod refreshes once a year). I'm not sure the Impresario knew much more than he told me (and Ichabod is a tight-lipped little bastard) and, having found me, he had no intention of engaging in a lengthy apprenticeship. The moments I remember of him were his haste, showing me something once, twice, maybe three times if it was especially complex or I was being especially obtuse, watching with impatience as I demonstrated what I'd learned. Muttering *Got it? Yes? Good.* Then onto the next lesson.

And as I said, not much meaning given – none at all, really, just the way to do things, how to summon the circus, to find the little lost souls who form the troupe, knowledge of when and if they might be freed. That, at least, has nothing to do with me – if their murderer were to be found then they'd be gone the next time the circus materialised. Once, Ichabod whispered when he'd had too much to drink, one of the fliers had disappeared mid-performance, mid-air. He told me that and the rule that I couldn't interfere, no matter what I might know or find out or deduce. Our purpose was to provide a home for the darling dead, the unwanted babes, for as long as they might need it. Not to give justice.

Someone needs to be their Impresario – their shepherd, really. Not a ringmaster, no, that's Ichabod, who reminds me time and again he's the original and the best. He's got no intention of relinquishing his role. But the shepherd must find the lost ones, and show the way, feeling the beat beneath the asphalt. And the shepherd needs very specific qualifications: must be in the between, the space that's neither life nor death. A conduit. Someone who can follow the hollow ways. So, when the Impresario found me – when his shoes and the rhythm of the road led him to where I lay, washed up on that riverbank – he found me mostly dead, but just a little bit alive. Like he once was, and whoever came before him in a long line of the mostly-dead.

And when he discovered me, when he realised what I was... well, all he saw was escape. A replacement. I hated him for a lot of years, but as I grew – and strangely enough, I did grow, dead-alive though I am – I began to understand it. I've been doing this for nigh on seventy years and I would give anything to bequeath the mantle. Make someone else the shepherd. I've been looking for a new me for at least two-thirds of my half-life. Still, no one. Or at least no one in the right state, or no one who's been willing or able to say *Yes* when I asked them. Not yet.

Maybe I was just an idiot. Because when he lifted me out of that suitcase, I – having been thrown in the river and floated, unexpected and Moses-like, downstream – I was very far from home. Maybe it was the rush of oxygen after so little for so long. Maybe it was seeing the light when so many hours had been spent, mostly dead, in the darkness of a bag. Maybe it was sheer desperation. But when he asked if I wanted to go on, to live again, I said *Yes*. Just like an idiot.

And a deal's a deal, right, when someone's pulled you back from being extinguished, even if they didn't explain the fine print. Because you didn't ask for it, did you? In my defence, I was only eight, but I probably knew enough about adults by then to know not to trust them.

Though I rambled the streets of Pleasance a good while this afternoon I couldn't find the place where the pulse beneath my feet led. Frustrating, but it probably meant that the lost one was still moving around, although not by their own volition. Eventually I had to give up, trust that somehow they'd find their way to us, even though we can stay for no more than one night. People might notice us; might notice that in the morning light only a single wagon leaves a town when just hours before there was a whole community of youngsters smiling and laughing and joking. Children with nothing to fear because the worst had already happened to them.

Cars begin to park by the side of the road, then along the dirt track, then people stream through the gate I hitched back earlier so no one else would get splinters. We don't charge admission, which makes us damned near irresistible. Small family groups, parents and children, some of whose faces I recognise from the schoolyard. Some see me and whisper and point, draw their parents' attention to the pretty brunette sitting there grand as you please. I smile, clench my fists, then throw them upwards as if they might leave my wrists, open my hands at the last moment and rainbow glitter flies everywhere, catching the light from the circus. The parents laugh and nod – they *know* it's a trick, how could it be anything else? *No such thing as magic*, they'll whisper to their offspring. The kids know better, but it's a fight they can't win. They'll hang onto the memory of the moment until the day the switch flicks and they become grownups themselves, then they'll decide *Yes, a trick, there's no such thing as magic.*

Soon the field is filled with moving forms, chatter, laughter, *oohs* and *aahs* as the fire-eaters weave through the crowd, gradually herding the spectators, did they but know it, along the main avenue and into the Big Top, gripping bags of candy and fatty foods on sticks, things that will harden arteries in short order – although folk will feel strangely hungry in a few hours, as if they've eaten nothing at all. I watch until the last of the assembled have disappeared into the tent, and there's no one left to spend their coins at the booths. The carousel is empty, the music suddenly tinny. Then the heads of the Tissot Family Circus troupe turn as one towards me, seeking permission. I nod and they drift like spiderwebs towards the entrance to the Big Top. I wait a moment, then clamber down from my post, intent on taking in the show with the rest of them.

The moment, however, my feet hit the grass, I sense it. The thud and beat of the signal. Close by, so close by. Almost like someone's drumming their heels on the ground. I take a tentative step forward, feel it weaken, then right, then left – that's it. Left, left, lefter.

Towards the cars parked on the dirt road. Past the trucks. To the only sedan, newer, well-kept, clean and polished. The rhythm is like an earthquake here, like I can barely keep my balance though I know I'm the only one who's being thrown about by the tremors. But there's no sound. No noise of heels beating against the floor of the trunk. I just know it's there.

Finger to the lock, I press hard, breathe a single word, and the lid flies open.

A small body, a blonde girl, maybe six. Eyes open and glazed, unmoving, pink dress, one sneaker. Two fingers broken. Mostly dead; so much mostly dead. But there's a spark and a thud I can hear, so faint, so faint. I touch her face – cold! Stiff and still – and I call quietly. Call her to come back, just a little, just a smidge. And the world's not around me anymore, the field is gone, and I feel more than see this tiny person standing in a dim corridor, pausing, uncertain, half-turning towards my voice.

And all I can feel is that greed – the hunger to be free – and I think that when she's here, when she's looking up at me with trust and hope, then I will ask her if she wants to go on, to live again, and maybe, just maybe she'll say *Yes*, just like the idiot I was. Just maybe she'll take my place and I'll get to sleep once and for all.

And she's almost turned around in the long dark tunnel, she's almost facing me, her feet might begin to move in the right direction and I might just put out a hand to guide her, draw her on, encourage her…

And I can't.

Can't say the words I want.

Instead I whisper *No. Go back. It'll be okay.*

And I watch as she walks towards actual death, true death, and I feel the rhythm of the road fading beneath my feet until there's nothing left, not the slightest tingle. And then she's gone from the tunnel, steps through the brightness at the other end, and I close my eyes for long seconds.

When I open them, I'm in the field, in the world, her wispy little ghost beside me. Properly dead, nothing that might be fooled into being the next shepherd, the Impresario. But a something, a someone who could at least have a better time of it with the Tissot Family Circus, for a while, or forever.

I look at the car – the vehicle someone chose to drive here while this child lay in the darkness like forgotten luggage – and I know that I can't interfere. But, oh, I look into the trunk, at the physical body lying there unmoving. I know that I come from a long line of non-interfering Impresarios. I can't meddle. But I *can* fail to close the lid. I can set a few fairy lights, blue and spectral to highlight the open maw, something to draw the attention. Who knows? The little one's time with us might be short. Might be very long. Who knows?

I sigh, offer my hand, and say, "Do you like carousels?"

MR THIRTEEN

BY M. R. CAREY

1

After Jo Ramsey died, and then French William, it somehow became Lot's job both to set up the room and to host the meetings. The two things had always been separate before, entrusted to two different people, but the group had taken a wound very close to its heart. It wouldn't need much, Lot felt, to push it over the edge of the catastrophe curve into a total collapse. So without anything being put to a vote, or even discussed, she took Jo's place in the chair and collected the key to the store cupboard from William's widow, Henriette.

"I really want to thank you," Henriette said when Lot arrived on the doorstep. "The group was such a comfort to him in these last months."

"I'm glad," Lot said. And then, in the interests of full disclosure, "It was hard to know what William was feeling. He hardly ever spoke at the meetings."

Henriette gave a sad little smile. "He hardly ever spoke at home, either. Most evenings I'd knit him up again while we watched *House of Games* or *Family Fortunes*, and then when I was done he'd go to bed. I don't think it was being able to talk about it that he liked. I think it was putting out the chairs and making the tea. He was happiest when he had something mindless to do."

Well that puts me in my place, Lot thought glumly. She took the key, on its Pokémon keychain, and went back to the church hall. She'd always wondered about the keychain. William and Henriette had never had any children, because William's curse was one that transmitted down the male line, so where had the keychain come from? Had William even known what a Pokémon was, or had he just picked the chain up out of a bargain bin somewhere? Most likely the latter, she thought.

Unravelling was a cruel curse. It took you at its own pace, getting a little worse day by day, month by month, year by year. At first it was just a finger, an elbow, or an ear that frayed, easily pinned or sewn or knitted back together by someone with deft fingers. The pieces that unravelled became dry but supple, like string or loose elastic, but they became flesh again when they were reunited with the rest of you. And then the next day they'd come away again, and the next day and the next and the day after that, a little quicker and a little further every time. How had Henriette decanted her dead husband into his coffin? It was a question to which Lot hoped she would never learn the answer.

Jo Ramsey's death had been quick and merciful by comparison. Her curse wasn't one she was born with but one she literally walked into by accident – a magical effluvium lingering in the air where a warlock's house had formerly stood. The theurgist she consulted had told her she would die at the end of three years unless she passed the malediction on to someone else by whispering their own name three times into their ear while they slept. Jo had slept alone every night of those three years. Oh, she had taken the odd lover while the sun was up, but she'd always kicked her partners out of bed long before nightfall. She didn't want to be tempted. She wanted the curse to die with her, and it had.

The group had given her a good send-off on her last night. Jo was adamant that she wanted a party and warned everyone that she'd drop on them like a ton of bricks if she caught them getting maudlin. "I've had a good innings," she said, despite being only fifty-seven, "and I'm not complaining. In a lot of ways, knowing when you're going to go is a blessing. It takes away some of the sting of it." That wasn't true at all in Lot's experience, but she respected Jo far too much to contradict her.

So now the group was down to a round dozen, and very few of the ones who were left had curses that were actually terminal in any direct way. Rhona Cave had a wound on her foot that gave off a fearful stench like shit, rotten meat and vomit all mixed together. "Like that poor chap in the *Aeneid*," she'd say when she was asked about it. "Unless it was in the *Odyssey*. They exiled him on an island. I just have to wear three pairs of socks and sit by an open window, so I'm not doing too bad." Mark Mackay's tattoos rearranged themselves on his face to reveal his thoughts and feelings, usually with ironic commentary. Subira Hassan's sweat was red wine, which meant that her clothes slowly became saturated with vivid purple stains over the course of a few hours. She brought a change of outfit to every meeting so she would be decent and unremarkable when she left.

And so on. And so what? There were a dozen groups like this one in South Hertfordshire alone. Not all magic was malevolent but anyone with enough hate in them could find a magical means to express it if they looked hard enough, and once uttered, curses tended to have a lot of staying power.

Lot's was a gift from Ronnie Miles, an ex-boyfriend whose fragile ego she had somehow bruised when they broke up. He called her two-faced, said she'd led him on knowing all along that she didn't intend to stay with him. His curse had been about both those things, in a way – having a second face and having foreknowledge – but it wasn't clear whether he'd known how it was going to come out. And he had been stupid enough to hang around after he'd passed the curse on to her, which meant that he was the first to experience the full effect of it. Served the bastard right, in Lot's opinion.

She had found the curse afterwards – or at least the *residuum*, the physical object that had transmitted it. It was a piece of vellum, actual calfskin, on which some words had been written in very old, very faded ink. Ronnie had slipped it to her when he came around to collect a few CDs he'd lent to her during their time together. Then he'd stood there watching her, grinning a nasty little grin, and told her that what went around was likely to come around.

Lot had taken the scrap of parchment to a theurgist afterwards and got it identified. The language was Sumerian, apparently.

Very old, the theurgist said, and very powerful. It translated as:

Whether you wish or whether you wish not
Speak, speak of them, the things that will be.
Whether your life is long or whether short
Speak, speak of them, the things that will end.
Two and seven, nine and fifteen and twenty-four,
Speak, speak of them, the pains of passing.
Two and seven, nine and fifteen and twenty-four,
Numbers of great power that cannot be stayed.
The hunger once awakened has no end.
Speech comes, truth comes, laid at your feet
In white linen like the dead,
In white linen dressed for the grave.

Lot hadn't needed to ask what any of that nonsense meant. She already knew by then. As she stood there staring at Ronnie's stupid, grinning face she had felt a tearing in her shoulder. She thought she must have pulled a muscle but when she slid her hand inside her t-shirt to massage the sore spot, sharp teeth closed on her fingers and bit them hard. The second mouth that had opened just above her left breast had no intention of being gagged, even accidentally. It began to speak in an eerie parody of her own voice. It told Ronnie Miles how he would die, and when.

Ronnie had staggered away in a state of shock, too stunned even to weep. Anyone hearing that voice – and Lot had tried her best to keep the number as low as she could – knew without question that the words it said were true. There was something in the tone and timbre of the voice that told you it was speaking from outside time and space; that it had looked down on you from an utterly inhuman vantage and seen your life in its entirety. There was no appeal, and no possibility of mistake. From the few friends they had in common, Lot heard that Ronnie had got blind drunk that night and hadn't really been sober since. *Pussy*, she thought sourly. His death wasn't even going to be that bad when it came – just a car accident, a few days in a coma and then clickety-click, the life support going off. Plenty of people had it worse.

But none of that altered the situation. Lot's curse made it impossible for her to be with anyone – romantically, sexually, intimately. Her second mouth responded to extremes of emotion. In Ronnie's case that had mostly been irritation arising from the sight of his smug, smirking face, but even that had been enough. Sexual arousal created a much stronger and more immediate effect. Lot was even more alone than Jo had been in that respect, because she had to steer clear of situations where she might start to feel attracted to someone even in the most casual way. The lead time, once the curse kicked in, was very short indeed.

The group meetings were her lifeline. But even she was forced to admit that sometimes the unvarying routine could get a little dull. Tuesdays were mostly personal testimonies, Fridays were all about the steps and the affirmations. But the twelve of them knew each other well enough by this time that they could have recited each other's testimonies by heart, and the steps and affirmations were never really what it was about. Not for Lot, anyway. It was about contact, in the constrained and limited ways in which contact was possible for her.

So she was ready for change when it came, for something new and unexpected. Not hungry, although sometimes it felt like that, just ready. Ready to embrace it, whatever it was, in the hope that she might somehow figure out a way to climb up out of the pit she was in and get a glimpse of the horizon. It didn't have to be much. She had long ago stopped hoping for love, or even for sex. But she would have killed for a little novelty.

Mr Thirteen came in one Friday evening out of a fog so dense it was as though the air had turned to milk. Jack Serkevksy was in the middle of his testimony and everyone was half-asleep because however strange and grotesque Jack's curse was, they were all extremely familiar with it. "So I ordered the salad," Jack was saying, "and I managed to get three mouthfuls down before it started to turn to ash. It seems to be happening a lot faster now, but I'm getting better at switching off my taste buds so I can force a fair amount down when it's sort of half-and-half. The trick is knowing when to stop. If I eat too much of the muck I just bring it right back up again, and then I'm hungrier than ever. Plus, you know, the lining of my throat…"

This was the point when Mr Thirteen arrived. As he stepped over the threshold of the little church hall he seemed almost to be coalescing out of the fog, his long black coat a tongue of shadow that had clung to him and congealed. He was tall and in Lot's eyes extremely good-looking, with dark eyes and tanned skin that looked sun-baked and lustrous. The lines of his face had the perfection of a Greek statue. His crisply curled hair reminded Lot of grapes on the vine.

Oh fuck! she thought, bracing herself. *Oh fuck that noise so hard! Where's a cold shower when you really need one?*

But the mouth on her shoulder said nothing. Nothing at all.

2

Peter Cadmus paused on the threshold, letting his face and his presence exert their usual effect. He had looked up the group online, and knew the names of everyone in the room, but this was the first time he'd seen them in the flesh and he used the time to size them up.

He was more interested in the women than the men; it was much more likely to be a woman that he finally chose. A man would do just as well, of course, but Cadmus' standard line of approach was to pretend a sexual interest in order to get close to his target, and back when he still cared about sex he had been strictly hetero, so he knew the rules of that dance somewhat better.

There were seven women and five men. Cadmus recited their names inside his head as he looked from face to face. The one who had been speaking when he came into the room was almost certainly Serkevsky. Useless, Cadmus decided at once. The man looked both old and emaciated, his vital force probably a shallow, guttering flow. He would only be worth considering as a last resort.

The overweight woman with her leg in a calliper must be Rhona Cave. She could also be discounted. She stank of rot and death. Anything he took from her would carry that taint.

That left ten, all possibles. All with the smoky miasma of black magic coming off them in rich waves, so his own power would find a ready point of entry. Any one of them, really, would be acceptable. But he liked the redheaded one best of all, the one sitting at the far end of the room with the clipboard in her hand. He was almost certain she was Charlotte Temple, the woman who posted up the dates and venues online for the group's meetings. She smiled at him, a cheerful empty smile that went pretty well with the impression he'd formed of her from those posts. Vacuous, friendly, well-meaning, nothing much going on upstairs. In addition, given the nature of the look she was currently giving him, as horny as a stoat and as lonely as a Catholic at a Rangers match. That was plan A, right there, Cadmus decided.

"Hello," the redheaded woman said. "Are you looking for the support group?"

Cadmus glanced around the room again, letting his eyes rest on each face in turn. He gave the redhead the full treatment, staring at her for the longest and keeping his gaze fixed on her as he spoke. "Yes," he said. Just the one word. Playing into the mystery. He knew what he looked like, and he knew that these were people who were likely to get the raw simplicity of magic all tangled up with bullshit notions about tragic fate and inexorable this and that.

"Okay," the redhead said with another vapid smile. "Great.

You've found it then. Please, come on in." She jumped up and went off to fetch a folding chair from the stacks of them that stood up against the wall. She set it down for him between herself and an Asian man with an eyepatch. But Cadmus didn't move yet. So long as he stayed by the door all the eyes in the room were on him and the normal business of the meeting couldn't resume. He had no qualms about milking the moment.

"I hadn't realised that your meeting was already underway," he said. "I wouldn't want to interrupt."

A murmur went around the room, a dozen voices earnestly insisting that he come in and sit down. "You're not interrupting at all," the redhead assured him. "We're always happy to welcome new members. Please." She gestured to the chair.

Cadmus nodded at last, slowly and with a self-deprecating reluctance. He closed the door to and crossed the room, letting his long coat fall open to reveal the brilliant silver weave of his waistcoat. If a picture was worth a thousand words, the right prop could be worth a million.

3

The chair creaked very loudly under the newcomer when he sat down in it, suggesting that there was some serious bulk under the long coat. He didn't look fat, though. It must be muscle, Lot thought: muscle was very dense. The notion brought a shiver of interest that she did her best to suppress at once. There was (quite literally) no future in that.

"Welcome," she said. "We're in the middle of our personal testimonies right now, and Mr Serkevsky has the floor. But as soon as he's finished – and please take your time, Jack – we'll greet you properly."

"I think I've said all I wanted to say," Jack told her. Like everyone else in the room he was eyeing the new man with naked curiosity.

"Well then," Lot said, "if you're sure. Welcome to the Chipping Barnet Curse and Malediction Support Group, Mr...?"

The pause went on for longer than she expected. "I can't speak my name aloud," the man said at last. "There would be consequences. Unpleasant ones, for you and for me. Since there were twelve of you before I came, and there are now thirteen, perhaps it would be best to call me that. Mr Thirteen. Or you could invent a name for me that's more to your liking. I'm sorry. I appreciate that this is far from ideal, and works directly against the trust on which groups like this depend, but it's the best I can do."

"Thirteen, then," Lot said. "If that's all right with everyone?" There were nods and murmurs of assent around the group.

"You're very kind," Mr Thirteen said.

Lot explained to him how the testimonies worked, assuring him at the same time that there was no expectation that he should speak. "It's not a rule or anything. We hope that sooner or later you'll be prepared to confide in us and talk about your curse, but that doesn't have to be tonight. You can come as often as you like and talk whenever you feel you're ready to."

"Thank you," Mr Thirteen answered. "But really, I'm not chary of speaking. That's why I came here. I've lived with my curse a very long time, and never until today took the step of trying to share the burden with anyone else. I feel I'm more than ready. I'll wait my turn, and get the feel of how the meeting works, but if it's acceptable to you all I'd very much like to talk about my condition."

"Of course," Lot said.

In fact, three more people spoke before Mr Thirteen finally put up his hand. It was almost as though he had decided to be the last speaker of the evening, but he was probably just more diffident than he had wanted to sound. After all, how would he have known anything about the rhythm and customs of the meeting? He had said this was the first time he'd ever sought out a self-help group.

"Mr Thirteen," Lot said, "would you like to share?"

"I would. Thank you." In his thrilling voice the four words sounded like the prelude to a symphony. "The curse that binds my body also constrains my speech, so there are limits to what I can tell you. But I can say that I don't belong to this time or this place. I was born a great many years ago, in a country that doesn't exist any more."

"Is that why you talk in such a funny way?" Lexie Hemington asked. "Sorry, that came out a bit rude, but you know what I mean."

"You're perceptive," Mr Thirteen said. "The cadences of my speech are a little odd. A little archaic, perhaps. It's something I try my best to correct, because I don't want to stand out — quite the opposite. But it's hard for me to pretend to be something I'm not."

"That's more than most men can say," Subira Hassan observed to the room at large.

"The city of my birth…" Mr Thirteen resumed. "Well, not even its name is remembered now. And I can't speak it, any more than I can speak my own. All I can say is that it was a beacon of light in a great darkness. Beloved of its children, the envy of all the world besides. An earthly paradise, full of every kind of happiness. I hold it in my heart, and always will."

He stopped, as if he was momentarily overwhelmed, but when he took up his account again his voice was even. "I was a soldier," he said. "But my country, my polity, had never waged a single war. We didn't need to. Our knowledge was so vast that we could hold the world at bay without doing harm to anyone. In my city the work of a soldier was maintaining civil order and protecting ordinary citizens from any who would seek to harm them.

"As part of this work, I went one day to arrest a witch. Her name I could speak, but I choose not to. She doesn't deserve to be remembered. She had the reputation of being cunning and cruel, and she plied an illegal trade — murdering and maiming by magical means to feed her clients' grudges and further their conspiracies."

"Um… can I just ask?" Mark Mackay said, putting up his hand.

The stranger seemed annoyed to be interrupted, but after a moment's pause he waved his own hand to indicate that Mark could speak.

"Well it's just," Mark sounded apologetic, "if everyone was happy and all that, where did this witch get her customers from?" His tattoos were more explicit. Across his forehead and cheeks words in German blackletter type blossomed one after another: DOESN'T SOUND MUCH LIKE AN EARTHLY PARADISE.

"There are always malcontents, even in a perfect system," Mr Thirteen said tightly.

"Yeah but, you know, are there enough to guarantee a viable cash flow? If I was a witch, I'd set up somewhere that was really shit."

Mr Thirteen stared at Mark for a few moments in silence. "I don't," he said at last, "claim to understand the workings of her mind. Possibly it gave her more pleasure to corrupt something beautiful than simply to thrive in a dungheap."

"That does sound very witchy," Rhona Cave pointed out.

"It does if you get your idea of witches from Disney movies," said Mark. To Mr Thirteen he added, "Sorry, only my girlfriend is one. A witch, I mean. And she's a bit touchy about the representation side of things. I suppose it's rubbed off on me a bit. I'm sorry, I'll shut up."

"Thank you," Mr Thirteen said, with something of a heavy emphasis. "In any event, when I came to her house to arrest her, the witch responded with a volley of deadly spells. Three of the men with me died in the first few seconds, two from snake bites – although there were no snakes to be seen – and one because his blood had frozen solid in his veins.

"The rest of us rushed on her and pinned her hands behind her back. That left her unable to make the signs in the air that transmitted her evil intent, but she was still free to curse – which she did with a liberal tongue. My sergeant was left allergic to the colour purple, so that even to see it caused him the most appalling pain. My ensign, Edrom, found that his shadow now weighed as much as he did, becoming a burden that he must drag along behind him whenever the sun shone. And I – well, by this time I had wrestled the evil creature to the ground, and so I took all the venom she had left to spit.

"Three curses she gave me. The first was that anyone who heard my name spoken aloud would suffer the abruption of several major blood vessels. The second was that my family and all who loved me or even thought of me kindly would forget that I had ever lived. But the third was the cruellest of all." He paused and looked around the room, just as he'd done when he first came in, taking in all their faces one by one. "The third was that I should never know the balm of death, but must live forever."

4

And it was preposterous! The story had more holes in it than a colander. As for Mr Thirteen himself, he was worse than ridiculous, he was a cliché. The Wandering Jew without the

Yiddishkeit, but with a *Matrix*-style floor-length coat and a stilted call-me-Ishmael delivery that he kept forgetting to keep up.

But – and this was the crazy part – that last statement seemed to be true. In spite of the nonsense, Lot found herself drawn to the man's athletic build and only dark-eyed good looks. Her mind had gone there, imagining him naked, imagining herself astride him, and her tell-tale second mouth had only pursed its lips. It hadn't said a word, or even cleared its throat.

Which meant – which had to mean – that although the rest of his story made about as much sense as a fire escape in a bungalow, the immortality part was for real. And that in its turn meant Lot could fuck the man's brains out without any risk of doing his head in. There was no prophecy to be delivered, no fate to be sealed. If Mr Thirteen couldn't die, she couldn't predict it.

And he definitely seemed to be interested in her. They chatted amiably through the tea-and-biscuits part of the evening as the other members of the group trickled away one by one, until finally only the two of them were left. Subira gave Lot a wink as she said goodnight, and when she waved she let Lot see that her fingers were crossed for her. Clearly she'd picked up on what was happening and was hoping it would happen some more.

"I fear I've been monopolising you," Mr Thirteen said. "And keeping you too long."

"It's fine," Lot said. "I have to stay behind to tidy things away and lock up. You can help if you like."

"I'd be happy to."

"Great. You stack the chairs and I'll fill the dishwasher."

She hesitated, wondering whether to go for broke. Her libido struggled with her natural reserve, and for once it won. "Do a decent job and there's a pint in it for you."

Thirteen smiled a radiant smile. "I am suitably incentivised. Watch me!"

5

Cadmus disliked the business of murder, the mess and the blood and the overwrought emotions, but he had to admit there was a part of him that had been looking forward to the hunt. Normally there was a challenge to winning the target's trust, shepherding them to an appropriate venue and choosing the right moment to act.

But none of this was hard. None of it involved any effort at all. Charlotte Temple was so desperate for companionship, or perhaps just for sex, that she did all the hunting for him. They went to a bar, they had at least one drink too many, he walked her home. It was clear from the outset that when they got to her front door she wouldn't be sending him away.

Through all of this he tried his best to think of her only as *the woman*, not as Charlotte or − as she had invited him to call her − Lot. It was important to keep some emotional distance. It would help him later, when he was working on her with the knife.

"Would you like to come inside for a nightcap?" she asked. The smile she gave him removed any ambiguity from the offer.

"I have to go to work in the morning," Cadmus said. He wasn't sure where that had come from. It was a lie – smart investments and compound interest meant that he hadn't had to work in more than a century. Possibly he just wanted to sound out the depths of her need.

But it was a misstep. "Another time, then," the woman said, and began to turn away.

"On the other hand," Cadmus said quickly, "I can always call in sick. I feel a dose of the flu coming on."

The woman shot him a glance over her shoulder, arch and provocative. "You should come in out of the cold then."

In her tiny, pokey apartment she took his coat and laid it over the back of a chair. She sat him down on a sofa with a tawdry floral print. He couldn't help noticing that the carpet was frayed in places and that the pictures on the wall had a rim of dust where the bottom of the frame met the glass. She wasn't keeping the place up. Sometimes being cursed did that to you, induced a state of fatalistic passivity. Death was sometimes a mercy for such people, though the way he killed had very little of mercy in it.

The woman poured two generous measures from a bottle of Jameson's and then went into the kitchen in search of ice cubes. "What is it you do?" she called out to him as she rummaged and clattered.

"I'm sorry?" Cadmus said. He was preoccupied. His hands were a little sweaty, which made it hard to unscrew the stopper from the little bottle of cyclobenzaprine he carried with him.

"Your job. What do you do for a living?"

"Oh." He rummaged briefly through his small repertoire of stock answers. "I'm a lawyer."

"What kind?"

Was there more than one kind? He hadn't known. "General practice," he said.

"That's doctors, isn't it?" The woman returned, carrying the ice cubes in her cupped hands. She dropped two into his glass and two into her own.

"I mean," Cadmus said, "my firm handles cases of all kinds. My own specialism is crime."

"Crime?"

"Criminal. Criminal law."

"Fascinating." She touched her glass to his. "Cheers."

She took a long swig. Cadmus only pretended to. Dutch courage was all very well, but he needed a steady hand for the work that was to come.

"So," the woman said, "exactly how old are you?"

"Old enough. You needn't worry that you're leading me astray."

She laughed, then shook her head. "Oh shit," she said. "I really, really want to drag you into the bedroom right now. But if we're going to do this, there's something you need to see first."

"Oh really?" He set down his glass.

"Promise me you won't freak out. If this is a deal-breaker, that's fine. You just walk out the door and this never happened. But don't scream or anything."

"It takes a lot to make me scream," he told her truthfully.

She undid the top three buttons of her shirt and slid it off her left shoulder. There was a mouth there, red-lipped and pursed in a way that looked slightly disapproving.

"He does not," the mouth said, in a voice that was superficially like Charlotte's own voice but with a strange fluting harmonic on some of the vowels. "He cannot. He will not."

For a few moments Cadmus couldn't think of anything to say. If he had actually been planning to have sex with Charlotte Temple, he would have changed his mind right there and then. But he was stuck here until the drug kicked in, so he had to say something. "That's your curse," he managed.

The woman shrugged. "Part of it. 'Two and seven, nine and fifteen and twenty-four. Numbers of great power that cannot be stayed.' It's a whole thing."

"What is that, though? What kind of thing?"

"Honestly?" She looked pained. "If you weren't − you know, like you said at the meeting − immortal, then right now it would be telling you how and when you're going to die. But since you're *not* going to die, it's reduced to waffly stuff like that." She did the buttons up again. "There it is," she said, with another shrug. "You're welcome to finish your drink and leave if you want to. No hard feelings. I didn't want you to geph… geth infer… get into this without…"

She faltered, blinked a few times, and flicked her tongue across her lips as if she was tasting something strange there. "Hair in my mouth," she muttered. "Sorry, that was… Oh.

Oh, I don't feel..."

She slumped sideways onto the sofa's arm, her glass toppling from her hand. Cheap whiskey splashed across the frayed carpet.

"You won't," Cadmus said, "feel much of anything at all. I promise."

He picked her up and carried her into the bedroom. He laid her down on her own bed, which was unmade. It would be easier to work with her laid out properly on a flat surface. The ritual required a few incisions to be made with a certain degree of accuracy.

He went and fetched the knife and the inkpot from his coat. They were all the kit he needed, and he travelled light. He set about to remove the woman's clothes.

"What did you do to me?" she asked him. The words were slurred, but it was alarming that she could speak at all. Perhaps he should fetch the bottle and dose her a little more heavily. But this wouldn't take long and she didn't seem to be able to move at all. Better to push on and get the job done.

"I slipped a muscle relaxant into your drink," he told her. "A very powerful one. It acts as a sedative too, but perhaps you've got some sort of tolerance. Hence you still being awake."

"Why? Why would you do that? To rape me? We were going to have sex anyway." She sounded only bewildered, not aggrieved or afraid. He felt a grudging admiration for that *sangfroid*.

"No, no," he said. "I have no intention of assaulting you. I'm going to sacrifice you. I told you the truth about my past, Charlotte. I only lied about one thing. I'm not cursed. I paid the witch – a fortune! – to give me immortality and to make me stay young forever. But the spell needs to be fed. Regularly, at intervals of five to ten years. I need to give Death a sop, a bribe, to keep him from taking me."

"And I'm the bribe?"

"Yes. Obviously." She was naked now, and he began to paint the first of the three runes on her body with the tip of his finger. He felt no arousal at the sight of her. His interest in sex had waned centuries ago. Eternal youth, sadly, didn't stave off the boredom of eternal recurrence and repetition. Few things did.

"You've made a mistake, Mr Thirteen," Charlotte said. "A very serious one. But I'm glad you did, really. You might have taken one of the others home. This way is better."

"I'm glad you think so," Cadmus said. He painted the second rune, moved on to the third.

He stumbled on the third, feeling a stab of pain at the end of his index finger. Staring at the woman's lower belly, he realised that the black line he had been drawing had turned to red.

This was because the end of his finger had been sheared off clean. He was drawing the line in his own blood.

"Shit!" he gasped. He stared at the truncated finger in disbelief. Then down at the woman's body, at the grinning mouth where her navel should have been. Other mouths were blossoming all over her body. Dozens and dozens of them. Cadmus jerked back quickly but the mouths rose up from the woman's bare flesh like blossom shaken loose from a tree. They circled him, all smiling, all with red lips and shiny white teeth and black voids where their throats should be.

And in strict accordance with the curse, some of the mouths – the second, seventh, ninth, fifteenth and twenty-fourth – recited prophecy. "You will not die," they told him. "Even now, you will not. You cannot. But the state in which you live will be disaggregated. Dispersed. It will not be pleasant for you."

The other mouths didn't say anything. They were too busy devouring Cadmus, flesh and blood and bone, heart and liver and lights, and too polite to speak while they were eating. They ate after their separate fashions and appetites. Big, hearty bites, dainty nibbles, chunks torn off and chewed with relish, bones crunched and swallowed. At a certain point Cadmus' ability to reflect on what was happening to him largely fell apart, but his consciousness remained. It had to, because the spell he'd bought and paid for would not be gainsaid. It couldn't allow him to die.

So his awareness remained, atomised, spread thinly across a great many different places. It was an awareness that consisted entirely of pain and panic, the need to escape and the lack of any ability to move. It went on for a very long time. Forever, in fact. The heat death of the universe passed him by and made no difference at all to his suffering.

6

L ot had truly awful indigestion the next day, and a headache – mostly from the drug, but probably also from the booze

– that took hours and hours to wear off. But the mouths were very thorough, and they hadn't left so much as a drop of blood on her sheets. All of Mr Thirteen had been ingested.

The whole thing brought her out of a slump, really. She'd believed him when he'd said that his eternal life was a curse, and had been very much taken aback when he revealed that it was something he'd asked for. It made Lot realise that the whole business of curses was really more or less subjective. More or less a matter of perspective. Life was what you made it, and there was no defensible reason not to be getting on with it.

THE CONFESSOR'S TALE

BY SARAH PINBOROUGH

A wolf stole Arkady Melanov's tongue when he was ten weeks old. It crept into the village from the surrounding forest and followed the sound of his cries as if they were the scent of a fresh kill. Eventually, its pricked ears reached the Melanovs' tiny one-level dwelling at the back of the bakery where the boy's father worked. The wooden door had been left an inch or two open to allow any passing breeze to alleviate the stifling trapped heat of the ovens, and the beast simply padded into the house. The source of the noise found, it tore Arkady's tongue free from his screaming mouth before disappearing out into the summer night, leaving only a bloody trail of silence. When Arkady's mother ran into the bedroom and found her mutilated baby, she couldn't bear the weight of her own guilt at leaving him to cry. She stood by the crib and hacked at her wrists with the pin from her hair until she bled to death.

That was how the story went.

There was, as always, another, quieter story whispered in the narrow alleys and smoky cook rooms of the village. It poured from mouth to ear, accompanied by nods of knowledge and raised eyebrows. The gestures spoke of Arkady's mother, the dark Ekaterina, discovered over her baby's cradle, her rosebud lips full of blood and meat and her eyes equally red with the madness of too many sleepless nights brought on by her infant son's incessant rages against the world. The Boyar's men took her to the castle and, after he and his entourage had had their fill of her, with one last glance back at daylight she was buried alive in the flower garden, as was the fate of those unfortunates who broke the law in the region of Kashkent.

That was how the other story went.

By the time he was five, Arkady had heard the second version of events several times through the cracked walls of shops and houses; the words carried easily on the fresh, hot summer winds. They didn't affect him. He found he didn't care much at all which story was true; the outcome remained the same. He would never scream again, nor gurgle with laughter, nor utter a single word. Arkady had learned his lesson young.

When he was seven, Arkady's father died. This came as no surprise to anyone, not even the young boy. Whereas Mikhail Melanov had once been a strong and handsome man, he had aged and weakened since his son lost his tongue and those two stories were born. He was often plagued by coughs and chills, until eventually his broad chest crumpled into itself, a hollow space where only a broken heart lived. Arkady would watch his father's arms tremble as he lifted the heavy trays of hot bread, often nearly dropping them before the next bout of wracking coughs would hit him, the boy doing what he could to help and fetching his father water from the jug in their small home at the back of the bakery. Mikhail Melanov would take it and nod in awkward thanks to his silent son, and the young boy would pretend not to see the distaste in his father's eyes.

When the long winter of that year came, the temperatures fell far below zero as they did each cycle, but this time the breath of the cold blew hard, and in the face of the ice and the winds, Mikhail Melanov's lungs decided enough was enough and breathed their last. It was not without a sense of relief. Arkady dutifully held his father's hand as he passed, and then stared long and hard at the cooling body and wondered where the man inside had gone. With no outlet, the question stayed trapped inside the isolated boy.

It was natural that the widow Samolienko and her son Sasha, who had stepped in to help when it was clear that Melanov was reaching the end, should take over the running of the bakery, and most of the village were pleased with the transition. The bread no longer had a coating of germs, and the babushka and her son worked hard to make sure enough loaves were baked each day for no-one to go hungry. Young Arkady had a knack for kneading the dough and she kept him on, providing a small bed for him in the room where the wolf or his mother had stolen his tongue. Being neither sentimental nor unkind, she treated the boy with relative indifference. Having only ever lived with his father, who had never hidden well his unease with his son, this seemed perfectly normal to the young boy.

A few days after the widow Samolienko took up residence, she called Arkady away from his work. Arkady saw his father's few clothes and possessions had been piled up in the middle of the dusty floor. The babushka's weathered eyes appraised him.

"I need to make space for my own and my son's clothes."

Arkady nodded. He wasn't quite sure what the widow wanted with him. Her hands stretched out and nestled in their floury palms sat an oblong box.

"I found this hidden at the bottom of the cupboard. I think it belonged to your mother." She shrugged. "It has her name scratched on the lid anyway."

His eyes fell to the box.

"I think it is some kind of game. Perhaps a puzzle of sorts." She shook it, and Arkady heard the pieces rattle inside. "Anyway, it seems poorly made and can have no value, so it is yours if you want it."

Somewhere behind the hardness in her charcoal eyes, Arkady saw a hint of pity for the orphaned boy with no tongue. He took the box and gave her a rare smile. She nodded, satisfied, and sent him back to his work.

* * *

Arkady waited until the widow and her son were sleeping before he lit the tiny candle by his bed and pulled the rectangular box out from under his pillow. His breath formed a crystal haze in the night, even the heat from the cooling ovens not enough to keep the arctic winter at bay. He ran his fingers over the rough surface, feeling the strange shape of his long ago disappeared mother's name under them. He swallowed hard, his heart beating with an unfamiliar anticipation.

There were ten oblong pieces in all – carved and worked into uneven two-inch tiles – and he carefully took each one out of the box and placed it on the bed next to the one before it, creating a line, before picking the first up again and examining it more thoroughly. He swallowed, his throat dry. Its pale surface was smooth and cool and he knew with a certainty he couldn't place that it and the others were formed from the bones of dead things. Each piece had a distinct pattern carved into it in fine lines, the grooves stained with black ink. Arkady frowned, his eyes flitting from tile to tile as his numb hands rearranged them, finding each one that linked with the next. When he was done he sat back, vaguely disappointed. He'd expected more from seeing the finished arrangement. Being quietly shunned by the other children of the village whose mothers' superstitious natures saw too many bad omens in the one thus far defining moment in his short life, Arkady had little experience of puzzles or games, but he thought they should take longer to complete.

He looked at the linked network of delicate lines laid out before him. It felt unfinished. There was more to it; there *had* to be. His eyes recorded the curves and straights of the design. Even dull and dead as the tiles were, he felt some satisfaction in watching them. Had his mother felt this way? Outside, in the heart of the forest, a wolf howled. The desolate sound danced sadly with the icy blasts that wrapped round the village, seeking any form of company. Having known no different, Arkady couldn't share the creature's sense of isolation, but its interruption did break his moment of reverie.

The box and its contents were carefully replaced under his thin pillow, and where the shape should have disturbed his sleep, he found it brought him a quiet comfort.

* * *

Arkady heard his first confession two months later. The widow Samolienko had shooed him out of the house in order to greet the family of Elana Vidic. The last thing she needed while encouraging a good match for her son was the strange little orphan boy. Arkady didn't mind. He was as happy as he knew how to be when in his own company.

Winter still had the landscape in its grip; white knuckles peering through the grey skin of the fields. But the wind had moved on to pastures new, and wrapped in Sasha's overcoat and scarf, Arkady wandered down to the riverbank, where he thought he might skim some stones over its frozen surface to pass half an hour or so.

He'd picked a spot that was usually quiet, even in the hot summer months. It was too close to the dense forest and slightly too far from the village to be deemed safe for children to play at. Arkady felt at home there on the edge of things and whenever he had some time of his own, which wasn't often, as the widow was a firm believer that the Devil made work for idle hands, it was where he found his feet taking him.

On this occasion, he had been beaten to it. Ivan Minsk sat on the snow-covered bank, his knees tucked under his handsome chin as he stared at the frosted mirror of the muddy water. If it hadn't been for the stream of breath lingering in front of his mouth, Arkady might have thought the older boy was dead, he was so still. It was only when Ivan turned his head to see who had joined him that Arkady noticed Ivan's hands. They were covered in blood, a stain of guilt on the blanket of white that surrounded them both. He raised his wide eyes to find Ivan's cold blue gaze on him. The boy's perfect face twisted into a smile.

"You're Arkady Melanov? The boy without the tongue?"

Arkady nodded. He didn't look at Ivan's hands.

"You can't talk?"

Arkady shrugged.

"Can you write?"

Arkady shook his head. His father had had a basic grasp of a few words and, as much as writing would have been a useful tool for Arkady, there was no one except the church who had sufficient knowledge to teach him. And as the widow Samolienko would say, if there was no one able to read his words, then what would be the point of him writing any?

Ivan's smile stretched. "Do you know what I've done?" He looked down at his own hands, turning them this way and that, watching the pale sunlight sparkle on their crimson coating. He didn't wait for an answer. "I've killed a pig. One of Korkova's. Fat bastard probably hasn't even noticed it's missing yet. I took it into the forest and carved it up while it was still alive."

He looked at Arkady, expecting a reaction. Arkady felt nothing. He knew that to steal a pig was a terrible crime, and in winter, when all food was valued, then it would be even more so, but there were things in Ivan's eyes that he couldn't understand.

"I could feel its fear and pain. It was beautiful." Ivan seemed lost in the moment and Arkady shuffled from foot to foot, wishing that the other boy would just go and he could bounce the small collection of stones in his pocket across the river.

"And there was so much blood." The boy raised his hands to smell them. "I think maybe, next time, I might try it with a person. I think that would be better, don't you?"

He looked at Arkady and smiled. Arkady, of course, said nothing. After a few silent moments, he left Ivan to his reverie and found a different place to throw his stones, but his mind couldn't quite leave the perfectly handsome boy with blood on his hands who was sitting not so very far along the curve of the river.

Ivan Minsk was found dead the next morning. It seemed he'd been skating on the river down by the forest and the thick ice's surface had given way in a freak accident. The women of the village wailed and sobbed and the men's faces were grim at the loss of such a strong and handsome boy. The widow brewed hot tea in the large samovar she kept for special occasions, and with a plate of freshly baked sweet cakes between them, the babushkas gathered in the home behind the bakery to shake their heads and gossip under the guise of bemoaning the cruelty of the world.

Arkady took refuge in his room and wondered if he was the only one to notice the lack of ice skates on the blue and frozen body that was pulled through the grieving village. Probably. His fingers sought out the comfort of the tiles inside the box, and when the level of noise was such from the other room that he was sure he wouldn't be disturbed, he tipped them out onto the bed and proceeded to make the now familiar pattern.

As he turned over the first tile, his eyes widened. It had changed. Where the delicate carving had been inked in black, the pattern now was filled with red. Arkady stared, before carefully placing it next to the others, their surfaces still dull and dead. His heart raced with rare excitement. He had been right; the puzzle hadn't been complete. He thought of Ivan and his stained hands and looked back at the crimson colour that ran like blood through the veins of the tile. There were nine more tiles to go. And then... what?

That night, he found it hard to sleep.

* * *

Arkady never sought out the confessions. Having no method of communication beyond gesture, he grew into a natural pragmatist. As often as he wishfully turned the tiles over in his hands, he also knew that fate would roll her dice as and when she was ready. That part of the puzzle was not in his control. For the main of the years that followed, Arkady got on with the business of growing up and working hard for the widow, for Sasha, and for Sasha's new wife, Elena.

But the confessions found him all the same; eight more over the next six years. In a side street while trying to make a short cut on his deliveries for the widow, a sobbing fat man told him that his wife had not died of a fever the winter before as was believed, but that when it seemed that she might recover, he pressed a pillow over her face, not being able to bear the thought of more years chained to her natural misery. He'd seen her ghost though, every day since. Arkady nodded and passed the man by.

A drunk told him how he liked to creep into his small daughter's bedroom when she slept and slide his hand under her nightdress. One of the most respected wives of the village told him how she craved the rough skin of workmen on her body and paid them to service her and thus make up for her husband's impotence.

Each stranger that found him in those isolated moments poured out the dark sins of their soul. They were eager to be free of their guilt without having to truly face justice; that much was clear in their hungry faces. Arkady could see the burdens lift from their shoulders as his ears took their words. When he left, they were always smiling, just as Ivan had been down by the river. Arkady didn't begrudge them their happiness. By the third time, he knew what the next day's outcome would be. A heart attack, an unfortunate fall, a sudden pox.

He would listen out for the slow toll of the church bell before pulling the box of tiles out from their safekeeping in his bed. With each death, a fresh piece would come to life, its veins of pattern turning blood red. Arkady felt nothing for their deaths, but there was a quiet excitement that his soul couldn't deny each time his trembling hands revealed the changes in the puzzle. When it was complete, then so would he be. By the time he was fourteen, there was only one dark tile left. As the first crisp leaves of snow fell outside his window that winter, for the first time in his life he felt a glimmer of warm hope. The completed pattern would free him from this half-existence. He was sure of it.

* * *

When the summer came, it was obvious it was time for a change in the living arrangements at the bakery. Sasha and Elena's lively five-year-old twins were getting too big to sleep in the same room as their parents, and the baker's wife's belly was already growing a new sibling for the family. The house at the back of the shop was too crowded and the widow took it upon herself to rectify the situation.

"I have arranged a new position for you, Arkady." She smiled as she spoke. She had grown fond of the boy in her own way over the years; he was a good worker and had never caused her any trouble. This change would be good for him. It would bring him some security. The boy looked up at her blankly.

"You are to work for the Boyar. You will go and live within the castle walls as a manservant." She paused. "I think a young man like you will do well there."

Arkady knew what she meant. The Boyar could be considered a fair ruler as far as taxes and tithes were concerned, but stories that leaked from the high walls that surrounded his castle and the dwellings and merchants within told of excessive debauchery and pleasures taken in the most deadly of sins by their landlord and his knights and clergy. Those who were caught spreading the stories were often hung on crosses outside the castle walls, their beaten bodies soft for the buzzards that would circle and peck hungrily, tearing strips of flesh from the still-living victims.

To speak ill of the Boyar was a crime, and although there were great rewards to be had in the trust of the Boyar's employment, the risks concerning accusations of malicious gossip were high. It was, after all, an easy way to remove a rival. With no tongue, it was a crime that Arkady could never commit. The old babushka, who had lived long enough to understand the ways of men, knew that with both his pliable nature and his silence, Arkady could not fail to impress the Boyar, and perhaps one day he would see fit to reward the old woman and her family for this gift. It was not that much to hope for.

The Boyar's men came the next day and Arkady left, the puzzle tucked carefully into his jacket pocket. He didn't look back at the village, the horse beneath him carrying him confidently the few miles uphill to the high castle walls. It was only when the gates closed heavily behind him that he thought of the whispered stories of his mother's demise within these very grounds and at his new employer's hands. Arkady found himself still empty of any feelings. His mother was not even the memory of a scent, and as he had several times before, he found himself wondering whether the wolf that took his tongue had somehow taken his heart, or perhaps some small part of his soul, with it.

The more he watched those in the world around him play out their small stories, the less he felt a part of it. On those nine occasions when people had shared with him the darkest secrets of their sins, he simply found himself puzzled by the range of emotion presented to him; their passion, their lust, their greed, and the heavy weight of their guilt. He'd felt nothing but mild curiosity. It was only when he placed bone against tiled bone and watched the puzzle coming together that he felt anything at all.

* * *

Arkady settled into life within the castle, and the summer months passed easily. The Boyar had grown fat and gout-ridden as he crept into his middle age, but if anything, as his body degenerated, its desires increased as if, by feeding them, he could somehow delay his inevitable demise. There were plenty amongst his retinue who were more than happy to encourage his pleasures in order to satisfy their own. Screams echoed up from the dungeons where new tortures were devised to be carried out on local thieves and petty criminals.

Lithe young women, and sometimes older ones, roamed naked between the castle's bedrooms, herded in from the surrounding towns and villages and drugged with alcohol and herbal liquors brewed by the Boyar's apothecaries. If they were lucky, their moans of pleasure did not turn to howls of pain.

For the others, once they had fallen still and silent with relief, their deaths ensuring their ordeals were truly over, Arkady was always there with his bucket and hard wooden scrubbing brush to clear the floors of warm blood and then fill the baths with sweet-smelling water for the knights and their leader to bathe in.

The Boyar learned to appreciate his silent manservant, and Arkady quickly became invaluable to him. Arkady cleaned up after his excesses without a raised eyebrow or even the slightest dilation of pupil at some of the sights that he found in front of him. The Boyar always watched carefully for any such reaction in all his men, and he found that even amongst those that shared his delights, there would occasionally be a small tremor or a flinch of shock at some physical experimentation the Boyar had tried. He was so used to this that Arkady's indifference was like a soothing balm. He did not have to wonder what Arkady might be thinking, because he had a curious feeling that Arkady did not spend any time at all thinking about the Boyar's unusual habits, and coupled with the boy's inability to speak, this made him completely reliable.

Arkady was soon moved to the small bedroom annexed to the Boyar's by a discreetly hidden door in the rich wood-panelled walls. It was a vast improvement on his tiny room at the back of the bakery, but the luxuriously sewn silk bed coverings and the roaring fire in the grate failed to impress Arkady. The fire was not that different from the warmth of the bread ovens, and a bed was simply a bed. That was the truth of it. Sometimes, as he pulled the puzzle box free from beneath his soft pillow and emptied the pieces out, seeking distraction from the sounds in the room next door, he wondered if maybe he saw the truth of too many things. The Boyar himself was one such example.

Did the old man even know that his depravities had slowly become more extreme since Arkady had been in his employ? Probably not. But Arkady, despite his youth, could see it clearly, and also the way the fat lord would look at him when he came in to clean up. He would feel those piggy eyes bore into him, seeking out some kind of reaction. It was simple. The Boyar wanted to shock Arkady. Despite enjoying the freedom from guilt the boy's indifference gave him, his need to feel powerful made him want Arkady to be affected by his deeds. And that was the truth of it.

It was only in the delicately carved tiles that the truth evaded him. They remained simply a wonder; a vague promise of hope, of change, of some kind of new life.

* * *

He was absorbed in them on the evening that the Boyar burst into his small room, his robes covered with blood, the glint of relieved madness fading from him as the monster left and the man returned.

"Arkady, I fear that you may need assistance..." He paused, his eyes snagging on the box and its contents as Arkady tried to hide them away.

"Give that to me." The Boyar held out his bloody hand and Arkady found himself passing over his treasured box.

The Boyar stared at it, and then frowned before sitting slowly down on the edge of Arkady's bed. "Ekaterina." His finger did as Arkady's childish one had so many years before, and traced out the shape of the word. "The beautiful Ekaterina."

He looked up, as if seeing Arkady for the first time. "I remember her. She was different to the rest." One hand waved dismissively towards the door of his bedchamber and the bloody remains of whoever had been unlucky enough to find themselves called in for company that night. "She was… special."

He opened the box, tipping its contents onto the bedclothes, turning each tile over in his fat hands and almost absently placing it next to the one before. "Was she your mother, Arkady?" He didn't look up. "Of course she was. I should have known. A boy with no tongue from the villages. It had to be you." He shook his head, a soft smile stretching his bloated, too-red cheeks. "Why I did not think about it, I do not know. Too easily distracted, I suppose."

The Boyar let out a long sigh and looked towards the small window. Despite its being covered with heavy drapes, he seemed to stare out to the stars beyond, the puzzle pieces forgotten.

"Your mother distracted me…" he started softly. "She was exquisite. They had washed the blood from her mouth when she was brought to me, but I could smell it on her."

Somewhere in the distance, Arkady heard the low peal of a church bell ringing out. The lamp against the wall flickered as if a gust of wind had caught it unawares and threatened its existence. For a moment his entire being stilled. Unlike the Boyar, Arkady had not forgotten the puzzle. This was it. The final confession. Something pounded in his chest and he realised that at last, his heart was alive.

"She enjoyed the pain," the Boyar continued, as if he couldn't hear the terrible chimes that were calling to them both. "Almost as much as I enjoyed hurting her." He frowned. "She had no limits. Until her, my tastes had been base, *ordinary*, but she forced me to new levels."

Arkady wasn't listening. Something was happening with the puzzle and it echoed deep in the core of him. The final tile had shivered into crimson, and with shaking hands, he formed them into their pattern, his heartbeat and the bell and the Boyar's confession rolling into one hum of excitement in his head.

It was complete. The puzzle was finished. The red lines burst into life, glowing as if made from some insane phosphorus. Arkady rose to his feet, and as the wall in front of them cracked and dissolved, the Boyar finally stopped speaking, his mouth dropping open in awe and wonder. Arkady did not look at him. He was no longer important. The pieces clicked, twisting sideways, each a tiny box of its own, and hooks flew out from each one, embedding in Arkady's soft skin. They dug into his flesh, warm blood trickling as they pulled and tore at him, tearing him exquisitely, releasing his true self so long trapped inside. It felt wonderful.

Arkady stared at the doorway that had been the wall, aware that beside him the Boyar had started to scream and jibber and shake. His fear felt good. Hooks found his mouth, and as they ripped it wider over his teeth and jaw, he watched the two figures emerge. Behind them, the darkness hummed with pain and confusion and he felt it tingle in his every cell.

"Have you found your tongue, Arkady, the Confessor?" The being was scarred on every inch of its damaged flesh, its strange clothing sewn through its skin, never to be removed. When it spoke, a scent of vanilla and putridness hung in the air. Arkady sucked it in, relishing it. His eyes widened as thick, black tongues erupted from his torn mouth as if tasting the creature's breath, rippling as they did so like the snakes of the Medusa's hair. More hooks embedded in the back of Arkady's skull, leaving his mouth wide open forever, home for the swirling mass of meat that filled it.

The Confessor. He rolled the words round in his mutilated mouth, letting all his tongues taste them. It felt right. It felt good.

"You are Cenobite. One of us."

If Arkady's jaw had not been stretched apart beyond limits, his torn bottom lip pulled over it, it would have dropped at the beauty of the second speaker. Its voice was a soft whisper and every inch of it appeared tattooed, jewelled pins driven into its skin and skull at regular intersections on the network of grids.

"We have been waiting for you."

Arkady's hellbound heart split with joy, and stepping forward, he happily left his humanity behind. He was going home.

The Boyar had crumpled to the ground, and the fat man's head shook as he cried and sobbed and begged for mercy.

The door in the wall was closing, and reaching down with his own bloody hand, Arkady pulled the lord forward, the weighty frame as light as a feather. The gloom embraced him and he thought he saw a flash of Ivan's smile somewhere in the shadows of the endless night. No matter. He would hear the Boyar's confession first, and if it didn't come easily, then he would force it. He had all of eternity to introduce the man to the possibilities of pain and pleasure.

And he would enjoy it.

THE OLD STORIES HIDE SECRETS DEEP INSIDE THEM

BY MARK CHADBOURN

L isten carefully.

The ancient tales are spells disguised as entertainment. At the heart of the maze of the telling lies enchanted gold, a hidden treasure that will transform with one curious glance. This is by design. For the crafters of those stories understood this simple and profound truth: only knowledge earned can change a person.

Truths offered easily are forgotten or ignored.

The virgin girl in a cloak the colour of menstruation who trips through the dark woods, pursued by a wolf, who is not really a wolf, but a lustful man who wants to corrupt. The virgin girl who is offered a poisoned apple by an elder woman jealous of her youth and beauty, a girl who must be woken from a sleep like death into the life of a woman. By a kiss. A kiss which is not a kiss, but an act of physical love.

Hildy always wondered why the old stories had so many lessons to teach virgin girls. Why no truths for virgin boys?

Why?

As she stood on the edge of the dig; lightning flickering behind the hills and wind whipping in from the north, these things troubled her for reasons she couldn't understand. In front of her, the confusion of trenches reached out into the gathering gloom. Whatever secrets were hidden there remained buried still.

"Another storm," Victoria said, the lightning dancing in her grey eyes. "You know it's bad when every night you dream about sitting in front of the fire."

Hildy looked up at the darkening sky. "This bad weather. It's slowing us down too much. Patience is wearing a bit thin."

They flashed each other a look. No need to name names.

Hildy liked Victoria. She had an enthusiasm that even the grim North Sea weather couldn't dispel. Blue hair, Hildy liked that too, and the nose ring, and the tattoo snaking out from under the cuff of her yellow windcheater. Victoria looked interesting, and was interesting. In contrast, Hildy had the bland, studious look of an academic who didn't give a damn how they appeared. She had only one thing in her favour, though it was a big thing admittedly: she was remarkably good at what she did, and that was digging up the past.

She was happy with that. There was a deep comfort in reaching your potential and knowing that you were in charge of your abilities.

They'd come to the Isle of Rousay in the Orkneys six weeks ago, a wind-blasted, rain-soaked heap of rock and grass adrift in the lonely expanse of turbulent slate-grey sea. Barely two hundred people made their home there. Hildy understood why. The moment she stepped off the ferry she could feel the loneliness sinking deep into her bones.

The rest of the university's archaeological team didn't seem to mind. The student volunteers and the technicians and the few wise old heads were buzzing with the prospect of a big history-making discovery, and a camping holiday with the usual laughs, drinking and occasional bouts of debauchery. Winter had seemed far away then. They were not so jubilant now the season had started to bite.

Hildy paced around the edges of the trenches, hearing Victoria squelch behind her. The whole expedition had started with a story. Victoria, who knew stories better than anyone, had stumbled across an account while immersed in completely unrelated research. Serendipity, that great lottery for seekers everywhere. Somewhere in the depths of the browning bones and the masks and the totems of the anthropology department she called home, Victoria turned up a misplaced document with some fragmentary folkloric tales from Svalbard. She liked to tell everyone she knew what she had when she saw it, but it was intuition really. Victoria told Hildy never to mistrust that.

On their nights huddled around a beer-washed pub table, she'd often gush the same thing; different words each time, but it was clearly a guiding light for her. "Folklore and myths and legends aren't flights of fancy. They're built around truths. Lessons to be learned. Because if information is embedded in a story the brain recalls it. They were smart those ancients. Smarter than us."

And the story? It was a blood and thunder yarn about a Viking warrior, a witch and a curse. Who couldn't fall for that?

"Doctor Rose?" The student dragged her way out of the trench, smeared with mud like some grave-revenant. She shook her head.

"Nothing?"

Hildy felt her heart sink. When she glanced at Victoria, her friend only said, "It's here. I know it is."

Nothing about this place made sense. That story had identified the windswept grassland on the edge of the sea as the location of a ship-burial and the last resting place of the blood-drenched warrior king Ulf the Red. Though it had been a long-shot, one that Hildy had fought hard for in the funding committee, the ground-penetrating radar seemed to confirm it. Everyone had been excited to see the ghost appear out of the black on the screen.

But when the digger ripped off the protective layer of turf and they dug down with their trowels, nothing emerged. Not even the fading sigh of a ghost. How could that be? The grave was in the data. The radar didn't lie. But all that lay in trench after trench was soil and stone and failure.

Almost as if what was buried there didn't want to be found.

Victoria hooked her arm through Hildy's and said, "Look, I know we've got a lot riding on this personally—"

"Do you think?" Hildy felt a pang of guilt for snapping back. Sometimes she hated herself for being so thin-skinned. But every day in the department was a fight and it had got worse the higher up she'd risen. Some people just didn't seem to like her. They wanted her to fail. After all the obstacles she'd clawed her way over to reach her position, all the patronising, the faint praise, the 'pranks', the taunting, the lies designed to undermine, the unearned contempt, the sneering dismissal, she wouldn't give them that opportunity. "I'm sorry," she said. "It's been a long few weeks, and I'm not sleeping… and that's all bollocks, isn't it? I'm just sorry."

Victoria gave her arm a comforting squeeze. "You need to unclench, beautiful. Come on, let's get you some of whatever slop they're serving up tonight. At least it'll be hot."

Leaning into each other, they trudged around the trenches towards the tents. A constellation of storm lamps flickered to life on all sides.

The spicy scent of that night's stew drifted out of the golden glow inside the mess tent, welcoming after the hardship of a day hunched over in mud and rainwater. The canvas billowed and the lines cracked in the gusting wind.

Once Hildy stepped through the open flaps, she saw only two people were seated at the trestle table, mugs of tea steaming in front of them. Their raucous laughter drained away when they saw Hildy and Victoria, replaced by an uncomfortable silence. Dr Simon Lazar hooked his head to one side and flashed her a sly glance. His smile died on his lips. Ben Carpenter jumped to his feet and beckoned them over. He was younger than Lazar, good looking in that slightly scrubbed way of many academics. He'd been working on his doctorate for what seemed like an age, and Hildy had found herself growing quite close to him as she mentored. She'd started to feel he was the only spark of decency in that whole department.

Ben grabbed two more mugs of tea and Hildy and Victoria slipped on to the bench opposite them.

"How's it going, Hildegarde?" Lazar said.

Hildegarde. He never called her Hildy, rarely even dignified her with Doctor Rose. "Nothing to report," she said with a smile that was supposed to show she wasn't concerned.

"People are starting to worry this is all money down the drain."

"People?"

"You know. The Prof."

Professor Enson Grieve, the department's self-appointed king. A lifetime of published papers and as much impact on the world of academia as a leaf drifting onto a mill pond. Still, he held himself in high regard and that was probably enough for him.

"He's coming in today," Lazar added.

"Today? Why?"

"Wants to see the site with his own eyes. You know, make an assessment."

Decide whether he's going to shut it down. Hildy felt queasy. Easy to see how that would go. Grieve was the kind of man for whom no grudge was too small. He wouldn't have forgotten that she was getting the research grant that he thought had been guaranteed for him. But he had the power here, as sickening as that was.

"I'm sure Professor Grieve will listen to reason." Hildy felt worried her smile was becoming fixed and she didn't want Lazar seeing her true feelings. He was, after all, Grieve's *protégé* and, no doubt, spy within the camp.

"Of course he will," Lazar replied with a grin.

Ben leaned across the table. "But what if the grave isn't here? We always knew the evidence was thin."

Ship burials, where a ship was dragged onto the land and used as a tomb, were rare in this part of the world. There was only one Viking burial recorded on mainland Britain, though a boat burial had been uncovered on the nearby island of Sanday. That one contained the remains of a man, an old woman and a child along with various grave goods. One found here on Rousay would be a career-making discovery for any archaeologist. The island already had lots of finds to its name, including a Viking drinking hall, so Victoria's claim wasn't beyond the bounds of possibility.

"Ben's right," Lazar said. "All we've really got is a bit of local hearsay and an old story. The radar is clearly flawed. It's just a story, Doctor Clements."

Hildy sensed Victoria bristle beside her.

"Just a story. Don't talk bollocks, Doctor Lazar."

Lazar smiled. Nothing seemed to ruffle him. "Try to convince me. One more time."

Victoria stared down her nose at the academic. Hildy knew that look. The smile was meant to soften it, but the coldness in those eyes suggested Victoria was thinking about snapping his spine. "I'll try to make it really simple so this time you'll remember it."

Lazar winked at Ben.

"The story is about the great Viking warrior king, Ulf the Red. You'd have liked him. He was a manly man. It was said he could split an enemy in two with his axe. He claimed to have personally killed two thousand foes, you know, as men do. Ulf means wolf."

"I like him already."

"But the story isn't really about Ulf. It's about Hilda, the fighter."

"Hilda. That's nearly like your name," Ben chipped in.

"Maybe that's why you became so obsessed," Lazar said.

"Yes. That's why," Hildy replied. She wasn't going to rise to the bait of all that lay behind that line.

"Hilda was a volva," Victoria continued. "That means wand-wed, or staff carrier. All the leaders of the clans had them. Wise women, filled with knowledge and power who could guide them with prophecies and the whispers of the spirits."

"A witch," Lazar said.

"A witch," Victoria replied. "They practised seidr. That means to bind. Are you keeping up? The volva have been around for three thousand years, perhaps even longer. They wore colourful dresses and a hat and gloves made of cat fur—"

"Stylish."

"They could leave their own bodies and enter into an animal if they wanted to travel. A raven, say. Or an owl. Which, incidentally, is also attributed to shamans and witches all over the world, in completely unconnected cultures. So maybe it's true."

"If you believe there's any truth in stories."

Hildy looked from Victoria to Lazar, those fixed smiles, a patina of politeness, those hard, almost murderous stares. They were like competing species, waiting for an opening to strike and claim ascendency.

"A volva didn't usually live very long. All that passing between worlds took a terrible toll. But usually they'd be murdered because those leaders didn't like their prophecies. Men, eh? Always needing lies to keep their egos intact, right across the centuries."

"Well. Somebody has a chip on their shoulder." Lazar glanced at Ben and laughed. "Did some boy say you were fat at school?"

Hildy reached under the table to fold restraining fingers around Victoria's wrist. She didn't need to. Victoria was in control.

"And that's what happened with Hilda." Victoria didn't miss a beat. "Hilda had suggested that one of Ulf's raids wouldn't turn out as planned. This never happened. He always came back victorious. Simmering, Ulf decided to punish her for this. He was going to take Hilda on the raid with him and he would slit her throat in front of his men... to prove his virility, I suppose? I can't really get into that mindset. Perhaps as some kind of sacrifice to ensure a successful outcome for his endeavour? Whatevs. The spirits told Hilda what was going to happen and she made preparations to protect herself."

Victoria rested her elbows on the table and leaned forward. For the first time Hildy saw a flicker of unease in Lazar's face, as if he was unused to being challenged in such a way.

"Hilda prepared a spell in a charm she was going to give to Ulf. A curse, I suppose. The spell was known as 'You Will Do No Good'. It would have taken away his blood lust. His potency." Victoria shrugged. "His ability to maintain an erection."

Lazar drained the last of his tea, hiding behind his mug.

"Only it didn't work," Victoria continued, sitting back. "Hilda was betrayed by someone close to her. Ulf learned of the curse and turned it back on her. She was the one who was unpowered."

"So the big brute won." Lazar clattered his mug back on the table.

"That depends on how you define 'win'. Ulf slit Hilda's throat in front of his men. But his raid was a failure as Hilda had prophesied. Ulf died in battle, as did many of his men. Those who survived gave him the send-off he deserved, leaving him in his ship-tomb here in Rousay. And we know it was here because the story has descriptions of his journey and the islands around. Ulf was put to rest. With Hilda lying beneath his feet, to show his dominance over her for all time."

"Wow. That's a great story," Ben said.

"It is indeed," Lazar added. This time his eyes flickered to Hildy. "But everything we're doing here is based on your premise that those descriptions of the voyage were an actual account and not just colour for a fireside yarn to keep the kids occupied on stormy nights. We're not even sure Ulf and Hilda actually existed, that's the real truth, isn't it? And all the funding committed on this dig and all the time and effort of the volunteers was just a reckless gamble that your simple premise was right. I mean, all power to you. You somehow convinced the funding committee you knew what you were talking about. Possibilities are great until they hit reality, and that's out there in those empty trenches. There's not even the slightest hint of a ship burial—"

"Apart from the radar," Hildy said.

"Apart from the glitching radar. In fact, there's no evidence of anything at all. Nothing. It's just been a big, epic, time and cash suck." Lazar held out his hands. "Don't get me wrong. I don't take any joy in this. I know what it's going to mean for you personally. For your career. It's going to be hard to come back from that."

Hildy could see right through his words to the black heart of him. Of course he took joy in it. He was a rival. He hated her achievements, that she was getting more attention than he was. That she was going somewhere, purely because of her own abilities, not because she'd licked the arse of somebody higher up.

"I'm not done yet," she said.

Lazar only smiled and nodded.

* * *

Black clouds churned across the moon and stars, and the rain lashed the grassland. Hildy looked out across the dig, the storm lantern in her hand swinging in the gale so that the shadows swooped and fed. Where had she gone wrong? The pattern of trenches followed the data from the radar exactly. She didn't believe the radar could have failed in such a way – it never had before. Something else was at play here.

The storm drowned out the sound of the footsteps tramping at her back until they were almost upon her, and she whirled. Ben's face flared in the lamplight, a startled look as if he thought she was going to attack him. His expression settled quickly into the familiar lazy grin, but this time it was tinged with pity. She hated to see that.

"Don't let Doctor Lazar get to you," he boomed above the storm.

"I'm not. I know it's here somewhere. I just have to crack it."

"I have faith in you." Ben surprised her by reaching out and giving her free hand a comforting squeeze. At any other time, she'd have smiled and pulled away, but he'd caught her at a low ebb. A little warmth, some words of support, that's what she yearned for right then.

For a moment, he hesitated and then he leaned in and kissed her. She let him, enjoying the touch of his lips on hers.

When he broke the embrace, she saw lights carving through the dark and her heart sank. A car rumbled along the sole road circling the island from the direction of the ferry.

"He's here," she shouted.

They watched as the beat-up Peugeot turned off the road and fishtailed onto the muddy track into the field. It juddered to a halt beside the rows of billowing tents and Professor Grieve lumbered out of the passenger side. The car reversed with a spinning of wheels and a spray of mud and sped away.

Hildy hurried to meet him. Grieve was a big man, his belly straining against his windcheater. The hood was pulled tightly around his pink face and the lamplight glimmered in his rain-streaked glasses.

"Let me get you somewhere dry," Hildy said.

"Show me the dig." Grieve held her gaze for a moment and then pushed ahead of her to where he knew the trenches would be. Ben had slipped away by the time they reached the excavation and they stood together peering into the dark.

"Nothing?" Grieve asked.

"Not yet—"

"Nothing at all?" He didn't wait for Hildy to answer. "We'll break up the camp tomorrow. At least we might be able to salvage a little funding before you piss it all away."

And then he span towards the tents without another word. Hildy waited a moment, feeling the bitterness rise inside her, and then she followed.

* * *

Her sleep was restless. She dreamed of a woman with hair like gold and emerald eyes that gleamed, her dress the colour of a spring leaf, waving a wand of silver in her left hand. She leant over Hildy and said, "You are filled with light."

When Hildy woke before dawn with Ben still snoring beside her, she felt infused with a new hope. Wearing nothing more than her wellingtons and a wind-cheater, she plunged out into the fading dark and hurried towards the dig. The storm had blown itself out while she slept and there was a refreshing charge to the cold air.

Victoria staggered beside her, bleary-eyed. "I thought I heard you getting up, you mad woman. What's wrong?"

Hildy peered at the landscape creeping out of the gloom. "I don't know. I had a dream…" She bit off the words before she sounded too stupid. "There's something I'm missing, I'm sure of it."

"I thought Grieve had already taken the decision to pack up."

"He has. What does he know."

Hildy's attention drifted across the rolling hummocks to the area where the radar had shown there was rock just beneath the scrubby grass. In the thin grey light, shadows crept along faint indentations that would have been invisible to the naked eye during full daylight. "There's something there," she said.

Victoria followed her gaze. "We discarded that—" She bit her lip. "Okay. I trust my instinct so I'll trust yours. Tell me more."

Hildy felt her mind moving like quicksilver, as it always did when she was fired up, and then she had it. "If you transpose the radar information onto that section, it aligns with those patterns on the turf. Can you see them? They're so faint."

"I can see them."

"I don't know why that would be. There's no logic to it—"

"I've seen some weird things in my time, Hildy, drinking

ayahuasca with shamans out in South America. It stopped me questioning things that at first don't seem to make sense."

"Okay." Hildy reflected for a moment, then she felt a rush of exhilaration. "Let's do it."

* * *

Now the wind had fallen and the island was still, the clank of trowels on stones chimed like a symphony. Hildy watched the volunteers at work, holding herself so rigid she barely breathed. She'd whipped them out of their tents and set them to the task before breakfast to get a head start.

"What's going on here?" Grieve was scowling as he walked up from the camp with Lazar and Ben. "I told you we were closing the dig down."

"One more thing to try."

"That's outrageous—"

A cry from the other side of the dig cut off whatever the professor was planning to say next. Hildy hurried around to the volunteer who was pointing with her trowel at some encrusted object in the soil.

Hildy cupped her hands to her mouth and shouted, "We've got something!"

But when she looked across the bobbing bodies of the diggers, she didn't see any jubilation or relief in the faces of Grieve and Lazar. They looked almost angry.

* * *

Over the days the outline of the ship emerged from the earth like the rising sun burning through the morning mist. Finally, in the late afternoon, Hildy and Victoria stood on the edge of the pit and studied what they'd found.

"You were right," Hildy said, wagging a finger at the skeleton of the man and the second set of bones curled beneath its feet. "It's Ulf and Hilda."

"*You* were right. It was your call."

Ben wandered around the other side of the pit, chatting to the volunteers, but Grieve and Lazar had spent most of the time sequestered in the mess tent. They seemed to have lost interest in what was the biggest find the department had ever had.

"Not just a warrior king, but a volva too," Hildy said. She thought back on the other finds that emerged from around Hilda's remains, the silver toe rings, a gold-plated box brooch containing the residue of what Victoria had suggested was white lead, a poisonous powder, a purse containing henbane seeds, owl pellets and animal bones, a glorious silver wand. And there too was what Victoria had insisted was the curse-charm, a round metal frame smaller than the palm of her hand with owl-bones still fastened to it by twists of wire.

"How do you feel?" Victoria asked.

Hildy smiled. "Queen of the world."

* * *

The words wouldn't come. Hildy frowned as she stared at the screen of her laptop. She'd never had this trouble before but she'd been trying to put her report for the department together there in the mess tent for three hours now.

"You're tired. You've just been under a lot of stress," Victoria comforted when Hildy told her. But it felt worse than that. Her head seemed to be filled with fog. She'd read a sentence and half the time she couldn't even remember what some of the words meant.

Grieve was on her back constantly, insisting she send the report back immediately to release the last tranche of funding. Otherwise they'd have to close everything up. Hildy knew exactly what was at stake. She still couldn't finish that report.

The next morning she set off on a walk to try and get her head in the right place. She trudged across the grassy slopes, following streams until she reached the high land, and then she sat and looked out across the churning seat to the clouds gathering on the horizon. Another storm was coming.

Convinced she'd done what she needed to do to clear her head, she pressed back down the slope towards the camp. But as the hours dragged on, she found herself wandering across unfamiliar pastures and the tents never materialised. Increasingly exhausted, she stumbled on until the dark came down hard and she couldn't see her hand in front of her face.

And then she started to cry. She had no idea why. She hadn't cried like that in a long time. But that was how the search party found her, sobbing like a lost child as the torchlight played across her face.

In the camp, she heard laughter as they brought her back in, sodden and dejected. Victoria was waiting, her face filled with concern, perhaps even that pity Hildy hated. Before they could talk, Grieve stormed up, with Lazar scurrying behind him.

Once they were back in the tent, the professor roared, "What is wrong with you?"

"I got lost," Hildy stuttered.

"And why in heaven's name were you going out for a stroll when you have things to do here?"

Hildy tried to explain, but the words tumbled over each other, and she realised she was rambling as she watched the contempt grow in Grieve's face.

"You haven't finished the report," he said, "and now we're in danger of losing everything."

"It's worse than that," Lazar chipped in. "Some of the finds are missing. You didn't record them properly. They're likely out on the spoil heap."

"That is the most unprofessional work I've ever encountered," Grieve snapped.

"I-I did record them…" Hildy stuttered. She wasn't even convincing herself.

"I'm going to write the report myself," the professor said. "We can't wait for you to get over your moods."

"Leave her alone." Victoria thrust herself in front of the two men. "We'll sort all this out in the morning."

She took Hildy's arm and guided her out into the storm,

across the camp to her tent. In the dry, they squatted on the sleeping bag. Hildy stared blankly at the wavering light of the storm-lantern.

"What is it, beautiful?" Victoria breathed.

Hildy began to sob again. "I don't know what's wrong with me." She flopped back and her head bounced on her rucksack. She felt something sharp dig into her neck.

Puzzled, she delved into the depths of the waterproofs and warm clothes and felt her fingers close around something metallic. When she tugged it out, the charm from the ship burial emerged into the light.

Hildy stared at it for a long moment, trying to understand. "I didn't put this here," she began. "I'm sure of it. I stuck it in the finds box."

Silence followed her words and when she looked round, Victoria was staring at the charm. She made to speak, but only one word came out: "Fuck."

* * *

"What have you done to me?"

Hildy stormed into the mess tent, her rage burning so brightly she could barely see. She couldn't control herself at all, it seemed, her emotions swinging wildly. Victoria had tried to restrain her, but Hildy threw her off, consumed with the desire to confront her tormentors.

From the trestle, Grieve and Lazar looked up at her with incredulity. "What has come over you?" the professor said.

"This." Hildy tossed the charm from the ship-burial onto the table.

"Steady!" Lazar jumped to his feet, cupping his hands around the delicate find. "Good Lord!"

"You cursed me. With that," Hildy shouted.

"Cursed you? Are you insane?" Grieve pushed himself to his feet.

"'You Will Do No Good'," Hildy almost shrieked. "'You Will Do No Good'. It's eating its way through my mind. It's stealing who I am!"

Grieve stared at her with contempt and then said, "The strain's got too much for you. You're having a breakdown. Go back to your tent. We'll get you to a doctor as soon as we can." He turned to Lazar. "This is just what I feared."

The anger flooded away for no reason Hildy could tell and she felt the tears boiling up again. Before she embarrassed herself any further, she flew out of the mess tent and into the night.

Somehow she found her way back to her billet. Victoria was waiting for her. Her friend hugged her tightly, desperately, and then she said, "I've seen Grieve's report. He's claiming credit for your find. Saying he supported you all the way. You were ready to give up until he pressed you to shift your attention to where the grave was."

Hildy sagged. "I don't care any more. I don't care about anything. What is happening to me?"

Victoria rested her hands on Hildy's shoulders. "I've seen things like this before, in a couple of places. The Congo.

Mongolia. The curse is real, sweetheart. But it can be lifted. I'll find a way. I'm searching the archives online now."

"It's not all in my head?"

"It's not in your head."

"Thank you, thank you. You're a good friend." Hildy felt overwhelmed with a rush of gratitude.

"One more thing. I asked around the volunteers. Someone was seen poking around your tent earlier."

"Grieve?"

Victoria shook her head. "Ben."

"Ben? But why would he do this? He's not got any grudge against me?"

"It doesn't matter. Just stay in your tent. Let me sort this out and then we can sort Grieve out, that fucking little shit."

Victoria swept away into the storm. But Hildy felt her emotions seesawing again. She couldn't contain herself. She threw herself across the camp to Ben's tent and wrenched open the flaps. He was sitting cross-legged on his sleeping bag.

He jolted at the intrusion, but then that familiar smile crept back. "Hi."

Hildy felt rage again, then despair, then a pathetic self-loathing, but none of her emotions would settle. It was as if someone had her by the wrist and was dragging her through room after room in some crazed dance.

"You put the charm in my rucksack."

Ben seemed on the brink of denying it, but then came to some calculation and replied, "Yes."

"Why, Ben?" Her voice cracked.

He shrugged. "I don't know. I guess I just wanted to see you fail."

Hildy felt her jaw slacken with incomprehension and she knew she must have looked stupid because Ben was silently laughing at her expression. "Why?"

Ben stared into space for a moment, frowning, and then said, "Yeah, just seemed like something I wanted to do in the moment. You're always so good at things, you know. Always succeeding."

Hildy couldn't find the words, could barely comprehend what he was saying to her. She wanted to scream, "Why? That makes no sense! You ruined me, and for what? What do you gain?"

But it was pointless. Everything was pointless.

She pulled herself out through the entrance of the tent, watching Ben in that golden glow of the storm lamp, watching him smiling at her, watching him until the dark swallowed her. The thunder cracked and the lightning flashed and another storm raged in her head, one that swept away all reason, that blasted out whatever remained of Hildy, of her brilliance and her thoughts and her memories and her life. And then she was staggering away into the night, screaming until her throat was raw, until she was nothing more than one agonised howl.

But as the last cry died on her lips, she heard a voice, not in the night but in her head, a kind voice, a loving voice, a strong and powerful voice, and it said, "You were filled with light and you will be again."

* * *

Hildy looked up into Victoria's face. It took her a while to realise where she was; her thoughts seemed alien creatures crawling inside her head. But gradually she realised she was nestled in her friend's lap, smeared with mud. The dawn sky glowed silver behind Victoria's head.

"Don't worry," Victoria said. "I've thrown away the tea."

Hildy blinked.

Victoria chuckled silently. "Don't try to think it through, beautiful. It's early days. You'll be yourself soon enough."

She eased Hildy's head out of her lap and tugged her to her feet. Hildy looked round, bewildered, as Victoria took her by the hand and led her away from the dig, past the still slumbering camp, across the road and on to the stony beach.

Three bodies sprawled on the slick black rocks ahead of the receding tide. Hildy recognised Grieve, Lazar and Ben.

"Why anyone would go swimming during a storm at night I'll never know," Victoria said. "I found henbane seeds in the tea they were drinking in the mess tent."

Hildy shook her head. "Henbane? You mean… what we found in the purse in the dig? They wouldn't be toxic after all these years, would they?"

"Probably not." Victoria shrugged. "I mean, don't ask me. I just dig up old curses for a living." She paused. "Did you go back to the mess tent last night?"

"I don't know. I can't remember what I did. Can't remember anything at all."

Victoria nodded. "Of course. This is a terrible tragedy and nobody would have wished it on them. But one thing I can say with utter conviction: people who mess with wise women get their fingers burned."

"Shouldn't we call the emergency services?"

"Yeah. But. Not much of an emergency, is it? Why don't we just sit here and watch the sun come up?"

Hildy sank down onto the stones at the edge of the beach and Victoria slipped an arm around her shoulders. The waves crashed in cascades of white and the gulls wheeled across the sky, shrieking.

AWAKE

BY LAURA PURCELL

Sleep was not the curse. It was only the beginning.

Waking up was meant to be my happy ending. It was meant to be a second chance. But when they pulled me out of that coffin, I rose to a living death.

The guards stare straight ahead as I sweep down the corridor, ermine skirts whispering at my heels. A ghost of a smile touches their stern lips. They see my beauty, their kingdom put to rights by my marriage, and that is all.

No one else glances at the chequered tiles and sees the long, scorched trail of burning footsteps. This sight is reserved for me alone.

My shoes clip steadily; a truer, stronger beat than my pulse. A princess must push on, whatever the horrors of her mind. Duty, always. The people require a calm exterior, a face as impassive and serene as the one displayed in my glass coffin.

"The Queen!" Halberds are crossed over the doorway to the great hall, but at the sight of me the guards part their arms. "Make way for the Queen."

I battle an instinct to flinch. They are not referring to my mother now; I have taken her title. I am She.

The door creaks open and I sail through. The path of blackened footsteps continues over the threshold, unchecked by our human barriers.

Tearing my eyes away from the tracks, I survey the great hall. A fire roars beneath the mantelpiece, just as it did that night. Long windows look out onto frosted grounds. The cold has made patterns on the glass, like breath steaming the panes. As though there were something invisible out there, panting for admittance.

All the peers stand when I enter. Before them is a feast of chicken, goose, peacock and swan; all the birds that may be snared in a net.

A footman pulls out a velvet chair for me and I take it with a smile. "Forgive me. I am late."

My husband beams indulgently from the head of the table, all glossy black hair and gleaming epaulettes. "But worth waiting for."

His companions take their chairs once more, place their napkins onto their laps, watching me. I am the only lady present. Even if there were dozens, every eye would still be trained on my face. I do not say this with vanity, it gives me no pleasure. Beauty makes my charade more difficult. Not a moment passes unobserved, in which I might fail.

We begin to eat.

I never realised before how revolting our human rituals

are, how primal it is to tear flesh with our teeth. Grease shines on the duke's plump fingertips. The earl bites into a piece of chicken skin, bubbled and crisp from the oven.

My stomach turns.

Mother's feet blistered that way in the red-hot shoes. It is an image, a *smell* I never shall erase. She danced. Oh, how she danced in her clogs of iron. She is dancing, still.

"Fine fowl, this year," the duke comments through a mouthful. "Plumper than ever they were before."

"Such wonderful seasoning!" The earl picks at a bone.

My husband smiles his handsome smile. "The kingdom heals. Even nature is restored." His fond glance drifts to me. "I see my queen favours the roast partridge. I must try some myself."

I favour nothing, with the taste of apple always on my tongue, tart and sharp as a snakebite. But I tell him the partridge is delicious and signal for the servant to place some on his plate.

A wing hits the porcelain with a moist slap.

"It is the new queen who brings us fortune." This from a baronet, red wine staining the corners of his mouth. "She is spotless, pure, as pale as the moon." He clears his throat self-importantly. "I have composed a poem in her honour."

Another one.

Of course they all want to hear it. Of course I assemble my most gracious, flattered expression and press a hand to my chest. If I could blush, I would do so, but blood no longer rises to stain my cheeks.

"You are too kind."

Again I hear of the beauty which drove my mother mad. They speak of my burden as though it were a blessing to be greatly desired. There are verses on my white, translucent skin, my unusually dark lips. The baronet does not understand what these signs foretell.

My husband takes my hand and presses it. "The queen is a jewel."

"A jewel," the others toast.

A corpse, I think. *A corpse.*

We return to our plates, where the meat has cooled. It does not matter. Whatever I eat it is apples, apples.

Partridge squelches in my husband's mouth. I picture my mother, greedily devouring the meal she thought was my lungs and liver. It made no difference, in the end, that we tricked her back then. The huntsman ought to have known that Mother's wishes were always granted.

She wanted me dead. I am certainly not alive.

* * *

The silver-backed brush flashes, shooting stars through the ebony night of my hair. He insists on a hundred strokes before bed; it is his pleasure to perform the task. His hands are gentle yet deft. I see his reflection in the glass, the pride on his face, the dawn of his arousal.

Could I have loved this man, were it not for the shadow between us?

The candlelight dips. Our eyes meet in the mirror. At least, that is what he must see: my own eyes, wide and frightened as they always were. I am forgetting their true colour.

"Why did you choose shoes?"

His expression flickers. "I beg your pardon?"

"For the evil queen's punishment? What made you think of the hot iron shoes?"

"Ah." He comprehends, now, and his chest swells with pride at the memory. "Did you not understand? It was a fitting end for a vain woman. She wanted to be the belle of the ball, the lady every man watched, and I granted her that wish. Fine gowns and shoes were her delight. I let her own apparel stand in judgement upon her."

There is a poetry to his justice I cannot deny. I wish that it had worked. My husband thinks he avenged me, and I allow him to go on believing, as if somehow that could make it true.

"Was it wrong?" he asks humbly. "Do you think me too cruel?"

I am honest. "Nothing was too cruel for her."

He nods and returns to his strokes. They say he kept my coffin with him always: while he ate, while he slept. I wonder if he ran his fingers through my dry, dead locks.

I must keep talking – at least it is still *my* voice. "She tried to kill me with a brush, once. I suppose it was more of a comb. I still feel the poison, leeching deep into my scalp with the teeth."

He is appalled. His face drops, the brush falls slack in his hand. "I had no idea. I thought it was only the apple."

There are things I should never tell, things I can never forget.

No one wants to hear of a princess' pain. She is to dismiss the past and live happily ever after.

He keeps watching me in the glass. The spark of desire has been snuffed like a candle flame, replaced with shock and pity.

"It was not only the apple," I say, by way of brevity.

He places the brush on the dressing-table, turns me around and kisses my forehead. It is better to see him as he truly is, instead of reversed.

"You have been through such great hardship, my love, but you are safe now. I shall let you rest."

He is the perfect prince, the perfect king, he wants the perfect queen. I smile as if I am the doll he bought and there is not something rotten lurking at the core of me.

"Then I will wish you good night."

He bends in a practiced, courtly bow. His cloak swings as he turns, creating a draught that sets the candle wavering. I swivel back to the glass, stare deep into the hectic, flashing image, hoping to find myself. This is no magic mirror. Yet when I look into it, or any other in this castle, I see only her wicked face.

* * *

It is always the same dream.

Warlocks and wise-men used to visit Mother and instruct her in the dark arts. Although I was never permitted near them, I used to hear their voices, bouncing off the stone walls and travelling down to the damp bowels of the castle where I was kept. One man articulated more clearly than all the rest.

He spoke as if each sentence were a summons from another realm. "Every dream," he said, "has its stem in a memory. Good or bad, whatever we see behind our closed eyelids was already there, inside."

The dream that haunts me night by night is no exception. The events really did take place.

It goes like this. Sunlight blazes into the cottage. Birds twitter through the open window and the air is flavoured with the scent of baking pastry. A woman crosses the threshold, her shadow stretching before her. She is my mother, though she wears another's face.

Laces dangle from her gnarly fingers, each string as lurid and tempting as a venomous snake. I never see the trade take place, never hear the chink of coin. In the blink of an eye the lace is threaded through my bodice and the woman is pulling tight, tight.

I see myself turning blue. Empty lungs burn inside my chest. Yet I can also sense the laces taut in my hands, silk squeezing blood from my fingers as the girl bucks and writhes beneath me.

I do not know if it is her memory or my own.

The image melts, as it always does, into the present day. Still I cannot breathe. I am laid beneath the canopy of my sumptuous royal bed, a swan-down coverlet pulled up to my chin.

Mother is sitting on my chest.

The weight of her is unbearable. My ribs seem to crack and cave in. The same hands that pulled the laces worm beneath the coverlet to seize my throat and choke what is left of me away.

121

She leans in, close, her breath warm against my cheek. It tastes of rotten apples.

Darkness begins to draw in. I would welcome its release. More than anything I want to return to the coffin of silver glass where I rested, finally at peace. But, of course, I start awake.

There is no sweat on my skin, no pounding of my heart and I do not pant for breath. My body is still a corpse, untouched by my emotion.

I left the candle on the dressing-table. It has dwindled to a stub drowning in its own wax, but it burns valiant, still. A flicker refuses to die. I take courage from its light.

Struggling out of bed, I make my way to the dressing-table stool. Her image rises once more from the depths of the glass. This time, I will strike back.

I grip the silver-backed brush and smash it into the mirror. Fractures spread in a spider-web. The last thing I see before she shatters into a million pieces is her wicked, wicked smile.

A glass shard sparkles in the candlelight. I drive it deep into my cheek. The pain is dulled but still there, making me gasp as though it were pleasure. Again. Skin catches as I drag the point heavily across my forehead. The blood that wells up is as warm and red as any mortal's.

At last I feel. The panic and the horror are sweet.

This is what she wanted all along, what I should have done years ago. It was not really my heart and lungs that Mother wanted, but my face.

Blood loss makes me giddy. A roaring fills my ears and dark spots threaten my vision. I lie back on the bed and watch apple-red bloom across the white sheets. Her poison is finally spurting out, she is trickling away.

I close my eyes, luxuriate in my warm, crimson, coppery bath. At last, I think I shall sleep without dreams.

* * *

Daylight plays across my closed eyelids. I hear sounds of the forest and for one delightful moment I think myself back at the cottage with the miners. Maybe that was heaven after all – or as close to it as I shall ever draw.

But then there is a jolt. The same jolt as when the prince's servants dropped my coffin and dislodged the apple from my throat. I start awake.

Blood has dried in rusty stains across my nightgown. When I shift, I leave a russet imprint of myself on the bed. There is no pain, now. Not until I raise a hand and cup it around my cheek.

The skin does not hurt; rather, the pain comes from deep down within me. A shriek somewhere at the bottom of a well. For my face is smooth: soft, cold and untouched.

Shambling out of bed, I pass to the mirror and of course it is flawless. Both the glass and my flesh have been magically repaired. My mouth hangs open as I drop onto the stool to see her smiling still.

"Why won't you die?" I hiss.

Then I remember she whispered this to me.

We are bound together, always. My mother formed me from a simple wish upon blood and snow. We shared a body as I grew and now… now it is my turn to carry the burden of her.

* * *

I walk up on the battlements. This is a fight I shall never win, but it feels better to be out in the air, away from my husband, away from mirrors.

The kingdom stretches out golden and green before me, a land of hills and tall pine. Somewhere to the east it joins with the country in which I was born. There is peace, at least for the people, and that is no small feat. My suffering serves some purpose.

We all thought the apple was meant to kill me. I know better now. Her dark power was deeper and more cunning than even I imagined. The white half for her, the red half for me. She made the apple so she could live.

The wind is a distant cackle in my ears. As it sweeps up my hair and fans it behind my back, I turn to the north where they say there is another princess who sleeps. Time does not touch her. Years pass but she remains the same, forever captured in the moment she pricked her finger and fell into an enchanted slumber.

Someone must have loathed her as thoroughly as my mother hated me. I should feel a connection with this princess, but all I have left in my heart is envy for her.

The leaves on the trees below me will drop and fall. These battlements, already hazed with moss, will gradually crumble away. My husband will die, cobwebs will form and everything will decay.

In the end, who will be left apart from me and this other, deathless princess?

She may sleep comfortably on.

But I am awake, chained to the wickedest woman of all, and there shall be no rest for me.

PRETTY MAIDS ALL IN A ROW

BY CHRISTINA HENRY

Maura's left eye was gone.

"Oh, no," Terry said, dropping the mail. She took Maura's face in her hands. Terry's hands were liver-spotted, the blue veins under the skin protruding. "Oh, no, what happened to you?"

Maura didn't respond. Her right eye – frozen, shiny, gleaming with some secret sorrow – stared back at Terry. Her mouth, a faded pink Cupid's bow, was parted slightly as if Maura were about to speak. No words came out. Maura couldn't explain this catastrophe.

Terry released Maura's face, brushed her fingers over Maura's lace dress and scanned around for the missing eye. She had to find it. Maura was the first line of defense, Terry's best soldier.

Terry shuffled forward, her shoulders hunched inside her brown cardigan. Her slippered feet kicked the mail aside, heedless. She squinted at the ground. She'd left her other glasses in the kitchen, the distance ones, and the readers tucked in her cardigan pocket wouldn't do her any good. She'd taken the readers so she could look at the mail, but bills and junk didn't matter now. Putting Maura back together was the only thing that mattered.

If Maura can't look out for me then all my soldiers might fall, and then what?

Terry clutched at the pendant she always wore, day or night. It was a small silver molded hand and wrist, the second and last finger forked while the other fingers folded in – the sign against the evil eye. Harold had given it to Terry years ago, warning her to never take it off. She never had – not when she slept, not when she showered. She knew what would happen if she did.

It had been the least Harold could do, really, considering he was the reason she was in this fix in the first place. The vengeful spirits should have dissipated when he died. He was the one they'd wanted. But apparently such spirits believed that guilt rubbed off on those in proximity to the guilty. Not that Terry was completely sure that Harold had done all those terrible things, never mind what the news said. Everyone knew those TV anchors lied. He'd always been so sweet to her, the best husband in the world.

Terry's foot nudged a stack of bundled papers under Maura's chair. Something gleamed there – was it the precious glass she was looking for? She bent her knees, just a little, because there was always the terrifying possibility that if she knelt on the floor she wouldn't be able to get up again. In the last few years her body had started to break down, break off, an old car rusting bit by bit. It was humiliating to rely on other people to help her, to feel that she couldn't manage things on her own.

Worst of all was the nagging sense that her son and her two granddaughters thought that her *brain* was rusting too, that she was "confused" or "mixed up". Terry hated the way they spoke to her like she was a child who didn't comprehend language. Well, Jessie didn't, not all the time. But still. There was nothing wrong with her mind.

The muffler might be scraping the ground but the engine is just fine, she thought. She did acknowledge, though, that she probably shouldn't have mentioned the spirits to her family. That had triggered some sideways glances they thought she hadn't seen. But they *would* keep asking her about her soldiers, as if it were anyone's business but hers what she kept in her own house.

They were all there, lined up on three shelves that ran along the hallway wall behind Maura's chair. Lots of porcelain dolls all in a row, mostly Madame Alexander dolls that Terry had kept for years and years. Tiny little porcelain faces with wide glass eyes fringed by long lashes, eyes that watched and warned. All her little girls, all her brave girls in their dresses, all her soldiers. All had their eyes turned toward the front door, the most dangerous potential breach.

There were some dolls in the kitchen, too, noses pointing toward the back door, and two at every window, perched on the sills. They stared out into the world, frightened the spirits away. Spirits feared clear sight, feared the gaze of the innocent, and Terry's soldiers all had that. But Maura was the best – she was the oldest, and the strongest. She'd been Terry's friend and companion all her life. Terry needed her.

Terry put a hand on Maura's chair as she lowered closer to the ground. The chair wasn't meant to hold much weight, not even Terry's own slight pressure. It was made of some lightweight wood and the seat was wicker weave, perfect for Maura but nobody else.

The chair wobbled a little as Terry hunched, scrabbling at the place where she'd seen that marble-like gleam. Her fingers groped around the newspapers, little puffs of dust following in their wake. Terry reached back further, sure that Maura's eye was just out of reach. A thin-legged spider scuttled over her hand, its touch lighter than air, and Terry whispered an apology for disturbing it.

The chair wobbled again, the feet scraping the floor as it shifted.

I should just go get my glasses from the kitchen, Terry thought. But it always took her so long to get from point A to point B, her arthritic knees only capable of shuffling steps, her already-once-broken hip stiff and unyielding. It would be faster just to reach, just to feel around until she found the eye.

Besides, she couldn't leave Maura with a blind spot for even a few moments. The spirits could sneak in that way. Once they'd breached the perimeter it would be harder for her to defend against them.

Harder, but not impossible. Harold had left her with a few other things besides the evil eye pendant. Again, the least he could do after leaving her behind to deal with this curse.

She bent her knees a little more, wished she was able to take ibuprofen for her arthritis pain. It wasn't good for her stomach, though, and the ice compresses that her doctor recommended were for the birds. They didn't do a thing, as far as Terry was concerned, except make her knees cold.

He'd also recommended that she try Tai Chi and she hadn't been able to control her eye roll. Terry was not going to stand in the middle of a public park with a bunch of old people and practice waving her arms very slowly.

She bent her knees a little more, her grip tightening on the edge of Maura's chair. Had she just felt the slip of glass under her fingertips? Maybe it had rolled behind the newspapers and gotten caught under the pages.

The chair shook. Terry felt her knees buckling beneath her. The wood seemed to disintegrate under her palm, a cracking thunderclap of doom. A splinter slid underneath her skin, pricking blood.

Terry saw Maura tip to the side, her white face falling in slow motion, the Cupid's bow mouth now hanging open in surprise. Terry's shoulder slammed into the floor and she cried out, but it wasn't her own pain that concerned her.

Maura crashed into the ground as Terry watched in horror. A web of cracks appeared in Maura's cheek. Her remaining eye rolled away.

"No," Terry moaned, reaching for Maura. "No, no. Don't worry. We can fix it. Don't worry."

Terry felt bile in the back of her throat, a curdling of saliva on her tongue. Something skittered over her face – no light-footed spider this time, but something that felt like a touch of draught.

Her skin iced beneath that touch. She knew what it was.

One of the spirits had breached the perimeter. Maura had fallen, and now this.

Someone knocked on the back door, three hard knocks. There was only one person in Terry's life who knocked that way, sure and clear.

Jessie, Terry thought. *Thank God. Jessie will help me. Jessie will understand.*

She liked Jessie better than her other granddaughter, Erin. Her son, Harry, said that she shouldn't say such things, but it was true. Erin wore her contempt for Terry a little too openly, made it clear that her love was an obligation to be met. Jessie might be secretly worried that her grandmother was losing her marbles, but she hid it better than anyone else. And Jessie really seemed to love Terry as Terry loved her.

And because Terry really loved Jessie the first thought that followed *Jessie will understand* was *No, Jessie, don't come in. They might get you. They might hurt you.*

Three knocks sounded again, and Terry thought of fairy tales, of three wishes and three nights to weave straw into gold and three bears and a cock crowing three times and all the magic hidden inside three, for good or ill.

Once more three knocks, three times three, and Terry closed her eyes and hoped that Jessie would be protected, that her granddaughter had sealed herself against harm. Because

Jessie was coming inside and Terry couldn't stop her. She heard the key turning in the back door lock.

"Grandma?" Jessie's voice, as strong and clear as her knock, floated through the kitchen and into the hall.

Terry tried to sit up but the pain in her shoulder stopped her. She whimpered, looking from Maura to the doorway. She had to get Maura's eyes back in and get her on the chair. It was the only way to stop further incursions. Jessie had to be kept safe.

"Grandma?"

Terry heard Jessie close the back door behind her, stride across the kitchen floor in her heavy boots. A moment later she was in the hall doorway – much taller than her grandmother, and sturdy with it. Terry envied her strength, wished she'd been that capable when she'd been Jessie's age. Terry had always been small and slight. Harold had preferred her that way, called her "his little doll".

Harold had a type. That was what the prosecutors had said.

"Grandma, what happened?" Jessie said, running to Terry's side.

"Maura," Terry said, moaning. "You have to fix Maura."

"Don't worry about Maura," Jessie said impatiently. "You're what's important. Now, is it okay to move you? Do you feel like anything's broken? Did you hit your head?"

"No," Terry said. "My shoulder... may be sprained or bruised. But we have to fix Maura. It's the only way to keep you safe. She can't watch with her eyes gone."

"Do you think you can sit up? I can help you," Jessie said.

It was like she hadn't heard anything Terry said about Maura, or worse, was ignoring it. Her family didn't understand about the spirits, didn't believe in them, didn't take them seriously.

"Come on," Jessie said, putting her arm under Terry's shoulder and lifting her to a sitting position.

Jessie wore denim overalls over a black sleeveless tee shirt and the suspender buttons clacked against the clip as Jessie moved. The sound seemed unnaturally loud in the silence of the hallway. A cloud of dust had kicked up after Maura's fall, and Terry saw movement between the motes, something shifting silently through space.

A spirit, she was sure of it. A tiny one that had snuck in while Terry collected the mail. And it had somehow plucked out Maura's eye. Terry followed the gust of air through the dust as it rose to the top shelf of dolls in the hallway, then she lost track of it.

There was nothing for it now. The spirit was inside, and bent on causing mischief. Terry needed to cleanse the hallway before it let in any more of its compatriots.

"How do you feel?" Jessie asked. "Dizzy? Nauseous?"

Terry felt none of those things, but she couldn't cleanse anything if Jessie was in the house, fluttering over her like she was a broken baby bird. Jessie wouldn't just leave after finding Terry on the floor like that.

She really is a good girl, Terry thought, though a touch of impatience followed. She didn't need Jessie to be a good girl at the moment. She needed Jessie to go away so she could make the house safe again. So Terry played along, careful not to overdo it. The last thing she needed was for Jessie to call Harry, or worse, an ambulance.

"Just a little dizzy," Terry said. "Can I have some water?"

"Sure, be right back," Jessie said, standing. She had very dark curly hair cut short to the nape of her neck. The curls on top of her head bounced as she stood. She pointed a finger at Terry, a finger tipped with short nails covered in bright blue polish. "Don't move. Don't try to stand up without me. I mean it."

Terry waved her hand. "All right, all right. I promise."

Jessie stomped into the kitchen and Terry immediately began scooting around on the floor, searching for Maura's eyes. Her gaze fell on Maura's face – on the empty sockets, the web of lines radiating over her cheek.

"I'm sorry, baby," Terry said, a spasm of grief in her chest. "I'll make it better, I promise. I'll fix you."

Terry patted the ground and a sharp pain lanced through her palm. She turned it over and saw the large splinter that had pushed under her skin, and then realized in horror that she'd bled on the floor of the hallway.

"Blood," she said. The spirits could use her blood, use it against her. Even a drop would allow them to bypass her sentries, come directly at her. Hopefully the little spirit that had snuck in hadn't noticed yet. She bent over her knees, tried to get closer to the ground. Terry took the corner of her old brown cardigan and rubbed at the spot of blood on the hardwood.

Out, damned spot, is what she said and I need this spot to come out, but all she appeared to be doing was smearing it around on the floor.

She heard the water running in the kitchen. When the faucet stopped she called, "Jessie? Would you bring me a damp sponge when you come back?"

Jessie appeared in the doorway again, holding a glass of water. "Why?"

"There's blood on the floor. I want to clean it up before it stains the hardwood."

Terry realized a moment later that she'd said the wrong thing, because instead of going back into the kitchen for the sponge Jessie rushed toward her.

"Blood? Where are you bleeding? Is it your head?"

"No, it's not my head," Terry said, trying to keep the irritation out of her voice. Why must they always think there was something wrong with her head? "It's a tiny splinter, and it bled on the floor, and I want to clean it up. So please, please, help me do that."

"Let me see," Jessie said, kneeling beside Terry and placing the glass of water on the floor. She took Terry's hand in hers, examining the injury.

Terry yanked her hand back in irritation. "Please, Jessie, listen to me. Don't ignore everything I say just because you think you know best. I'm not a child."

Something flickered in Jessie's eyes, something that Terry was sure she read rightly as *Then why do you act like one?* but her granddaughter, to her credit, did not say it out loud.

"Okay, Grandma," Jessie said with a little sigh. "I'll get you a sponge if you drink this water."

"I will," Terry said, and watched Jessie stomp back into the kitchen.

Terry immediately resumed her search for Maura's eyes, but they seemed to have disappeared.

They have to be here somewhere, Terry thought. One little spirit couldn't cause so much damage in such a short time.

Jessie ran the faucet in the kitchen for a moment, which reminded Terry that she'd promised to drink some water. She lifted the glass to her lips, and her head tilted backward. As she did, a movement caught the corner of her eye, a movement sliding smoothly up the wall, inhuman, alien.

A thin-legged spider with a tiny brown body, making an elevator of its silk. She exhaled in relief. Every movement in the house was not fraught with sinister implication. Sometimes a spider was just a spider.

The spider caught the bottommost shelf of dolls, shimmied easily over the edge, and Terry lost sight of it. She hoped that it found something delicious to eat.

Jessie joined her again, handing out the damp sponge. Terry carefully scrubbed the floor until there were no remnants of her blood anywhere. She'd mop the hallway, just to be safe, after Jessie left.

"All right, are we done with that now?" Jessie asked. Terry ignored the put-upon tone in her voice. "Can I clean and disinfect this splinter?"

"Yes," Terry said meekly. The sooner she submitted to Jessie's ministrations the sooner Jessie would leave, and then Terry could address the more important matter of the spirits.

Jessie helped Terry to her feet. It wasn't lost on Terry that her granddaughter was being extra gentle, no matter how impatient she might feel.

As Terry stood, her eyes shifted to the shelves of soldiers again. The spider she'd seen earlier was crawling over the green pinafore of her Italian girl doll. The Italian girl was her second-favorite, with her colorful dress and her little straw bonnet and her black hair and eyes.

Terry wondered idly where the spider was going when it stopped on the doll's blushing cheek. Its legs reached toward the girl's dark eye and somehow, though she knew it couldn't be physically possible, the eye began to spin in its socket.

Noo, Terry thought. *Nooo, spider, spider, why did you betray me? I never sweep you out of corners, I never stomp on you when you pass before me.*

"Nooo," she said aloud, and Jessie stopped trying to shuffle her toward the kitchen.

"Are you okay? Does something hurt? Do you feel sick?"

"The spider," Terry said, trying to wrench away from Jessie, but her granddaughter held firm – not hurting Terry, but not letting her go.

"What spider?" Jessie asked. "Since when do you care about spiders? They're living rent-free all over this house. There are some big ones in the attic, too. Erin won't even go up there."

Terry didn't care about Erin's feelings on the subject. All she cared about was stopping the little traitor before it did any more work for those trying to hurt her. "On my Italian girl. It's trying to take her eye out. It's working for the spirits, *colluding* with them."

"Grandma," Jessie said, in that "I'm-trying-to-be-patient" tone that made Terry wild. "There are no spirits after you. We've talked about this."

"There *are.* Jessie, I love you but you don't understand. None of you do. Now please, please, let me stop that spider before it hurts my Italian girl like it hurt Maura."

Jessie loosened her grip, just a little, like she wasn't certain about what to say or do. It was enough. Terry swept her hand toward the spider. The miserable little turncoat was too intent on its work to notice. Its body brushed under Terry's fingers, flew away from the doll onto the floor. Its legs scrabbled in the air for purchase for a moment, and then Terry's slipper came down on it, hard.

"Ha!" she said, triumphant. "There'll be no more of that, thanks very much."

She wondered how the spirits had recruited the spider in the first place. They must be frustrated if they were forced to use the local arachnid population.

"Oh, no," she said, realizing what this meant. "They're using the spiders now. They could use more of them."

She'd have to clean the whole house of spiders. They were in every corner, under every piece of furniture. She was always careful to vacuum around them, to let them live as they pleased.

All her little friends and companions, all the neighbors that had kept her company when her human neighbors turned away – they would have to go. They'd turned on her, like all the others.

The scandal of Harold's arrest, the allegations that had come up in the trial, the conviction that followed – it all meant that people who'd known Terry for years would turn away when they passed her on the street, would pretend they didn't see her in the grocery store. The spiders had been a comfort to her. They'd listened without judgment. They'd filled up her home with their tiny little children. She'd kept them safe.

But the spiders were like Judas, ready to turn their backs on her. She hardened her heart against them.

"We'll have to clean out all the spiders," Terry said. "Can you stay and help me?"

Jessie's eyes slid away from Terry's. "Grandma, we just have to worry about your injuries right now. You cut your hand. You said you might have sprained your shoulder. I think maybe I should take you to the urgent care clinic, just in case."

Terry ground to a halt. "No, I'm not going to the clinic."

"Grandma, be reasonable," Jessie said. "I'm not trying to hurt your feelings, but you aren't young any more. Even a little thing like a fall could have serious consequences."

"It's not the consequences of the fall that I'm worried about."

"All right, Grandma. Enough with this spirits nonsense. There are no spirits coming to get you. I know you don't want to admit it, but Grandpa Harold was a terrible person. You're not responsible for what he did, but he was a terrible person. Clearly you feel some guilt or something related to that, but there are no vengeful souls trying to drag you to hell by association. You have to stop saying things like this. Dad is talking about putting you in a care home. He thinks it's not safe for you to be by yourself, that you've lost touch with reality."

Terry waited patiently through most of Jessie's speech, until she got to the part where Harry wanted to put her in a home.

Another traitor, she thought with a spurt of anger. Her own son, trying to remove her from the home she'd shared with his father.

He'll probably get twice its value when he sells it, Terry thought bitterly. *The home of an infamous serial killer.*

She shook that thought, and the attendant bile that rose with it, away. It wasn't time to worry about what Harry might do to her, or what his father had done...

(but he had done so much he killed all those girls he killed them he killed them all those girls he called his little dolls just like me pretty maids all in a row just like my soldiers on the shelves except they died)

... it was time to worry about the spiders, about the potential rebellion within her own walls.

Jessie was looking at her expectantly, and Terry recalled that Jessie had been talking before.

"Your father won't put me in a care home," Terry said. "And I'm not crazy, Jessie, whatever you may think."

"I don't think you're crazy, Grandma. Just..." Jessie trailed off, looking uncomfortable.

"Just confused? Just a little mixed-up? It's all right, Jessie. You don't have to believe me. But will you help me? Help me clear the house of spiders?"

"Because the spiders are working with the spirits," Jessie said, doubt in every syllable.

"It doesn't matter why," Terry said. "All of you have been complaining for years that I let the spiders run rampant in the house. Wouldn't you love to see them evicted?"

"Well," Jessie said, rubbing the back of her neck. "I don't know. I always kind of liked them – or at least, I liked that you left them alone."

"But I can't now," Terry said. "So, will you help me or not?"

"If I don't you're just going to go through the whole house on your own, aren't you?" Jessie said.

"Yes," Terry said.

"Fine," Jessie said. "But first I want to look at your shoulder and make sure it's not swelling or anything."

"My shoulder is fine," Terry said.

"Grandma."

"All right," Terry said, submitting. She was going to get her way, so she could play along for a little bit. Jessie would help her clear the spiders, and then Jessie would go home, and Terry would find Maura's eyes and cleanse the hallway of that lurking spirit, and everything would be fine again.

Everything would be fine.

If she kept telling herself that over and over, then maybe it would be true.

Jessie was as good as her word. She took out the vacuum and went after Terry's eight-legged tenants with a thoroughness that her grandmother admired. They went all through the house, hunting under every piece of furniture and into every corner. They stopped when they reached the attic door.

"Should we do upstairs, too?" Jessie asked doubtfully. "I feel like you might need an exterminator for those."

Terry thought, weighing the risk. It was possible that the spirits might get into the attic, recruit from the population there. On the other hand, they *were* a bunch of lazy lobs. The attic spiders hardly moved at all. Surely they wouldn't come all the way down from the attic just to pluck out the eyes of her little soldier dolls.

"No, I think it will be all right," Terry said. "Thank you for helping me, Jessie."

"Sure," Jessie said, bringing the vacuum downstairs.

Terry followed her slowly, carefully. Stairs were a source of constant anxiety. She gripped the banister and tried not to think about falling.

By the time she reached the bottom, Jessie had already put the vacuum away in the hall closet.

"Can I make you some lunch?" Terry asked.

"Peanut butter and marshmallow fluff?" Jessie asked hopefully.

Terry laughed. Even though she was twenty years old, Jessie still preferred her favorite childhood sandwich. Terry kept a jar of marshmallow fluff just for Jessie's visits.

Terry made the sandwich, and watched Jessie eat it, and

tried not to grow impatient with her granddaughter's continued presence in the house. Terry had work to do, a spell to cast to cleanse the house of the spirit's incursion. She couldn't do that while Jessie was here. Terry felt she'd already reached the limits of Jessie's tolerance in relation to the spirits.

"You know, Grandma," Jessie said in a casual way that told Terry it was not casual at all. "Maybe I'll stay here tonight, in the guest bedroom. What do you think? I could just run home to get my overnight bag."

I think you've been texting your father while I was putting fluff on bread for you, you little traitor, Terry thought. *I think you've decided I need looking after because I've been having an "episode."*

But she didn't say this, or let any of her bitterness leak through in her tone. If Jessie wanted to go away for a while, that would be enough time for Terry to take out the book Harold had given her, the book of witchcraft to keep her safe.

Harold had always wanted her to be safe, even if he broke all his other dolls.

(and you knew oh yes you knew what he was up to but you weren't bothered about it so long as he took his obsessions elsewhere and stayed sweet to you then you didn't care)

"That sounds fun," Terry said to Jessie.

"A girls' night!" Jessie said, a little too heartily. "We can watch a movie and make popcorn."

Terry couldn't eat popcorn anymore. It played havoc with her stomach. But she went along and nodded, as if she was excited about the prospect.

"I'll be back in an hour or two," Jessie said, glancing at her watch.

"Sure, sweetie," Terry said, but in her mind she thought *Traitor.*

As soon as Jessie went out, Terry hurried to the armoire in the living room. She kept her book and her materials for her spells on the second shelf in there.

Terry threw open the doors of the armoire, her brain already feverishly moving ahead to the ritual she'd need to cast.

The second shelf was empty.

For a moment Terry stared, thought wildly that Jessie or Harry or Erin had taken her things, tossed them out in a fit of pique.

But then she crouched a little so that her face was closer to the shelf, balanced her reading glasses on her nose, saw the gossamer silver strands trailing across the surface, noticed the unmistakable marks of tiny featherlight feet.

"Traitors." Terry moaned. "Traitors, traitors, TRAITORS!"

This collusion with the spirits had clearly been going on for some time if the traitors had already hidden her books and herbs. When was the last time she'd checked this cabinet? When had the spirits convinced the spiders, brought them over to their side despite all of Terry's many kindnesses?

Terry was happier than ever that she had cleared the house of them. They didn't deserve her mercy. But it was a blow, a terrible blow. How would she cleanse the hallway now?

The tinkle of something hard and marble-like falling to the floor filtered through her anger. Terry followed the sound to the two dolls that stood sentry in the east-facing living room window. A bright blue iris rolled along the baseboard beneath the sill, arrowing directly for the corner.

"No!" Terry shouted, running after the eye.

It disappeared into the tiny hole in the floor where the walls joined, disappeared as neatly as a billiard aimed for a pocket. She was sure she saw the tiny almost-clear body of a baby spider behind it, pushing the eye out of her reach.

"No, no, the babies, we forgot about the babies." Terry stood over the hole, wringing her hands. Everything was going wrong all of a sudden, all her defenses falling one after another, *click-click-click* like dominoes.

The babies were too small to hunt. They hid in the cracks between the floorboards.

Oh, no. The floors.

Terry had dismissed the slow-moving denizens of the attic but she hadn't thought about the floors, or what might be underneath them.

There could be hundreds of traitors down there, thousands of their spawn running free, hiding the eyes of her pretty dolls, her soldiers.

"What should I do? What should I do?" Terry grasped the pendant around her neck, the pendant she never, ever took off.

All around the room she heard the *tink-tink-tink* of doll's eyes hitting the floor, saw them rolling in different directions toward cracks and holes she'd never noticed before.

Then the sounds from the hall began. Terry wanted to run to her soldiers but she couldn't. Her body was too old;

it was turning on her just like the neighbors and the spiders and her own son. So she shuffled as fast as she could, but she already knew it was too late. She heard the sound of eyes falling steadily and continuously, like a hailstorm on a summer night, and the sound grew louder and louder as a storm would until it reached a crescendo.

Terry limped into the hallway, breathless, and saw all the eyes of her pretty dolls popping from their sockets, falling to the floor, rolling away to some secret fastness far from her.

"Why?" Terry shouted over the din. "Why are you helping them?"

The front door flew open. There was nothing to stop the spirits now.

In came the girls, all the pretty girls, all of Harold's pretty little dolls, one after another.

Terry held up her right hand, her left gripping her pendant. "Stay away! I didn't do anything to you. I didn't!"

But the girls couldn't see her hand urging them to stop, for all the girls were missing their eyes. Harold had always taken their eyes, at the end.

"I didn't do anything," Terry said, weeping. "I didn't."

The first girl stopped in front of Terry, and all the others behind her paused. She tilted her head to one side, like she was listening for something. Then she said, "But you knew."

"You knew, you knew," the other girls chanted.

"You knew and you didn't stop him. You knew and you let him go on," the first girl said, and Terry remembered that her

147

name was Grace, and that her mother had wept and screamed during the trial.

"I didn't," Terry said, but her lie sounded like a lie now. There was no force behind it.

"You did," Grace said. "You couldn't have saved me, but you could have saved the others."

"He was my husband," Terry said. "What was I to do?"

"The right thing," Grace said. "And now, so shall we."

Grace reached for Terry's face, and Terry screamed.

* * *

"Grandma?" Jessie called, opening the back door.

The house seemed unnaturally quiet. She wondered if her grandmother was sleeping. Jessie walked quietly through the kitchen, peeking into the living room first. The doors to the armoire stood open, but there was no other sign that Terry had been there.

She stepped into the hallway and stopped. The hall was empty, but the front door stood open.

"Grandma?" Jessie called again.

No answer. It was so still. Even the air seemed hushed, breath tucked away.

Jessie ran up the stairs, the first stirrings of panic in her throat. At the top of the stairs she saw the attic ladder hanging down.

The spiders, Jessie thought in relief. Her grandmother had just wanted to do a thorough job with the spiders she was suddenly obsessed with, and had gone up in the attic to clean.

Jessie climbed the ladder stairs, ready to chastise Terry for exerting herself.

But Terry wasn't exerting herself. Terry was lying on the floor in the middle of the attic, face to the ceiling.

There were two empty sockets in her face. Her mouth was open and several strands of gossamer silk trailed away from her lips.

On the floor there were two large spiders, the size of tarantulas, dragging Terry's eyes away.

THE VIRAL VOYAGE OF BIRD MAN

BY KATHERINE ARDEN

I used to beg people to hear me. I had to. A hundred years ago, no one would give me the time of day, but I had to tell my story anyway. I would plead. Threaten. Terrify. And now here you are. You know you're the fifth person tonight? I can't even go to a damn bar without someone recognizing me, sliding over, offering me a drink – a fine ale, this, thank you – and asking for my story. I should make you pay me for it.

And why do you even want to know? You know what happened anyway, or you wouldn't be here.

Well, I suppose you're here now. Sit there. Don't interrupt.

Oh this damn story. I must be drunk. You know, in a hundred thousand tellings, my story has never once made sense? Stories need logic, don't they? Cause and effect. Well, mine doesn't have it.

I used to think that if I said it over enough times, I'd finally understand, and then I could stop. But the more I told, the less I understood. *And*, I told the whole world once, or almost. It wasn't enough. But I'm getting ahead of myself.

That's unusual. Tell the same story a hundred thousand times, and you get it down perfectly. Everything in order. The turns of phrase. The embellishments, the *bon mots*. The little elisions and exaggerations. It becomes a face you hand to the world, immutable as a stone mask.

Not anymore. But I'm getting ahead of myself again.

I killed a bird. Just one bird. Why? Christ, who knows? No, I wasn't hungry. It wouldn't have been good eating anyway. It was an albatross, all wings and bones, so purely white that the foam on the sea looked yellow when the creature dipped to the waves. We'd come south, on the *Swallow*, out of Cork, a hard voyage, below the fortieth parallel, and we were in fog near the mountains of ice. The albatross was playing all round our masts, as though to mock the anxious eyes we kept turning from wind to tide. It was beautiful and it was free and I was bored and I shot it.

I just wanted to see what would happen. How those wings would crumple, how it would sound, when it thumped on the deck. And indeed, the wings fell like trailing laundry and it hit the deck with a satisfying thud. My shipmates cheered. Said I'd done us all a favor. That the albatross was an unlucky beast, had brought the fogs and chancy winds, and the loom of the ice under our lee.

So we tacked the albatross by its wings to the mast, and then the southerlies blew up and ran us north again, north and north, out of the region of ice mountains and cold fog. We were well pleased. We'd a hold fat with blubber and whale-oil, a goodly share for every man. So we made a fine run, north to where the sun lay like a mirror on the unmoving sea. All was well, all was as it should be and it never occurred to me to care for an instant that I'd shot that damned bird.

Then our wind failed. Day after day the ship turned round, pointing now east, now south; with the sea like a hot mirror below us, the ship wallowing in her own filth. Surely, we thought, a wind would come, or a squall of rain, to tide us over, the last piece of luck on our lucky voyage.

But none did. My shipmates, those louts, started to blame me. Said that it was my fault, that I'd killed the albatross and angered some vengeful spirit of the sea. I didn't believe it. You'd think the vengeful spirit of the sea would be a little brisker, wouldn't you? Not hang fire all the way to the doldrums. The albatross' wings were shriveled on the mast; what took their *vengeful spirit* so long? But they wouldn't hear my arguments. Just glared at me, and glared and glared.

And then we had no water.

They took the bird off the mast and hung it round my neck. Maybe they thought my shudders, at the touch of flaccid, rotting wings would appease their sea-spirit. Make it take me and not them. Christ, I wish it had.

It didn't though.

There was still no air, and then the crew started dying. They died hating me. I hope it comforted them, having to hate, so they wouldn't have to be afraid of how capricious it all was, life or death, wind or no wind.

I was the last alive, dying of thirst myself, wits astray, my shipmates lying heaped around me, dead in the doldrums when a ship hove into view. I used to tell people that Death was on that ship, with a girl called Life-in-Death, and the two of them played dice for our souls. That was a time when people liked that sort of idea. When I put it into verse, women would clap their hands.

It's all rot though. I should like to have seen a beautiful girl in the doldrums. The truth is I don't know who was on that ship. I was dying. It could have been anyone. I remember voices, someone laughing, a hand, blue light. That's all. It could have been *The Flying Dutchman*, a flying circus, a whaler with a kindly captain. We were nothing if not salvageable, with our pristine hull, packed full of oil, and all the crew dead but me.

All I know is that I was dying, and a ship came and the wind came with it, and I didn't die. I was delirious, though, and I do not remember the voyage home. Perhaps it was a ghost ship, crewed by angels. I told people that once.

It is not, you must admit, a story worthy of a hundred thousand tellings. A little superstition, crumpled wings, a deck full of dead men, delirium, a valuable hold, someone's lucky salvage.

But that's not the whole story. Two things happened, after I got back to Cork.

Rather, one thing happened, and one thing failed to happen.

First, I *had* to tell that story. My gut burned with agony if I didn't. It was like I had to vomit, but it was words inside me, and not my supper. From crossbow to ghost ship, every third person I met – I had to tell that damned nonsensical, pointless tale.

That was the first thing.

The second thing failed to happen. I didn't die. I just went on. On and on. Like that voyage knocked me out of the world and brought me back a story with legs and a story is immortal.

Oh, I tried not to tell my story. I tried living in the woods, far from the sound of the sea, in case it really was my shipmates' sea-spirit, causing my trouble. Not dying has a few advantages. I could lie out in the rain and not sicken. I could walk through thickets and the wolves wouldn't kill me.

Living wild, I grew to know the birds and the beasts. I remember how the trees soared, like cathedral arches, enclosing me in green light, and the smell of the loam in the summer rain. I stayed in the forest as much as I could. I didn't have to vomit up my story to every third person in a place where there were no people. But eventually I always had to go back. For food, for company. And then I'd be choking out the wretched tale all over again.

I got it polished and pat, even added a few rhymes – told it in meter for a few years, just to change things up. But the arc of it stayed the same – and so did I. The days piled up like snowflakes, became drifts, became years, became centuries, and I learned the alarm-call of a rook before a storm, and I buried a hundred dogs, who loved me with their whole souls.

It's not as easy as it sounds, being a walking story. I'd give some poor sod the old flaming glance, and say "heed me, lest you become me" or some rot of that kind, even though I had no idea *what* I had become, or why I was there at all. And sometimes the poor dupe would cross himself and listen. But mostly people would laugh at me or spit at me, or worse, try to reason with me: *but sir, how is it that an albatross killed at the fortieth parallel would lead to a curse falling upon you in the doldrums and all this seems a bit thin, for immortality. I'd like to be immortal. Maybe I should kill an albatross.*

Fools.

I used to think if I could just understand why I kept failing to die, then I could be done. But I could never. People do what I did all the time. You take something that flies, that's whiter than foam and you want to break it. Just to see what happens. What's wrong with that? If breaking things that are beautiful was enough to make a man immortal, well then we'd all be, and I wouldn't be talking to you and the world would have a lot more people in it.

I tried repenting for the murder of the albatross – went to confession and so forth – but all my confessions were more annoyed than anything, and it didn't work.

I tried getting myself killed. I'd walk the tracks of robbers, join the army. But the knives never quite came out, the bullets never quite struck home. And all this time I'd have to tell my story. Do you think I understood it *better* after a hundred years? I didn't. The opposite was true. By that time it was words utterly without sense, sliding featureless between my lips.

I don't know when I first noticed that the wild places had gotten smaller. I remember wanting to stand again beneath the vaulting trees, and bathe in the green light beneath. But they'd all been cut for masts. I remember wanting to see where the wolves denned again, and watch their puppies play in the sun. But I couldn't find them. There were only towns, towns, everywhere towns, and every day I had to bore some scowling crofter with my tale, until I thought I should go mad.

I went north and north and north again, half-hermit and half-madman until finally in desperation, I crept onto a ship going west.

Back when I was a man and not a walking story, I loved the sea. I remember one day at dawn on the last voyage of the *Sparrow*, we found ourselves in a pod of ten thousand whales, the whole surface of the sea alive with spouts: fin whales and right whales, and murderous whales and the vast great whales that no one can take. They stretched from horizon to horizon, a city in the sea. I stared until my eyes hurt.

But on that voyage there were no whales for me. There was no horizon at all. Only the stifling dark, and the way fear crept through the men as I whispered my story in their ears. They were too afraid to even try to kill me but flung me ashore the instant a boat could touch and shrived the ship afterward.

And then I was in a new world, and the forests were vast again. I saw great cats in the ancient gloom, pigeons that filled the sky like a river. I walked into the trees alone, resolving never to see another man.

But soon enough the woods were ringing with axes and hammers and sawmills, and the wild places began, once more, to shrink. The railroads were cut and the pigeons were killed, and I fled west and the whole industrious world came after, so I had to tell my story more and more and *still more* and *I was still alive.* Do you hear what I am saying? *Oh, God, I was still alive.*

I am still alive.

No, I'm all right. Just give me a moment.

It was the radio that gave me the notion first, but it was only an idea, entertained and laid aside. I was in a rooming house in Massachusetts, their resident madman, and I remember the landlady's excitement when she turned the dial. I remember how a thin voice, authoritative, came wavering out of that big wooden box. And I remember thinking what if that was my story, there on the radio, what if there were a hundred million radios in a hundred million homes, telling my story, what if *everyone knew*? Then maybe I wouldn't have to tell it anymore. There wouldn't be anyone to tell it to.

I disabused myself of the notion. Not everyone had radios. I didn't have any idea how to get my voice into that wooden box. The next day I got up with my bundle and left the rooming house and went to go look at the sea, churned with ships and the cod all gone. But the notion stayed in the back of my mind.

That wasn't a good century for an absurd story like mine. People had more important things to do than listen to me. The world was gray with war, riddled with absences. And I still had to walk around and try to persuade people to listen. Sometimes, hard-faced men would say, *Ha, that's your sin? Good on ya pal, here's mine*. And they'd tell me a story that iced the blood in my veins. That was after the war.

Or I'd tell my story to long-haired people that smelled of patchouli and they'd listen with their hair in their eyes, nodding. Then they'd say something like, *that's rad, dude*, or *the bird, you know, represents, virginal nature and the arrow was the phallus that violated her and*—

Everyone's got an opinion, haven't they?

They had started laying down hard roads by then, for their machines to run, and then some bastard invented electric lights. I hated the lights worst of all. They faded the stars, made the world bright and small. I felt like the only mystery left anywhere, skulking in the shrinking dark, with nowhere to hide, and the same old nonsense spilling from my lips.

And I still couldn't die.

The century turned again. No, I don't remember the year. I lost track of years a long time ago. I remember that it was hot and green, that it was spring, and it was evening, and I was in a park. One of the things they build in places where the fields and forests are gone, and men realize there is nowhere to raise your face, in reasonable silence, to the sun.

I could feel my story like a coal in my throat, and I knew I must tell it soon, again. Not for the first time, I was wondering if I could take refuge in madness.

I don't know why I chose the girl. Her hair was short and smooth and brown. I don't know how old she was. Everyone looked like well-nourished children to me anyway, by then. Not their faces, but their eyes. Have you looked in mine? Look now. I know I don't look a day over fifty. But you can see the years in my eyes. Afraid? Good. You should be. Stop talking. I suppose I'll give you the old line: *heed me lest you become me.*

You don't want to become me.

Anyway, I remember liking the serenity in the girl's face, the book in her hands. I didn't think she'd be afraid of me or try to argue with me, at all, and that was all I cared about. I'd learned to choose my hearers by then.

She was reading alone on a blanket, and when I dropped down beside her and told her I'd a tale to burn her ears, she stared at me, and said, "Is that like the weirdest come on ever?"

I could tell my story in every language of men, but sometimes, in those days, those languages changed too fast even for me. I said austerely, to cover my confusion, "It is a story that I must tell."

"Why?" she said.

I had to start telling it soon. My stomach burned, the words felt like they were going to come straight out through the skin of my throat. "I don't know," I managed.

"'Kay," said the girl. She pulled out her telephone – like a tiny radio with lights, I've always thought, although I have never understood how they actually work – and said, "Why not? You're something else, you know. I didn't think eyes could actually blaze, you know, in real life. Contacts? Can I get a video?"

I was taken aback. People didn't want anything of me, except for me to go away.

160

"Why?" I said, hearing my voice rusty, trying to recover my stride, wondering when I'd last asked someone else a question.

"Oh," she said. "To post."

I didn't know what she meant, but if whatever she wanted happened to kill me, I'd sing her praises forever, so I nodded.

She pointed her shining oblong thing at me. "Go ahead."

I still didn't understand, but I let the well-worn words out, and felt the brief relief of it.

After I was done, she put down her telephone, and said, "Huh. Damn. That was pretty cool. What's your name?"

There was a time when I would have drawn myself up impressively and said, "I am the ancient mariner," and then disappeared into the dark. But the dark was all but gone by then, there were lights by day and lights by night, and so I said stiffly, "It doesn't matter."

"Sure it does," said the girl. She looked at her telephone, and said, "Do you do this kind of thing a lot? Performance art? 'Cause you're killing it." She turned her shining thing around and I blinked and saw myself, small, thin, shabby, a little grizzled, telling my story with eyes that burned with savage confusion.

I didn't know what was making her happy, exactly. It didn't seem like it was going to kill me, more's the pity. I thought to go. But then she smiled and looked down and said, "Damn, comments *pouring* in, just like I thought, everyone *loves* you, you're so *authentic*." Her eyes were bright and sharp and so, so young, with that close-focused look that people had in those days, who spent more time indoors than out.

That was when I remembered my long-ago thought, at the Massachusetts rooming house. "People are hearing my story?" I asked her. Clumsy-tongued with hope, I added, "Will many people hear?"

"For sure. I've got tons of followers, and I mean, you've got such a *vibe.*"

The grass was hot and the sun was hot, and I had no idea what she meant or what she saw when she looked at me. She was looking back down at her telephone. "Incredible," she said with satisfaction. "You're *impressive*, for sure. So nice to meet you. Where you staying?"

Nowhere was the answer. Everywhere. What did she take me for? I hadn't *lived* anywhere, really, since the *Swallow*.

I just looked at her.

"Well," she said. "I need you to not be weird, but do you want to crash with me? For a few days? You can have the couch and maybe we can make a couple more videos? You can tell me more of your stories and stuff?"

"Crash—?" I said.

"Stay," she said. "Do you want to stay?"

I don't know how long I stared at her. I couldn't *stay* anywhere. I had to tell my story. But it occurred to me then, that I didn't want to. That I had no impulse to get up off her blanket, and go and harangue anyone else. That I couldn't remember a time when that was true. I dared to wonder then if her *post* was working. If it was somehow telling my story so I didn't have to.

"All right," I said.

I stayed on her sofa that night – stop leering at me, young man, it was just her sofa, she was like a bright-eyed child to me – and it *was* working, what she'd done with my story, *posting* it, because I had no impulse to leave her, to find someone else to tell it to. I just slept on her couch and then sat in her kitchen like a ninny, flattened with the most painful sense of relief.

That morning she came up to me and said, "Do you have any other stories?"

"A—what?" I said.

"Another story!" she said. "Your other one was great. Just – weird and good. And it's gone absolutely viral. People are begging for more of you."

"I already told my story," I said, bewildered.

"You don't have another story?"

No. I *was* that story. Dead albatross, doomed voyage. A bolt, a thud, thirst. But she was frowning with disappointment, turning away, and I thought of losing this place – her cluttered kitchen, the smell of coffee and bread, the shocking sense of stillness after all my wretched, wandering centuries, and so in some desperation, I remembered the island.

"Yes – I remember – it was – before the albatross," I said.

She turned back to me, pulled out her telephone, nodded encouragingly. I licked my lips. My words flopped gracelessly over each other. Raw, awkward, bits of sentences. But I forced them out. "The roaring forties, we used to call that ocean. Easy to sink there. You broach-to, get side-on to a wave, and go to the bottom. Or you'd go overboard – ship would get crosswise

163

to a wave, and you'd be thrown clear, or you'd slide out of the rigging and down. There'd be ice on the ropes, your hair frozen solid, you're trying to take in sail and there's water like a mountain, tall as a hundred ships coming towards you—"

"Yeah," said the girl, earnestly. "Yeah, uh huh. That's cool, that's good. Like – context, you know. For your persona. Bird Man. Can we call you that?"

Maybe I'd taken the habit of storytelling too deep, for I didn't answer her question, just went on talking. "The first time the waves died, it was like we'd come to another world. Ice mountains, blue and pink and green and white, and we shipped a bow-grace, to keep them from the hull. The ship had been battered by the passage; we were pumping the hold watch and watch, and the master pricking his chart and shaking his head. The island saved us."

"What island?" the girl asked obligingly.

"I don't know," I said. "It wasn't on the charts. It had a deep bay, though. With high walls, and—"

Apologetically, she broke in and said, "Cool story, but do you mind singing a sea-shanty? I think it would really work for you. Ancient sailor vibes and everything. People don't really care about islands. We want the human connection, you know."

I was about to plow on, realized I didn't have to. *This* story didn't have me by the throat. I opened my mouth, closed it again, suddenly adrift, without the compulsion to speak. She was looking impatient though, so I cleared my throat, opened my mouth awkwardly and began "The Ladies of Spain," at full voice, if rusty.

But she stopped me halfway through, shuddering. "Dude – what? That's not cool. Don't just – I mean that song is objectifying those ladies. I love your old sailor vibes but come on. In fact, maybe no sea shanties."

I didn't understand. But it didn't matter. She and I were *still* talking and I hadn't gotten up to tell the story to anyone else. She had a small mole by her mouth, and something was strange about her eyebrows. I was staring at that girl like she was the first human being I'd seen in three hundred years.

But maybe I had the habit then, of telling stories, because I surprised myself by saying, abruptly, "About that island – there were seabirds nesting on the beach, by the bay, and seals on the shore, and they'd never seen a person before. Even once."

She gave her phone a resigned look but humored me. "No?" she asked vaguely. "How'd you know?"

"Because they didn't run," I said.

She looked up at me then. "Run?"

"When we killed them," I said. "They didn't know what was happening. They'd never seen men before. You could smash a sea-bird's egg and she'd just blink at you…"

I hadn't thought of that island in three hundred years. Abruptly I wondered what had happened to the *other* birds, the thousands of albatrosses nesting there, too many to kill.

The girl put her telephone down hastily. "No, no, no that's all wrong. You're – that's not your *vibe*. You're like, repentant.

You know, you killed the bird and now you're cursed to wander the earth *forever.* We can do better. How about a different story."

She mashed her finger against her telephone and held it up to me again. I said, "Once I saw ten thousand whales, a pod bigger than the horizon, all of them blowing at once, like a cloud on the sea."

"Ooooh," she said, with pleasure. "What'd you do?"

Strange, how all my stories ended the same. "We harpooned the nearest," I said, frowning at how strong the memory was rising, as though my one story had enfolded a thousand and I was just now noticing. "She'd a calf. The men laughed at its swimming, round and round the ship, and trying to get under its mother's fins, where we'd lashed her to the side."

The girl made a moue of distaste, and put her telephone down again. "Well, I can edit this a bit, I guess," she said, and went off.

I sat there – I don't know how long. I am sure the girl thought me a madman, just sitting there limp. But that stillness was the most beautiful thing I'd felt in hundreds of years.

I didn't move the rest of the day, and she left me alone. She was in her room, talking to herself, talking to her phone. But that evening, she came out again, looking pleased. "I edited your island story," she said. "Added the nice bit about the baby whale. It's great. People still love you. Can we take some photos maybe? You in your cool coat, with your creepy sailor vibes? By the lake? It's sort of like the sea, isn't it?"

She lived not far from a lake. I could see it out her window.

Grass running down to muddy water, in the light of the setting sun. Heard my own voice, strange. "It's a little like the sea."

* * *

I went to the water with her, and she pointed her telephone at me a good deal, with the light on it shining, hurting my eyes. It was the light that made me say, "I miss the moths."

It was night by then, and there were no stars. Well, there might have been. But the lights were brighter.

"Moths?"

"There used to be moths," I said. "They would have been there, not too long ago. There, around that big light. They're gone now."

"We have moths," she said. "See, there's one." She was looking into her telephone again.

I wasn't sure why I was so determined to make her understand. "There ought to be a thousand around every light. There used to be. Whole globes of moths. Worlds of moths. But they're gone now."

She wasn't listening. I could see in her young, intent face, that she had no use for moths. Her telephone was much brighter than the absent stars.

"Sorry – just posting these pics," she said. "You're so cool-looking – can't you tell a more, you know – upbeat story? I dunno – do you have a lost love?"

"Lost?" I said. I tried to think what had been lost. Love, no. There was Blew, on shipboard, we'd touch each other in the hold, sometimes. And there were girls, in port. But what had I loved? What had I lost?

I don't know what made me say it. "Sometimes, in the southern ocean, the sea would glow – the ship's wake would glow – a medico of ours called it phosphorescence. And I'd stand at the rail and it would be as though the stars had come down to the sea."

She said, "No – that's not super relevant, yeah? We need to focus on narrative here. You're Bird Man. It's working. We just need to embellish. Kind of dark but not too depressing. You're always going on about sad stuff. Moths and stars and dead whales. What am I supposed to do with that? How about a lost love? Maybe I look like her and that's why you stopped to talk to me."

"You don't look like anyone I knew," I told her. "People now don't look the same as they did."

That brightened her up. She pulled out her telephone again. "Tell me more. How were people different then?"

"Smaller," I said. "Different eyebrows. Worse teeth. Saw further. The eyes, you know. And happier."

She was shaking her head. "No – *no* – like, just be upbeat for *one second.* People weren't happier three hundred years ago. Didn't even have electricity or anything."

My answer, to my despair, surged to the tip of my tongue, with all the intensity that I'd ever felt for the story of the albatross. I had to tell her. *Have you forgotten, I had to ask. Have you? Have people everywhere forgotten? How low the stars can seem, how many fish were in the sea, how the birds darkened the sky, how the moths came to the light?*

Heed me lest you become me. Hah. Well, everyone's becoming me. I was alone on a ship with men dying all around me. You're all alone here on this shrinking world, and it's dying all round you. And you've forgotten how it was. Stars, whales, seabirds. You've forgotten. But I can tell you. I have to tell you.

The second everyone heard my old story, I realized I had a new story.

Fucking curse.

Anyway, I got up.

"Where are you going?" she said. The moon was rising.

I said, with pain, with utter desperate agony, "I have to tell my story."

"But you told me!" she said. "You killed the albatross."

"Yes," I said turning away, wondering who had really been on that ship that night, and what they'd said, what they'd meant for me. Wondered who hadn't bothered to tell me that *forever* wasn't a strange effect. Forever was the point, and the story was never going to end. "I killed the albatross."

THE ANGELS OF LONDON

BY ADAM L. G. NEVILL

Still a little surprised such things were tolerated in the city, Frank stared at the mess.

At the base of the lamppost on the street corner, rubbish bags spilled their entrails across the pavement. Someone had once dumped a bin bag. Others followed their example until a pyramid of refuse rose up the lamppost to waist-height. The core of the structure had since rotted as if the body of the king that the pyramid honoured was poorly embalmed. A mattress had been thrown against the pile too. Rusted springs were visible and watermarks formed continents on the quilted fabric. Now a broken pushchair, with canvas rags hanging from the aluminium frame, augmented the installation. A disturbing element of squalor and human fragility, something London's occupants became immune to or a part of. He wasn't sure which of the two paths he would follow: indifference or collaboration.

He thought of submitting the entire mess to the Turner Prize but never had the energy to smile at his own joke. And he had no one to share it with.

Above his head the pub's sign creaked. It was wooden, the mounting of iron nearly rusted through. He wondered how long it would stay up there. It was amazing how many old and broken things just kept going in the city.

The actual picture of The Angel of London was painted on the wood inside the corroded frame. The paint had weathered and given the picture a wholly different aspect from the one originally intended. With its scaly-looking face, tight skullcap and wreath of leaves, the angel now resembled something Francis Bacon might have painted. Whenever Frank saw the hideous peeling face he knew he was home.

The pub was dead, had been closed for years. Through the grimy window panes he could see the silhouettes of wooden chairs placed upside down upon tables, a bar that resembled an unused plinth inside a dusty tomb, and a poster for a long-expired competition connecting rugby to Guinness.

Indicating a high turnover of tenants in the rooms upstairs, a mass of uncollected post was slung upon a shelf inside the door next to the bar. Why was the old post not forwarded to past residents? Or did the current tenants operate a wilful resistance to the outside world? Few of his questions about people in the city were ever answered.

There was no post for Frank. Someone was taking his mail; not even junk reached him.

After four months as a tenant in a room above the derelict bar, Frank acknowledged that he was vanishing from the world entirely. Becoming a thing withered, gaunt and grey, shabby and less substantial. Anxiety about money, finding the right kind of work, his future, isolation – all of it was intent on reducing him to a ghost. And one that only a few dimly remembered.

He wondered if his image in photographs was disappearing too. If he didn't find a better job and get out of the building, he imagined himself disintegrating into a stain on the murky wallpaper of his wretched room. He'd already disappeared from the social radar of his two friends. A relocation to London to catch up professionally still hadn't landed him a job anywhere near the film industry. His plummet to the bottom had been immediate.

London had golden rules. Never take the first accommodation you view, but he had done so because the room above The Angel in Dalston was the only place he'd found on Gumtree at £100 a week, all that he could afford. Never take the first job you're offered, but he had done so because the one grand he came to town with was gone in a month. He worked security in Chelsea, on shifts, which was nowhere near Dalston. Poorly paid jobs for the semi-skilled were plentiful, but affordable accommodation in the first three zones was scarce enough to not exist.

Frank wearily made his way up through the dimly lit dilapidation to his room. Familiar smells engulfed him: damp carpet warmed by radiators, cooking oil, an overflowing kitchen bin.

When he reached the first floor, Granby was waiting outside his room.

Frank jumped. "Fuck's sake."

Fright subsided into loathing. Granby knew what time he came in from work, had surreptitiously learned his movements by watching him from inside the building. When a tenant came out of their room, if he listened carefully, Frank would always hear the click of Granby's door on the third floor. Like a spider behind a trapdoor the landlord appeared to do little but watch his captives. Frank had never heard the murmur of a television, or music, coming from Granby's attic room; had never seen him prepare food in the sordid kitchen either, or even leave the building. The landlord was so thin he didn't appear to eat.

"Right, mate," came the whispery voice out of the gloom. Granby's bony face, watery eyes and peg teeth were barely visible. The figure sniffed, was always sniffing hard up one nostril. Frank knew what was coming.

"Need to speak wiv you 'bout the rent, mate." Granby had no conversation beyond insincere small talk and attempts to scratch money from the people who barely existed within the building.

Frank had come to wonder whether The Angel was an abandoned building that utility companies had forgotten to disconnect. Maybe Granby had assumed proprietorship of the rooms upstairs. Whatever was going on was some kind of dodge, and it contributed to his doubt that Granby had any right to charge rent for the squalid rooms. He'd once attempted to start a conversation with Granby, but the shifty creature never revealed any details about himself, or the property, beyond claiming that The Angel had been in the hands of his family for years.

After deductions from his wage packet, Frank took home nine hundred pounds a month. Nearly half of that went to Granby. Food took another two hundred, and credit-card debt one hundred. That left a hundred for transport. Frank saved as much of the remaining hundred as possible for a deposit on a room he hoped would be less wretched than the one he lived in at The Angel.

ATM machines informed him he had saved three hundred pounds, but Frank hadn't seen a bank statement in four months. He suspected Granby was opening his mail to learn about his finances. Which would mean the lies he had told Granby about his savings his landlord would now be wise to. Granby must know about the one hundred he saved each month and wanted it for himself.

The small figure moved in front of his door as Frank released his keys from his jacket pocket. "Ain't just you, mate. Times is hard for all of us. But fings go up, like. For everyone." The weasel's harassment was predictable.

He had no idea how old Granby was. He could have been thirty or sixty. His movements were agile, his voice wasn't aged, but his face was worn. The eyes had seen too much. The spirit inside them was blunted and only occasionally enlivened by feral intent when money was being discussed; acquiring money was his only purpose. The same vulpine self-interest applied to the teeming millions in the city.

But what was most remarkable, or memorable, about Granby's features was that they reminded Frank of a particular kind of working-class face: the type you saw leering out of a black and white photograph taken during the Second World War. Granby's face was not contemporary at all. But the white sport leisure wear and curly hair were utterly incongruous and made Granby look ridiculous. He was like a person from the forties masquerading as someone from the eighties.

"That right?"

Frank's irritation cooled when he detected a tension in Granby's wiry arms, and a narrowing around his eyes. When angry, Granby paled in a way that was horrible to behold. Resistance to Granby took things to a new level, quickly. When his loquacious wheedling for money fell flat, physical confrontation never seemed far away. Frank suspected there was a great capacity for violence in the man. Granby communicated the sense that everything was at stake, that he would be ruined if Frank didn't meet his demands.

Frank intended to leave The Angel anyway, and within four weeks. But four weeks was an eternity in the same building as a man determined to make life a condition of incremental blackmail, with insinuations of terrible consequences if his extortion was not placated. But, for once, Frank's inherent caution around unstable people took a back seat. "We've been through this before, Granby. There's no shower. One bathroom. I'm washing in a sink."

Granby didn't like the disadvantages of The Angel being pointed out to him by the tenants. "Everyone has to put up wiv it, mate. That's life. What you fink you should be in, some top hotel for a hundred a week? You is having a laugh, mate."

"What improvements have been made that can justify another rent hike?"

Granby was also a firm believer that if a conversation remained one-sided for long enough, then the tenant would see his point. His Cockney voice rose to drown Frank out. He started bouncing on his heels like a wiry puppet, or something much worse: a bantam-weight boxer. "I gotta look after my family. My family's the most important fing in the world to me. If our personal financial situation is freatened, I tell you something, mate, I don't know what I'd do. What I'm capable of."

Frank had never seen any evidence of this "family". The hard-pressed "family" had initially been used as a sob story during the second month of his tenancy, when Granby first asked him for more money, with tears in his doleful eyes. Frank had only enjoyed one harassment-free month to get settled in. Something that also stank of a well-rehearsed tactic.

"What fucking family?"

Granby's fists clenched; Frank sensed they would feel like wooden hammers against his face. He lowered his voice, but kept an edge in his tone. "There are four tenants in this building all paying you four hundred quid a month. For what? Half the lights don't work. The furniture's either totally wrecked or barely serviceable. My post isn't delivered. Or is it? And you've got nearly two grand a month coming in. For what?"

"What you mean, two grand a mumf? Vat's got nuffin' to do wiv you." Granby started walking backwards and forwards. He took his white tracksuit top off. Rolled his head around his shoulders as if preparing for physical exercise. "Nuffin. Nuffin. That's personal. Now you is going too far."

"There's no inventory. No contract. Cash-in-hand. Do you even have a right to collect money on this place?"

"What you talkin' about? Eh? You're freatening me? You is freatening my family. You need to watch your mouf. I've warned you."

"I'm leaving. This last month's rent comes out of my deposit."

"You're going nowhere. Free months' notice. We agreed."

Sleep deprivation from night shifts, three hours a day travelling on the bus to and from work with a dark shabby room at the end of the journey, the ever-present sight of his clothes on the floor because there was no chest of drawers or wardrobe, the endless trips to the laundrette, the indifference of strangers, being dead on his feet, never having any money, the fidgeting anxiety that accompanies failure like a crowd of persistent children, the cold terror about his future: all of this rose through him and became a terrible pressure. It would soon release in a steam he could no longer cap.

"Agreed? We agreed one hundred a month! In my second month you try and hike the rent twenty-five quid a week. So am I to stay here for as long as you decide, while you keep upping the rent? And making threats? Do I subjugate my life to your 'family's' financial security? You don't scare me, Granby. One visit to the police, the DHSS, whoever, and your little operation's over. I bet you're signing on too, eh? You've not done a day's work in your life, have you?"

By the time he'd finished, Frank knew he'd gone too far; he'd tripped every wire in the little man's mind by using off-piste words like "subjugate", by sub-legal diction like "rights", and adopting a sarcastic tone about the man having a family. There was no place for a concept like fairness at The Angel. The Angel was an extortion racket, run like a prison, and the tenants were inmates.

Granby circled him. "I gotta go. I gotta go. Get out my fuckin' way." He made for the stairs. "You is taking me for a cunt. A cunt! There'll be trouble. There'll be trouble if I don't go right now."

At first, Frank assumed Granby was all mouth about not being held responsible for his actions, and was possibly backing off. And he felt triumphant as if a bully had been faced down, a petty tyrant dethroned. But Granby's bloodless face and glassy eyes, the muttering of the lipless mouth, the repetition, also suggested that Frank had committed a terrible offence.

Granby had just barked at him as if he were less than human. "Cunt" wasn't just a word to Granby, it was a statement of an unfairly conferred status, a belittling judgement. Frank's protest would surely be countered with the most severe reprisal. Frank understood this in a heartbeat. Once you'd taken someone like Granby for a *cunt*, anything could be done to you. That's what the word meant down here. In places like The Angel.

He also had a suspicion that direct action, one-on-one, might not be Granby's style either. Frank's neck prickled at the thought of his throat being slit in the night. Or maybe the curly head would move swiftly through the dark, with peg teeth grinning, before the steel went deep into the meat as Frank bent over the sink to wash his armpits.

What a time to realise this now. Frank's words could not be taken back or ameliorated.

Granby had keys to his room.

He should leave now.

But what about his stuff? If he abandoned his CDs and books they were gone for ever. They were all he owned. And where could he go? Were there any couches he could borrow? Three nights in a London hotel was his limit, so what came after?

"Look, Granby. Hang on."

Granby was on the staircase and rising to the second floor. Was he going back to his room to get a weapon? Recent news stories of people burned alive, of acid thrown in faces, of knifings, closed Frank's throat and made him feel sick. He wanted to make amends and hated himself for being craven.

Granby's feet bumped up two flights of stairs. At the top of the house a door slammed.

Frank let himself into his room.

In less than a minute there came a gentle tapping at his locked door. Sat immobile on the end of his bed, Frank swallowed but failed to find his voice.

"Frank. Frank." It was the Irishman, Malcolm. An old decorator with haunted astigmatic eyes, who hung off the payphone in the entry most evenings, muttering into the plastic handset, usually in defence of his involvement in some protracted dispute that Frank only heard one side of. The two men were on nodding terms, but rarely spoke despite sharing the first floor. London was that kind of place. The other tenants of The Angel were either uninterested in him or wary of a new arrival.

Frank approached the door. "What?" he whispered back.

"Can I speak with you? It's all right, Granby's back in his room."

The insinuation that he was hiding from Granby behind a locked door made Frank ashamed. He opened the door. His hand trembled on the handle.

"Can I speak with you?" The man's eyes looked in two directions and the skin of his face was yellow-grey from smoking. The first floor reeked of hand-rolled cigarettes, amongst other things.

Frank let his neighbour inside, closed the door and locked it as quietly as he could.

The small man spent a few seconds looking about the room, studying the walls. There were no pictures, just wallpaper thick with paint the colour of sour milk. There was little else to look at, if you discounted unpacked boxes of possessions, and the incongruous office chair before a sash window that overlooked a yard, the space filled with broken furniture.

Without looking at Frank, the man said, "Oh, you're all right, son. For a few days. And he won't come down to sort you out. Don't operate like that here."

"Then how does it operate?" The question was out of his mouth before he could consider it.

Malcolm turned to face him. Frank didn't know which eye to look at. He chose the one that wasn't dead and bulgy and always directed at the floor. "You want to be careful, son. You don't want to mess with Granby. You might have a day or two to straighten this out, but not much more."

"I'm not letting him rob me. We agreed a hundred a week. He tried—"

"I know. I heard."

"So?" Frank held out his hands, questioningly, at the man's presence in his dismal room. If he'd just come to reiterate Granby's threats he might as well leave.

"Take it from one who knows, my friend, you best pay the man what he asks to avoid trouble. Serious trouble. He's very upset now."

Frank opened his mouth to protest. Malcolm held up one thick-fingered hand. "You have to adapt. You're with the Angels now, my friend." The man's use of "with" confused Frank, as if his neighbour was suggesting he'd joined a community established around angels. "With the angels" was also a phrase that had an uncomfortable association with death.

"I'm leaving. So there won't be any trouble."

Malcolm smiled. "Oh, they won't let you leave, son."

"What do you mean, 'they'? Granby can't stop me."

"No, true. But they'll come and find you to collect the debt."

"There is no debt."

"In your mind, son. But not in theirs."

"What? Who's they?"

"It's been decided. See if it hasn't, my friend."

"This is crazy."

"I'll tell you what I'll do. You've a good heart, son. I can tell. So I'll go and—"

"No. I'm not mixed up in anything. I took a room. A piece of shit in a broken-down building. And now I'm leaving it because I am being threatened. Simple."

"I wish it were, son. But at The Angel there are different rules, ones we've all had to learn."

"This is getting silly."

"Oh, no, son, it's deadly serious. You can trust me on this. I shouldn't even be here. There'll be hell comin' down those stairs if he knows I'm in here, talking like this." The way the man mentioned the stairs made Frank's legs feel weak.

"He's bullying you all. Robbing you."

"Oh, it ain't just Granby. No, no, son. It's those he has the ear of, if you know what I mean."

"I don't."

The man whistled between what was left of his brown teeth and raised an eyebrow. "Granby works for others. A bad lot. Very bad. He's the last of your worries."

"What, loan-sharks?"

"No, no. Worse than that, my friend. A family. A very old London family. Granby don't have much say in things. He just does favours for them."

"You mean organised crime. Like the Krays?"

"No, son."

"I'm really not following. I appreciate the heads-up, but—"

"I'll tell you what. You give me the money and I'll go and see Granby about the disagreement."

"What?"

"Before it gets out of hand."

Frank shook his head. The old scratcher was trying to get a cut of Granby's scam. More threats from Granby delivered by a patsy. "No way. I'm not giving you any money. I'm not frightened of him."

Malcolm smiled at the lie. "It's no place to go taking a stand, my friend. Not here. Won't get you anywhere. I've seen what happens. And as I said, it ain't him you need to worry about." Malcolm dropped his voice to a conspiratorial whisper. "It's them others he's got up there with him at the top of the house. They's running things. Always have done. Granby's a go-between. But he has their ear, like I said."

Frank swallowed the lump in his throat that tried to shut his voice off. "He's alone up there. Surely?"

Malcolm shook his head, his expression grave. "No, my friend. You don't want to go believing things like that. And it's best to keep them up there. Keep the peace, like."

"So… what… what do you mean? They attack people, this family?"

"When Granby came here he brought a bad lot with him. An old family that's been in this city a very long time. Long before Granby and most of them out there." The man waved one hand at the windows. "This used to be a different place, I can tell you. Was once called The Jerusalem. Clean. Good sort of people lived here. We used to drink in that bar when it was open. Even women lived here. But there's not been a woman here in fifteen years. Not since they come and changed the name. It all went downhill when Granby brought them here."

"Fifteen years. You've lived here for fifteen years?" He nearly added, "Jesus Christ" to add weight to his horror.

"Twenty," Malcolm said.

Frank could see the man wasn't joking.

"I used to be upstairs. On the second floor. Better room. But Granby moved me down here. I couldn't pay enough, see?"

Frank slumped more than sat on his bed and tried to comprehend what the man was alluding to: some kind of hierarchy of favouritism connected to the rooms and rental rates. "You mean…" He couldn't form the words.

"What, son?"

"He demoted you from the second floor. Because you wouldn't pay more rent?"

"Couldn't keep up with the cost. Down here I can manage. But think of this, son. You're on the first floor. Where can you go that's further down? There's no rooms on the ground floor. Nowhere to live. So you're already on your last life."

Frank thought of the dusty, abandoned bar, then became irritated with himself for even considering the man's nonsense.

Malcolm nodded. "You can't afford to make enemies when you're already at the bottom."

"I can't believe you put up with this. Do the other two upstairs?"

"Oh, yes, we all keep to the rules, son. There's no other way. I've been here long enough to know that. Jimmy on the second floor still works in the City, and he's been here as long as me. He's the only one left who has. So why do you think a man like that lives in a place like this? You think he chooses to?"

Returning from night shifts, Frank often saw an elderly man in a suit. He always left the building early. They'd never spoken and the man refused to meet his eye. "How much does he pay?" Frank's curiosity had taken over.

"That's between Jimmy and Granby. You never discuss money here. They don't like it. That was your first mistake."

"Oh, they don't like that? What a surprise. This just gets better and better. So some guy in finance is trapped here and has been shaken down by Granby for fifteen years? Fuck's sake. This is unbelievable. What about the drag queen?"

Malcolm didn't return Frank's grin. "The fella who dresses like a woman, Lillian. That's what he calls himself now. And that's a bad business right there, my friend. Oh, Lord. But it shows how bad it can get if Granby is upset about rent not being paid."

Frank had caught sight of a frail and elderly cross-dresser more times than he wished to remember, but never outside the building. A habitual haunter of the bathroom and its speckled mirror, the cross-dresser often clattered around inside while Frank waited on the stairs to use the toilet. "Lillian" also played opera records and made the stairs stink of perfume. Frank didn't know anything else because they'd never spoken. The man may

THE ANGELS OF LONDON

have once been a convincing female mimic, as he was small-boned, but now looked haggard and was always drunk.

"He was an actor once," Malcolm said.

"What?"

"Oh, yes. On the stage. West End. Long time ago. Work dried up and he couldn't keep up with Granby. That's when he made the change. To go on the game."

"Game?"

"Whore."

"No…"

"These days he sucks cocks down The Duchess to keep up with Granby."

Frank started to grin. He was close to screaming with hysterical laughter.

"It's terrible. He lost everything. Now he drinks. He let this place get to him. But you can't afford to let it get to you. Never. You have to learn to adapt if you want to enjoy any kind of life here. This is how it is once they let you inside. Lilly can't keep up with his rent now. He'll be the next to go, unless he gets your room at the reduced rate."

His visitor never intended the story to be amusing, but Frank couldn't stop grinning. "Go? Go where? Where will Lillian go if he doesn't get demoted into this shit-tip of a room?"

"What I am trying to tell you is that I've known others here too, who also thought like you, and who held out on Granby. But they're not around now." Again, Malcolm dropped his voice to a whisper. "But they never left either." He winked the eye Frank had been looking at. "Granby will give anyone a few months to make arrangements and you've had that. But then the collecting goes to others. And Granby don't like that because it makes him look bad. And they are all he's got going for him. If he can't collect they have to get involved. They come down. You follow? And them coming down to sort things out makes them very angry at being disturbed. Angry at Granby, angry at us. And I'd guess we're close to that time now."

"He and his imaginary family up in the attic are not getting another penny from me. I'll be gone in four weeks, or less."

"Oh, son, don't go getting ahead of yourself. There'll be no four weeks. Like I said, you have to pay now. That's how it works here. To keep them others up there. And no one leaves unless *they* say so. That's the arrangement."

Frank had heard enough. "OK. OK. I appreciate the advice. But I know a racket when I see one. This is bullshit. Do you honestly think I'll stay here and let myself get threatened? Maybe for fifteen years, while Granby takes my money, whacking up the rent whenever he wants to? And if I can't pay then I have to put on a friggin' dress? Christ almighty, what is wrong with you people?"

Frank briefly entertained an image of himself as an older man, wearing a dress in The Duchess, wherever that was. He wanted to howl with laughter.

He stood up and unlocked his door. Malcolm understood it was time to leave, but hesitated. "You're in The Angel now. You're in their house."

"Yeah, yeah. Thanks. I get it. But no thanks."

The old man stepped out of his room into the half-darkness of the corridor. The one begrimed window of the stairwell let a little light through. A silvery-grey infusion illumined half of the decrepit old figure's silhouette, which stood perfectly still. Without blinking either of his mad eyes, Malcolm watched Frank's door close.

Outside his room, Frank heard a trace of opera music. A muted fanfare. He shuddered.

* * *

Night fell and Frank paced his room, from the windows to the radiator, back and forth. The carpet looked as if it had been worn down by the similar movements of previous inmates.

Neither of his friends, Nigel or Mike, would help him out with a sofa to sleep on: girlfriends were cited as reasons in both cases. *Cheers.*

Frank had twelve-hour shifts across the next three days, so looking for a room was not an option he could pursue in the morning. As a temp he could not afford to lose the money by taking a day off work. He'd have to stick it out at The Angel for a few more days. Maybe return to his room late after work and keep a low profile for a bit. When the shift pattern concluded he could find a new place and split.

Worn out by his nerves and thoughts, Frank placed the office chair under the door handle and flopped onto his bed.

Sleep came quickly. Sleep hectic with dreams.

He saw a fat man stood by a window that opened above the pub's sign. The room must have been situated at the front of the building. The man fed pigeons and shouted, "Bitch, fucking bitch" at most of the women who passed in the street below.

In another room similar to his own, an old man crawled in circles on the carpet. His false teeth were lost and the host of a quiz show spoke about angels to him through the window of an old television.

In a chaotic and nonsensical carousel of what resembled excerpts from a seemingly unending collection of ethereal footage, his own room was featured several times. The carpet was brighter and the walls not so sallow in each brief episode. In one scene he vividly dreamed of a bearded man with a thickly haired body lying on the bed. A yellow candlewick bedspread covered him to his stomach. In one hand he held a two-litre bottle of vodka. The man stared at the ceiling with what looked like revulsion and terror.

In another dream a yolk-eyed drunk also appeared in the same bed. This time the mattress was partially covered by a tatty purple sleeping bag. The man sang a music-hall song while someone shouted "Cunt!" through the door. In that scene there was a strange sound too with no visible source. It sounded like a large bird was stuck inside the room and was beating the walls with its wings. Either that or the creature was desperately trying to flap its way inside.

Frank awoke and sat up in bed. His face was wet with tears. He was exhausted. Shaken by the dreams, he didn't go back to sleep. He got up and dressed in his security guard's uniform.

It then took him a few minutes to summon enough courage to open the door of his room and to enter the dark passage outside. He urgently needed to empty his bladder.

As he came out of the bathroom, and before his scrabbling fingers could locate the switch and turn the timed light back on, he realised that he was not alone in the corridor that passed between his room and Malcolm's.

At first he thought the scuffling sound was being made by a dog. But thin bluish light, falling through a sash window on the stairwell, illumined something that was not a dog, rising from the floor outside his room, until it was standing on two thin legs.

Someone frail, with unkempt hair. Perhaps an elderly woman. What may have been a nightgown fell to the form's scrawny knees. But the arms of the figure appeared to be too long for a person of any age. And behind it something that sounded like a pair of broken umbrellas was being shaken with fury and thrashed at the air.

Frank whimpered and slapped the light on to reveal an empty corridor. Paper peeling from the walls, red skirting boards, faded green carpet, but no sign of life.

He stood still, stunned. The thud of his heart filled his head. His thoughts groped for an explanation. The light clicked out, leaving him in the dark.

* * *

At work, Frank was often stood before the plate-glass doors, at the entrance of the residential building he guarded. Staring at the forecourt of Clarendon House, without really seeing the parked cars, he contemplated the hallucination and his dreams from the night before. He wondered if the building was some kind of hellish trap, where alcoholics and the unstable came to die. Or maybe the actual building damaged the occupants enough for them to see things, to hallucinate.

By the end of the afternoon, he'd more or less convinced himself that the tourniquet of stress constricting his life had tightened and led to the dreams and the *episode* endured the night before. A growing sense of entrapment, Granby's threats of violence, and Malcolm's elliptical suggestions of a sinister "family" housed within The Angel had all played their part. The resulting strain had caused him to half-glimpse the remnant of a nightmare in a dingy, unlit corridor.

After Frank clocked off, he whiled away four hours in Islington, sipping beer that he could ill afford to buy, before making his way back to The Angel.

At 10 p.m. he inched open the front door, removed his shoes and crept up to the first floor. He used the sides of the stairs to reduce the noise of his ascent. Despite his best efforts to move silently, once he reached his room, with his keys at the ready in one hand, he heard the distant sound of Granby's door opening, two floors up. The idea of something slipping out of that attic room was too horrible to entertain, and Frank eschewed all attempts to keep quiet in his haste to get inside his room, before locking the door behind him.

From 10 p.m. until midnight, the total absence of Lilly's opera music, the lack of a mutter from Malcolm's television, and no sign of any congress in the communal areas beyond his door, Frank interpreted as unwelcome signs of anticipation, if not apprehension, among the other occupants of The Angel. Something was about to happen. And the suggestion by his neighbour the previous evening that something would come down from the top of the house to "collect" rent from him no longer seemed as absurd to Frank as it had done during daylight hours.

He managed to stay awake in the large silent building until 2 a.m., when sleep overcame him.

At 4 a.m. he sat up with a small cry, convinced that the group of thin figures who were standing around his bed had actually come out of the dream with him and were now present at the bedside.

He removed his hands from his face and sat still in the darkness. The figures from the dream faded quickly.

Some ambient light from a distant streetlamp distinguished his thin curtains from the surrounding walls. The rest of the room remained dark. Which was galling because the sound of scratching from the wrong side of the ceiling, directly above his bed, was not something he could investigate with his wide open, beseeching eyes.

He turned sideways and scrabbled for the switch of the bedside lamp. He was so frightened, and his cringing among the bedclothes impeded his movement to such an extent, that it seemed to take about a minute for him to get the lamp switched on.

During the appalling wait for light, he'd imagined that something was hanging from the ceiling by its feet, and that a face was no more than a few inches from his own. Moments before the room was lit, he'd also heard the sound of determined wings beating against the plaster of the ceiling. He'd imagined that an animal was struggling to squeeze back through a small hole.

With the overhead light on, as well as the bedside lamp, the noise ceased. Frank could see that there was nothing on the ceiling either, and no evidence of any intrusion to account for the commotion above his bed. But he was left with an enduring fear that something within the building was now determined to show itself.

He dressed hurriedly and picked up his wallet and phone. He'd leave the building and wait out the remainder of the night, walking the streets if necessary, because that was infinitely preferable to staying inside the building.

Frank never made the stairs.

Once the door to his room was open, he became too afraid to enter the corridor.

Out there, on the staircase, the air was being cracked by the sound of dry wings. The noise of a dirty pigeon rising from the greasy cement of Trafalgar Square, but one hundred times louder. At the end of the passage, where a little light fell through the window over the stairwell, the silhouette was visible of *someone* who wasn't Malcolm, Jimmy, Lillian or Granby.

Nor could Frank be certain that the wizened figure's feet were even touching the stairs. He lacked the presence of mind to speculate how it was possible for the figure to hover like that, as well as flicker in and out of his sight. The image appeared and then disappeared before the window. But whoever, or whatever, it was, the intruder was in a state of great agitation at the sight of him.

What he could see of the form's outline shook a misshapen head about in the air. What might have been fingers at the end of the long arms repeatedly clenched into fists, then unclenched. The idea of turning the corridor light on and seeing the figure in more detail was something Frank found too unbearable to contemplate.

Cringing inside his doorway, he only found his voice after he'd swallowed the constriction in his throat. "Money. I'll get it. Please don't. The money. I'll get it."

Somewhere upstairs in the house he heard Granby's voice over the sound of the beating wings. "Cunt! Cunt! Cunt! Cunt!" the man screamed in a kind of mantra, as if he had entered into an animal frenzy, one part fury and one part intense sexual excitement at the thought of violence and blood within the wretched building.

Frank was sure he was about to be torn apart by the thing on the stairs. Or, even worse, taken somewhere else that the building offered access to, through the ceilings of its scruffy rooms. And it was at that point that enough clarity returned to his mind for him to make a suggestion. To offer a compromise to the noisy and foul air batting against his face.

He was never sure whether he spoke, or whether his offer was a thought or even a prayer to this unnatural thing that was moving from the window and up to the ceiling of the first floor. But he closed his eyes and made a pledge that he would collect money on behalf of the thing before the window. And he boasted that he would be better at collecting than Granby ever had been.

When a stench fouler than anything he had ever experienced engulfed his face and made him vomit onto his shoes – a miasma that might have hung over a cluttered battlefield, or a plague pit – Frank collapsed upon the hard carpet.

What revived him was the commotion of the old wings moving upwards and through the centre of the stairwell. This noise was soon followed by a series of screams in the attic, human cries made amidst a terrible thumping, that of a solid object connecting with a wall, and with tremendous force.

Gradually, the noises died away and silence returned to the building. A respite blessed to Frank's battered senses.

When he got to his feet he knew what he had to do.

* * *

The door to Granby's room was open, but Frank never entered. Instead, he peered inside from the doorway.

Frank never turned the light on either. What he could see of the room was half-lit by the residual streetlight shining through the skylight. That was more than adequate.

A ceiling sloped either side of a central roof beam.

Bulging black bin bags covered the floor. The nearest bag was packed taut with bank notes. He assumed that all of the other bags were filled with money too.

On the table under the window, wristwatches and items of jewellery glinted. In one corner of the room a large collection of shoes formed an ominous pile.

In the centre of the room, as if adored by the congregation of rubbish sacks, four stone rectangles stood upright. Each short column had a small stone figure mounted upon it.

Frank only glanced at the sculptures; he found himself unable to look upon them for longer than a second. But, as he stood in the doorway, he was in no doubt that they were rifling through his mind. Inside his thoughts, he heard a flock of little wings.

Being so close to the figures, for so long, must have driven Granby half-mad. Even though the inanimate quartet appeared to have been carved from rock, and had since become rusticated by a great age, for a man with more intelligence and imagination than Granby, cohabitation with the figures would have been a guarantee of the fullest insanity. Merely being in their presence assured Frank of this.

To withstand the angels for so long, Frank could only assume that Granby had sealed himself inside the old sleeping bag. It was rolled up beneath the table covered in watches and rings.

There wasn't much of Granby left to ask about the sleeping arrangements. What remained of him was mostly still inside the white tracksuit. The fabric was near luminous in the faint light – a sodium glow, occasionally supplemented with bursts of red from the flickering signage of the fried chicken takeaway across the street from The Angel. But the former landlord of The Angel had recently been rearranged into new configurations, fresh contortions of limb and posture.

The curly hair had been completely torn from his head, along with most of his scalp. The top of Granby's skull shone wetly upon the floor, directly beneath the closest column. It was not possible for the legs and arms of the living to bend in the way that Granby's limbs now did. The man's spine had come to resemble broken crockery covered by a handkerchief.

As Frank's eyes became more accustomed to the gloom, he was aware of the shapes hanging from the picture rail on wires. There were at least a score of them. At first he had mistaken the shapes for overcoats, but now realised that, although he had correctly identified at least two coats, their owners were still inside them. The other hanged figures were naked and had withered to not much more than bones. Not seeing greater detail was a blessing.

Inside the vast house below, Frank heard the first signs of life: Malcolm closing the bathroom door and running the only working tap over the basin.

On the second floor there must have been two empty rooms, and Frank was sick of the sight of Lillian, so make that three empty rooms.

Frank took one final look at the smashed figure of Granby, and noticed the man's teeth were also missing. He thought it a strange city that allowed its old gods to keep such odd tokens.

But now he needed to get the empty second-floor rooms occupied quickly. £125 a week seemed like a reasonable rate. At least to start with.

A CURSE IS A CURSE

BY HELEN GRANT

I saw him coming a long time before he ever reached the village. I was up on the roof, mending the thatch while the weather was dry. It was rather warm, and the sweat was trickling down unpleasantly into my bodice. I stopped to take a mouthful of ale, and glanced down, and there he was.

People down in the village think that Sarah and I have a special sense for when outsiders are coming – that there's something witchy in it. We don't disabuse them. In fact, there was a great tree that came down in the storm some years back, so that when you look down from up here on the hill there is a gap. You can see right out to the plain beyond, and since that's the only sensible way to reach this place, you'll usually spot any visitors approaching. If the villagers came up here, they'd know this, but of course they don't.

I sat back on my heels and shaded my eyes.

Probably not trouble, I thought. There was only one of him, and although he was mounted on a horse I could see neither the bright gleam of a cuirass nor the glitter of mail. He might be a pedlar, I supposed, or perhaps a travelling minstrel, though those didn't usually run to anything grander than a donkey. Once, we had an itinerant priest all dressed in black, like a crow; he rode in with a high fever, almost dropping off his horse, and at first nobody wanted to go near him. They put him in a disused house with water and a chunk of bread, and he died raving three days later. When they were sure he was really dead, they took him to the ruins of the church and put him under a stone with somebody else's name on it. I believe they ate the horse.

I could not tell what manner of person this was coming towards the village, not from that distance, but I could be sure it was a man. A woman would not ride across that lonely plain, alone and undefended. After a while I went back to my thatching. Inevitably he would find his way up here, to me and Sarah. There is no inn down in the village and most people do not care to take in strangers.

For about two hours more I worked. In one place I think a marten had got into the thatch, such was the damage, and then I had to go down into the house; human urine may ward the creatures off but I'd have struggled to produce anything after working so long out in the sun. So I asked Sarah, and while she was crouching over the bucket and I was staring out of the unglazed window, I said:

"There's a man coming. I saw from the roof."

Piss tinkled against the metal and then Sarah said, "Ah."

I hesitated. Then I said, "I'd like this one."

She was silent for a moment, so I added, "I'm eighteen, Sarah."

I heard a rustle as she rearranged her skirts.

"There's no hurry," she said.

"We don't know how long it will be until the next one," I pointed out.

"No," she agreed. "But don't you want to look first?"

"I suppose," I said. But I had made up my mind. Unless he was diseased, or too old, he would be mine. You have to make the most of what Chance offers.

In the meantime, I went back up onto the roof and carried on with the thatching. Nothing gets done without hard work.

* * *

I first saw him in the morning, but it was almost evening when he came up to the house. He was no longer astride the horse but leading it, picking his way carefully between the rocks and roots that clotted the path. When he first appeared, he was looking down, watching his footing, and I couldn't see his face, only his thick dark hair. He was neither fat nor thin, but somewhere in between, and around the ordinary height. When he looked up, I saw a lean brown face, clean-shaven and dark-eyed, not actually handsome, but not ugly either; and not old, though not as young as me.

He saw me standing outside the house, hands on my hips, and I saw the beginnings of something appear on his face – warmth perhaps, or curiosity. Then he saw the Wall, and that look was wiped out at once. He stopped walking, and the horse stopped walking, and I saw him glance from side to side, as if there might be somewhere else to go but here.

I sighed to myself, and then I started down towards him, with what I hoped was an encouraging smile on my face.

"Good evening, sir," I said. "Are you looking for lodging?"

He seemed somewhat troubled as to how to answer this question.

"Is this the house of Sarah and Maggie?"

"I am Maggie. Sarah is indoors."

I saw his gaze wander behind me again. "I did not know you were so close to the Wall."

"Well, we are," I said briskly. "But you need not concern yourself."

Still he stood there, not moving forward.

"Is the Wall... complete?"

I glanced back at the mossy stonework that reared up behind the house, overtopping the thatched roof. "Of course it is. Do you think we would live here otherwise?"

I waited.

Eventually he said, "The villagers..." and stopped.

"The villagers," I said, "have probably told you all manner of nonsense about why and how we live here. There is no witchcraft in our safety. The Wall is perfectly complete, and will probably stand for another two hundred years."

He considered. "I might perhaps walk the perimeter of it..."

"You most certainly will not," I said. "It would take you all night. Believe me when I say that you will be safer up here than you would be down in the village, where nobody will take you in anyway. It will be dark in a little time, and the next place is half a day's journey from here. You had better come inside, and be thankful of the shelter."

"I will." But I noticed that as he came up to the house, he kept looking at the Wall.

We put the horse in the little building adjoining our place and gave it water and hay, and then I took him indoors to Sarah.

She turned as he came in, looked at him and then looked at me and nodded.

He seemed taller now, in this warm, smoky little room with its low ceiling. He had to stoop under the bunches of dried plants hanging from the beams.

"Are you Mistress Sarah?" he asked.

"Just Sarah will do," she said.

"I am Luke."

"Luke of someone, of somewhere?"

"Just Luke will do."

Sarah began to put out plates. "There is partridge and root vegetables for dinner. How will you pay for your lodging, just Luke?"

"With this." He held out a silver piece.

She snorted. "That is better than the last travelling minstrel, who wanted to pay us with a song."

"I am not a minstrel," said Luke. He put down his pack and pulled out a chair to sit down.

"Then what are you?" She stopped to look him up and down. "Not a pedlar; you've been indoors a full two minutes and not tried to sell us anything."

He laughed. "Not a pedlar either. I am not sure there is an exact word for what I am. The nearest one is *sage.*"

"*Sage?*"

He nodded. "A gatherer of wisdom... and information."

Sarah made a face. "And how does that get you silver pieces? It seems to me that there is no money at all in that."

Luke put his elbows on the table, comfortably. "My master pays me to travel, and to seek knowledge."

"And who is your master? A king?"

"I suppose you might say he is a king."

There was a short silence.

"If this is true," said Sarah at last, "then your master is very foolish. But if it is not true, then you should know that neither Maggie nor I have anything worth robbing, and that we sleep fully armed."

He studied her for a moment. "I am not a robber, nor a murderer, nor a tormentor of women. I have one knife, and one bow, and you may lock them into the room with yourselves tonight if you wish."

"Very well," she said, and turned her back to fetch the pan of food.

I sat down opposite Luke.

"A *sage?*"

He nodded.

"And you think there is knowledge here, in this place? Something to be learned?"

"There is something to be learned everywhere."

His face was perfectly grave, his eyes watchful. I could not think of anything else to ask.

"I hope you will eat well," I said.

* * *

We put Luke into my small chamber, and I went upstairs with Sarah to the room under the eaves. Sarah carried Luke's knife and bow.

"I think we should lock ourselves in as he suggested," she said. Her brow was furrowed. "A *sage*, indeed. I don't believe it."

I walked a little way, turned and walked back.

"I'm going downstairs again," I said.

"Maggie." Sarah touched my shoulder. "Stay here."

"No," I said. I hesitated. "It will be alright."

"But if—"

I touched her hand but I did not look her in the eye. "It will be alright, Mother," I said.

Then I let myself out of the room and went back down the wooden staircase, treading quietly. The fire was banked up and in the low light I saw that the door to the small chamber was ajar. All was silent. I stood there for a moment but not for long because I did not want to think too much about what I intended to do. Then I went in.

Luke was lying on his back on the straw mattress. His

eyes were closed, but the instant I crossed the threshold they opened, and he sat up.

He said: "I have three more silver pieces. You can take them. Don't do what you were going to do. Just take the silver."

"I don't want the silver."

"Then what do you want?"

"I want..."

He waited.

"I want a child."

"What?!" Then he saw my face, and saw that I was in earnest.

"There's no guarantee, you know," he said.

"I know." I rubbed my hands together. "I want to try."

Luke was silent for a moment. "Are you sure?"

"Yes."

I went over to him and stood there, but I didn't know what to do, so he held out his hands to me and pulled me close. He smelled of the road, of sweat and dust, of grass wilting in the sunshine, and something else that reminded me of old parchment. None of these were bad smells.

"I may not come back this way," he said.

"I know."

"Even if there's a child."

"Stop talking," I said, and he did.

* * *

Afterwards, he drifted off to sleep, lying on his back again. I had only ever seen Sarah sleeping before, and so I watched him for a bit, wondering how he could lie there so confidently with his face exposed. I usually slept like a dormouse, curled into a ball. After a while I became bored, and shook him awake.

He looked fuddled. "You want to do it *again*? I'm not sure I can. It's too soon."

"No, I want to talk."

"*Talk*? Ye Gods, woman." But now he was awake and blinking, so with a lot of sighing he propped himself up on his elbow, facing me.

"Are you really a sage?"

"Yes."

"So someone pays you – silver – to travel around finding out about things?"

He nodded.

"Just... anything?"

"Well, not *anything*. There are some things that are pretty well known already, like how to grow the ordinary crops, and make bread, and dry things for the winter."

"What then?"

"Some of it is about understanding what happened in the past. Why things are the way they are. And the – the extent of things now. People don't travel much, you know; we don't know what's out there. Did you know that if you travel two hundred and ten miles from here you will come to a great body of water, so vast that you cannot see the other side, and nameless?"

I shook my head. "I've never been more than twenty miles from here."

"Well, it's true. I've seen it with my own eyes."

"I don't believe you."

"I have. It has a peculiar smell too – of brine."

I laughed, and shook my head again.

"Really, it does. And some people think that there may be land on the other side of the water, with people on it, just like us."

"If there are such things to be discovered," I said, "why did you come here?"

"Because of the Wall."

"The Wall? Why do you want to know about the Wall?"

This time he shook his head. "Before I tell you that, I want you to tell me what you know about it. What do the villagers say about it? Why is it there?" He put out one lean, brown hand and pushed the hair back from my face. "And you, who live so close to it, what can you tell me about it? Have you seen or heard anything?"

I looked down. "Sometimes. Not often."

"Tell me."

I frowned a little. "It's ill luck to talk of it."

"No possible harm can come from telling me."

I was doubtful about this, but he spoke with such sincerity that I decided to tell him anyway. Sarah and I have lived on the edge of ill luck forever, after all.

"It's a curse," I said.

"Wait – before you tell me, let me get my quill and my ink." And he actually climbed out of bed and went to rummage through his pack. I watched, bemused; it seemed impossible that what I said should be important enough to write down. There are people out on the roads who would rob you for clean parchment as soon as for silver pieces. But in spite of this, he fetched all his things and when he was ready, the point of the quill hovering over the ink, he nodded for me to go on.

"It's a curse," I said again.

"A *curse*?"

"Yes. And this is how it came about. Many years ago, too many to count, the village was a much bigger place, and it covered all this great hill. There were a lot more people living here then, and they lived in great luxury and comfort. They always had more than enough to eat, and nobody ever died of cold or hunger or overwork. And yet," I said, "they were not content. They always wanted more – more food, more entertainment, more life.

"Amongst the inhabitants of this village there lived a very great witch. She was so powerful that she could do anything; she even had power over life and death. So the people sent a deputation to this witch, saying that they wanted to live longer – even forever. They believed that she could do this for them, and they also believed that they merited it. Their arrogance knew no bounds. *Bless us with everlasting life*, they demanded.

"The witch knew that such a thing would not be a blessing; it would be a curse. She told them this, and she refused to do what they asked. But the people would not be satisfied. They argued and begged and insisted, and when she still said no, they laid hands on her and tortured her.

"For seven days and seven nights she endured the most terrible pains and then she gave in, not because she was tormented to it by the agonies she suffered, but because she became angry and believed that the people deserved to be punished. So she laid upon them the most terrible curse in the world: that they should live forever. And then she died."

I paused, and heard the scratching of the quill pen over the parchment. Then I resumed the story.

"Nobody bothered to bury the witch. Heedless and pitiless, they went away rejoicing at their good fortune. And for a time it certainly did seem that they were blessed, because they no longer lived under the shadow of death.

"But as time passed, and people began to age and their limbs grew weak and their eyes could no longer see properly, it began to occur to them what they had done. They would have gone back to the witch and asked her to make them young and whole again too, but the witch was dead, and her bones were whitening under the broad sky. So there was no help there.

"Some of the people acquired injuries over the years – they lost an arm or a foot or an eye – and of course they did not die of any of these things, but went on living, even if the damage turned gangrenous and foul. And at last their brains went too; the sharpest and luckiest amongst them lasted for over a hundred years, but in the end they were all as babes – understanding nothing at all, speechless and reasonless.

"Those living outside the village, who had not asked for the curse to be visited on them, became afraid of these shambling, undying creatures. And so they caused a great Wall to be built all around the village, so that the inhabitants would have to stay within and wear out their many centuries unseen by the rest of the world.

"Since that time, nobody has seen what is inside the Wall. But they say that those within continue to live, and that even if their bodies are worn away to nothing at all, or entirely consumed by fire, some part of them still does not die. And if you were to stand close to the Wall on a very clear, still night, and listen for a long time, you might hear those invisible ones as a groan or a sigh.

"And so," I concluded in the traditional manner, "it shall be until the end of time."

For a little while, the quill continued its scratching, spilling the words across the parchment, and although I have never learned the art of it myself, I thought the script looked very elegant. Then Luke put down the pen, shook a little sand onto the page to dry the ink, and put his materials away with great care.

"Fascinating," he remarked. "An original curse story."

He smiled at me. "And I am wide awake now. If you wish to make the chances of a child a little likelier, I could go again."

I considered this. The first time had not been the absolute living paradise that people led you to expect – but on the other hand, the idea had some merits.

"Yes," I said. "Alright."

* * *

At dawn I heard a quiet sound and opened my eyes a very little. Sarah was standing at the door of the small chamber looking at Luke sleeping and me pressing close to him. She rolled her eyes and shook her head, and then she turned away. A few minutes later I heard the outer door open and close, and knew that she had gone out.

I extricated myself carefully and padded out into the kitchen, where I looked around carefully. Sarah's big woven willow basket was not in its place, and I guessed she had gone out to gather herbs – a nice piece of tact, since it left me and Luke alone for an hour or two. I swept the hearth and made a new fire, and brewed tea. In a little box on a high shelf was our precious supply of sugar, and I broke off a tiny piece to add to the brew, although I knew Sarah would scold me later. I carried a cup through to Luke.

He propped himself up, and took the cup. He tasted it, and made a face.

"What is this?"

"Raspberry leaf," I said, a little piqued. "For fertility. We have one pot to brew in, so I made us the same."

"Perhaps you had better drink it then," he said, and handed me the cup back. Then, seeing my face, he added, "You added sugar, which was a great kindness, but I would rather you had it than me."

"You are the guest," I objected.

"And you may be carrying my child."

"Hardly yet," I said, but I couldn't repress a smile.

After a while, he said, "I must go today, you know."

"Today? You cannot stay a single night more?"

"No." He looked away for a moment. "But if you would show me along part of the Wall first, that would be a great help to me."

"Of course." I fidgeted. "Did you write down all that I said?"

"As closely as I could."

"Who will you show it to? Really a king?"

After a pause he said, "Not exactly a king."

"What then?"

Luke sighed. "The... head of research."

A flock of birds took flight in my gut, ice on their wings.

"And I have lain with you," I said, my voice thin and unsteady.

"Research is not what you think it is," he said. The way he kept saying the word, so frankly and boldly, made my stomach turn over.

"It is the worst of the dark arts."

"No, it isn't. Do you even know what it means?"

"It means things that even people like me and Sarah, whom the villagers take for witches, should not meddle with."

"But what *exactly* do you think it means?"

I shook my head. "Evil."

"It isn't." His gaze was level, unflinching. "It's simply another word for what I told you I did before – gathering wisdom and information."

"But those things are not wrong. Pointless, perhaps, and even idle, when there is so much work to be done. But not evil. You must be wrong about this. What you do cannot be..." I dropped my voice. "...research."

Luke sat up, putting his bare feet on the floor, and looked at me earnestly.

"Maggie, it doesn't really matter what you call it. It is a kind of work, and it has to be done, if we are ever to make progress – if we are ever to get back to where we once were."

"Why would we want to go back to the past? To the building of the Wall?"

"Because it wasn't just about the things that went wrong." He reached out and took my hand in his. His touch was warm and comforting, and the thought that this was not an evil man passed treacherously through my head. I didn't move nearer, but nor did I remove my hand.

"In my travels, I have seen things you would barely believe. Not just the great stretch of water I told you about, but things that people made. Many, many days' travel from here, there is a great palace, beautiful but well defended. It has windows that glitter in the sunshine, and rings of wall and fencing all around it – fencing too high to scale, with rows of tiny metal claws on top of it. I have been inside this place myself, because one gate lies open, pushed down by the passing of some great force.

"This palace has many rooms – perhaps a thousand. Can you imagine that?"

I shook my head again, fascinated in spite of myself.

"There are things we believe to be machines, although we cannot say yet what animated them."

"Spirits?"

"I don't believe so. I think there was some other principle, which we have not grasped. And there are rooms which are full of the tiniest vials you can think of, made of pure clear glass – rows upon rows of them. How the glassblowers managed to create such things, so absolutely perfect and regular, is a great mystery, as is their purpose. What could possibly be stored in something so tiny?"

"Better not to know," I said.

"So people have said, for a very long time. But we do not think so – not any more."

"But..." I tried to frame the right question. "If you have seen all these wonderful and peculiar things, why did you want to come and see the Wall, which is old and ugly?"

"Because..." He put his head on one side. "We want to understand what happened. Your story of a curse is very interesting – very inventive – but I don't believe it to be the literal truth. No – don't be angry. I think your story is very clever, and explains what happened very neatly. But do you know that there are other places – many other places – like your village?"

"There are?"

Luke nodded. "Some of them have Walls, like this one. There is one place where there is a natural island, with only one bridge onto it, and the bridge has been sealed off. And in some places, the living areas were burned to the ground, and fenced off to warn people not to go there."

"But..." I said, wrinkling my brow. "How did this happen? Were there curses in these other places too?"

"There was no curse," Luke said. "At least, not in the sense you mean – a witch's curse. We think that *people* caused what happened – that they made this kind of living death."

"But why would anyone do that?" I asked him.

"We don't know," he admitted.

"You say..." I lowered my voice again. "...that *research* is not evil. But that seems very evil to me."

He thought about it for a moment. "All I can tell you is: the kind of research I do does not cause anything like that. In fact, we hope it might stop bad things happening again in the future."

"You think so?"

"I do." He looked at me very gravely. "You're not afraid of me, surely?"

 I considered. "No. I suppose not."

"Well then, I shall get up, and then let us go and look at this Wall of yours."

* * *

We made breakfast with two brown eggs and the end of the bread, and then we went out to walk along the Wall. It is possible to walk right around it, although it takes a long time – perhaps a day, although it depends on the time of year, and the growth of plants or the covering of ice. We did not attempt this, but simply made our way perhaps two miles along it. It can be quite difficult going, especially for someone who does not know the terrain, as Luke didn't. There used to be houses and other buildings under much of it, so there are big uneven stones to climb over, and treacherous places where the spaces between the stones lead into chasms in the ground. Trees have thrust their way up too, and spiny bushes. The Wall is damp in places, and green with moss, but nowhere is it broken. The people who constructed it made it well.

We stopped in a place where there was water coming up from the ground, so that we could drink. It was very quiet: just the sound of the water bubbling up and running away.

"Is this safe to drink?" asked Luke, looking from the Wall to the spring.

I shrugged. "I've drunk from it all my life and nothing has happened."

"Well, then," he said, and knelt to drink, but I thought he looked ill at ease.

After, he said, "It's very quiet here. Do you ever hear anything from the other side?"

I opened my mouth to reply, and at that moment we both heard a thin shriek wavering through the air, very close by. Luke jumped so hard I almost laughed.

"A bird," I said.

He looked at me, his dark eyes wide and troubled.

"Really," I said. "Just a bird." I brushed my hands on my skirts. "I have heard things from the other side," I said, "but only rarely. Slow movements, a kind of grunt. It could be anything. Animals. A wild pig."

"Are there wild pigs in there?"

I shrugged again. "Who knows?" I could feel my mouth turning up at the corner. "You are easily frightened, for someone who claims to do... research."

"And you?" he said. "You are not afraid, to live so close to it?"

"No," I replied. "The Wall is sturdy. I told you, it will stand for another two hundred years at least. Whatever is in there, it cannot do us any harm."

"Let us go back," Luke said. "I have seen enough."

And so we did. When we came within sight of the house, there was smoke coming out of the chimney. Sarah was inside. I took the chance to pull Luke to me and kiss him before we went in. I knew I was kissing him goodbye. Then I started to walk towards the house, and he caught my arm and pulled me back.

"You know I have to go today," he said. "But despite what I said before, I think perhaps I can come back."

I looked up at him. "I wish you would."

He said, "I have to go north, but I could travel back this way. It might be a year, it might be longer. But if you have a child by then, I could see it. And if you don't have a child... well..."

"We could try again," I said softly.

We looked at each other and smiled. There was nothing more to say after that, so we went down to the house together.

* * *

Before the sun was overhead he left, leading the horse down the rocky path. Sarah had said goodbye curtly; her sharp eyes had noticed that the box with the sugar in it had been moved from its place. She was reckoning up the partridge and the vegetables and the sugar against the silver piece.

I stood outside the house and watched him go. Just before he moved out of sight, he turned and raised a hand, and I raised one back.

I wondered whether I ought to cry, but decided that there was too much to think about. I put my hands on my abdomen and rubbed gently, wondering if Luke's seed had taken or not, and whether he would really return. On the whole I thought he would. His stories about the world beyond the limits of the village seemed too fantastical to be believed, but even if those were untruths, I didn't think he was *that* kind of liar.

When I was sure that he was really out of sight, and that the only movements I could detect were leaves moving in the breeze, I went indoors.

Sarah was making bread, kneading the dough with irritable energy. The basket of herbs was on the other end of the table, so I started to sort through them.

"He says he'll come back," I said.

Sarah said nothing.

"He told me other things too," I said, and once I started talking I couldn't seem to stop. "He said that whatever is on the other side of the Wall, it wasn't because of a curse at all. He said there wasn't any witch either. He said that there are other places, lots of places, like this one – some of them with walls, and one on an island, and some all burnt away to nothing. And he went to a palace filled with thousands of tiny bottles, and nobody knows what was in them. Luke says it was *people* who caused the thing on the other side of the Wall. People. Not a curse."

Sarah stopped kneading, and turned to look at me. Then she shook her head, and gave a long sigh.

"A curse is a curse," she said.

DARK CAROUSEL

BY JOE HILL

It used to be on postcards: the carousel at the end of the Cape Maggie Pier. It was called the Wild Wheel, and it ran fast – not as fast as a roller coaster but quite a bit faster than the usual carousel for kiddies. The Wheel looked like an immense cupcake, its cupola roof striped in black and green with royal gold trim. After dark it was a jewel box awash in an infernal red glow, like the light inside an oven. Wurlitzer music floated up and down the beach, discordant strains that sounded like a Romanian waltz, something for a nineteenth-century ball attended by Dracula and his icy white brides.

It was the most striking feature of Cape Maggie's run-down, seedy harbor walk. The harbor walk had been run-down and seedy since my grandparents were kids. The air was redolent with the cloying perfume of cotton candy, an odor that doesn't exist in nature and can only be described as "pink" smell. There was always a puddle of vomit on the boardwalk that had to be avoided. There were always soggy bits of popcorn floating in the puke. There were a dozen sit-down restaurants where you could pay too much for fried clams and wait too long to get them. There were always harassed-looking, sunburned grownups carrying shrieking, sunburned children, the whole family out for a seaside lark.

On the pier itself, there were the usual stands selling candied apples and hot dogs, booths where you could shoot an air rifle at tin outlaws who popped up from behind tin cacti. There was a great pirate ship that swung back and forth like a pendulum, sailing high out over the sides of the pier and the ocean beyond, while shrill screams carried into the night. I thought of that ride as the SS *Fuck No*. And there was a bouncy house called Bertha's Bounce. The entrance was the face of an obscenely fat woman with glaring eyes and glistening red cheeks. You took your shoes off outside and climbed in over her lolling tongue, between bloated lips. That was where the trouble started, and it was Geri Renshaw and I who started it. After all, there wasn't any rule that big kids, or even teenagers, couldn't play in the bouncy house. If you had a ticket, you could have your three minutes to leap around – and Geri said she wanted to see if it was as much fun as she remembered.

We went in with five little kids, and the music started, a recording of small children with piping voices, singing a highly sanitized version of "Jump Around" by House of Pain. Geri took my hands, and we jumped up and down, bounding about like astronauts on the moon. We lurched this way and that until we crashed into a wall and she pulled me down. When she rolled on top and began to bounce on *me*, she was just goofing, but the

224

gray-haired woman who'd taken our tickets was watching, and she shouted, "NONE OF THAT!" at the top of her lungs and snapped her fingers at us. "OUT! This is a family ride."

"Got that right," Geri said, leaning over me, her breath warm in my face and pink-scented. She had just inhaled a cloud of cotton candy. She was in a tight, striped halter top that left her tanned midriff bare. Her breasts were right in my face in a very lovely way. "This is the kind of ride that makes families, if you don't use protection."

I laughed – I couldn't help it – even though I was embarrassed and my face was burning. Geri was like that. Geri and her brother Jake were always dragging me into situations that excited and discomfited me in equal measure. They led me into things that I regretted in the moment but were later a pleasure to remember. Real sin, I think, produces the same emotions, in the exact opposite order.

As we exited, the ticket collector stared at us the way a person might look at a snake eating a rat, or two beetles fucking.

"Keep your pants on, Bertha," Geri said. "We did."

I grinned like an idiot but still felt bad. Geri and Jake Renshaw would take shit from no man, and no woman either. They relished verbally swatting down the ignorant and the self-righteous: the twerp, the bully, and the Baptist all the same.

Jake was waiting with an arm around Nancy Fairmont's waist when we came reeling across the pier. He had a wax cup of beer in the other hand, and he gave it to me as I walked up. God, it was *good*. That right there might've been the best beer of my life. Salty and cold, the sides of the cup beaded with ice water, and the flavor mixed with the briny tang of the sea air.

It was the tail end of August in 1994, and all of us were eighteen and free, although Jake could've easily passed for almost thirty. To look at Nancy, it was hard to believe she was dating Jake Renshaw, who with his flattop cut and his tattoos looked like trouble (and sometimes was). But then it was hard to picture a kid like me with Geri. Geri and Jake were twins and six feet tall to the inch – which meant they both had two inches on me, something that always bothered me when I had to rise on my toes to give Geri a kiss. They were strong, lean, limber, and blond, and they grew up jumping dirt bikes and doing after-school detentions. Jake had a criminal record. The only reason Geri didn't have one as well, Jake insisted, was that she'd never been caught.

Nancy, on the other hand, wore glasses with lenses as big as tea saucers and went everywhere with a book clutched to her flat chest. Her father was a veterinarian, her mother a librarian. As for me, Paul Whitestone, I longed to have a tattoo and a criminal record of my own, but instead I had an acceptance letter from Dartmouth and a notebook full of one-act plays.

Jake, Geri, and I had made the run to Cape Maggie in Jake Renshaw's 1982 Corvette, a car as sleek as a cruise missile and almost as fast. It was a two-seater, and no one would let us ride in it today the way we did then: Geri in my lap, Jake behind the wheel, and a six-pack of beer behind the stick shift – which we polished off while we were en route. We had come down from

Lewiston to meet Nancy, who'd worked on the pier all summer long, selling fried dough. When she finished her shift, the four of us were going to drive nine miles to my parents' summer cottage on Maggie Pond. My parents were home in Lewiston, and we'd have the place to ourselves. It seemed like a good spot to make our final stand against adulthood.

Maybe I felt guilty about offending the ticket lady at Big Bertha, but Nancy was there to clear my conscience. She touched her glasses and said, "Mrs Gish over there pickets Planned Parenthood every Sunday, with faked-up pictures of dead babies. Which is pretty funny, since her husband owns half the booths on the pier, including Funhouse Funnel Cakes, where I work, and he's tried to cop a feel on just about every girl who ever worked for him."

"Does he, now?" Jake asked. He was grinning, but there was a slow, sly chill in his voice that I knew from experience was a warning that we were wading into dangerous territory.

"Never mind, Jake," Nancy said, and she kissed his cheek. "He only paws high-school girls. I'm too old for him now."

"You ought to point him out sometime," Jake said, and he looked this way and that along the pier, as if scouting for the guy right then and there.

Nancy put her hand on his chin and forcibly turned his head to look at her. "You mean I ought to ruin our night by letting you get arrested and kicked out of the service?" He laughed at her, but suddenly she was cross with him. "You dick around, Jake, and you could do five years. The only reason you

227

aren't there already is the marines took you — I guess because our nation's military-industrial complex can always use more cannon fodder. It's not your job to get even with every creep who ever wandered down the harbor walk."

"It's not your job to make sure I get out of Maine," Jake said, his tone almost mild. "And if I wind up in the state prison, at least I'd get to see you on the weekends."

"I wouldn't visit you," she said.

"Yes you would," he told her, kissing her cheek, and she blushed and looked upset, and we all knew she would. It was embarrassing how tightly she was wrapped around Jake's finger, how badly she wanted to make him happy. I understood exactly how she felt, because I was stuck on Geri just the same way.

Six months before, we had all gone bowling at Lewiston Lanes, something to do to kill a Thursday night. A drunk in the next lane made an obscene moan of appreciation when Geri bent over to get a ball, noisily admiring her rear in her tight jeans. Nancy told him not to be vile, and he replied that she didn't need to worry, no one was going to bother checking out a no-tits cunt like herself. Jake had gently kissed Nancy on the top of her head and then, before she could grab his wrist and pull him back, decked the guy hard enough to shatter his nose and knock him flat.

The only problem was that the drunk and his buddies were all off-duty cops, and in the fracas that followed, Jake was wrestled to the floor and handcuffed, a snub-nosed revolver put to his head. In the trial much was made of the fact that he had a switchblade in his pocket and a prior record of petty vandalism. The drunk – who in court was no longer a drunk but instead a good-looking officer of the law with a wife and four kids – insisted he had called Nancy a "little runt," not a "no-tits cunt." But it hardly mattered what he'd said, because the judge felt that both girls had been provocative in dress and behavior and so presumably had no right to be outraged by a little ribald commentary. The judge told Jake it was jail or military service, and two days later Jake was on his way to Camp Lejeune in North Carolina, his head shaved and everything he owned stuffed into a Nike gym bag.

Now he was back for ten days on leave. The week after next, he'd board a plane at Bangor International Airport and fly to Germany for deployment in Berlin. I wouldn't be there to see him go – by then I'd be moved into my dorm in New Hampshire. Nan was on her way elsewhere as well. After Labor Day she started classes at U of Maine in Orono. Only Geri was going nowhere, staying behind in Lewiston, where she had a job with housekeeping at a Days Inn. Jake had committed the assault, but it often seemed to me that somehow Geri was the one who'd received the prison sentence.

Nan was on break, still had a few hours on her shift to go before she was free. She wanted to blow the smell of fried grease from her hair, so we wandered out toward the end of the pier. A salty, scouring wind sang among the guy wires, snapped the pennants. The wind was blowing hard inland, too, coming in gusts that ripped off hats and slammed doors. Back on shore that wind felt like summer, sultry and sweet with the smell of baked grass and hot tarmac. Out on the end of the pier, the gusts carried a thrilling chill that made your pulse race. Out on the end of the pier, you were in October Country.

We slowed as we approached the Wild Wheel, which had just stopped turning. Geri tugged my hand and pointed at one of the creatures on the carousel. It was a black cat the size of a pony, with a limp mouse in its jaws. The cat's head was turned slightly, so it seemed to be watching us avidly with its bright green glass eyes.

"Oh, hey," Geri said. "That one looks just like me on my first date with Paul."

Nancy clapped a hand over her mouth to stifle her laughter. Geri didn't need to say which of us was the mouse and which was the cat. Nancy had a lovely, helpless laugh that went through her whole tiny frame, doubled her over, and turned her face pink.

"Come on," Geri said. "Let's find our spirit animals." And she let go of my hand and took Nancy's.

The Wurlitzer began to play, a theatrical, whimsical, but also curiously dirgelike melody. Wandering amid the steeds, I looked at the creatures of the Wheel with a mix of fascination and repulsion. It seemed to me a uniquely disquieting collection of grotesqueries. There was a wolf as big as a bicycle, its sculpted, glossy fur a tangled mess of blacks and grays and its eyes as yellow as my beer. One paw was lifted slightly, and its pad was crimson, as if he had trod in blood. A sea serpent uncoiled itself across the outer edge of the carousel, a scaly rope as thick as a tree trunk. It had a shaggy gold mane and a gaping red mouth lined with black fangs. When I leaned in close, I discovered they were real: a mismatched set of shark's teeth, black with age. I walked through a team of white horses, frozen in the act of lunging, tendons straining in their necks, their mouths open as if to scream in anguish or rage. White horses with white eyes, like classical statuary.

"Where the hell you think they got these horses from? Satan's Circus Supplies? Lookat," Jake said, and he gestured at the mouth of one of the horses. It had the black, forked tongue of a snake, lolling out of its mouth.

"They come from Nacogdoches, Texas," came a voice from down on the pier. "They're over a century old. They were salvaged from Cooger's Carousel of Ten Thousand Lights, after a fire burned Cooger's Fun Park to the ground. You can see how that one there was scorched."

The ride operator stood at a control board, to one side of the steps leading up to the merry-go-round. He wore a dress uniform, as if he were an ancient bellboy in some grand Eastern European hotel, a place where aristocrats went to summer with their families. His suit jacket was of green velvet, with two rows of brass buttons down the front and golden epaulets on his shoulders.

He put down a steel thermos and pointed at a horse whose face was blistered on one side, toasted a golden brown, like a marshmallow. The operator's upper lip lifted in a curiously repulsive grin. He had red, plump, vaguely indecent lips, like a young Mick Jagger – unsettling in such an old, shriveled face. "They screamed."

"Who?" I asked.

"The horses," he said. "When the carousel began to burn. A dozen witnesses heard them. They screamed like girls."

My arms prickled with goose bumps. It was a delightfully macabre claim to make.

"I heard they're all salvaged," Nancy said, from somewhere just behind me. She and Geri had circumnavigated the entirety of the carousel, examining the steeds, and were only now returning to us. "There was a piece in the *Portland Press Herald* last year."

"The griffin came from Selznick's in Hungary," said the operator, "after they went bankrupt. The cat was a gift from Manx, who runs Christmasland in Colorado. The sea serpent was carved by Frederick Savage himself, who constructed the most famous carousel of them all, the Golden Gallopers on Brighton Palace Pier, after which the Wild Wheel is modeled. You're one of Mr Gish's girls, aren't you?"

"Ye-*e-sss*," said Nancy slowly, perhaps because she didn't quite like the operator's phrasing, the way he called her "one of Mr Gish's girls." "I work for him at the funnel-cake stand."

"Only the best for Mr Gish's girls," said the operator. "Would you like to ride a horse that once carried Judy Garland?"

He stepped up onto the carousel and offered Nancy his hand, which she took without hesitation, as if he were a desirable young man asking her to dance and not a creepy old dude with fat, damp lips. He led her to the first in the herd of six horses, and when she put a foot into one golden stirrup, he braced her waist to help her up.

"Judy visited Cooger's in 1940, when she was on an extended tour to support *The Wizard of Oz*. She received a key to the city, sang 'Over the Rainbow' to an adoring crowd, and then rode the Ten Thousand Lights. There's a photo of her in my private office, riding this very horse. There you go, right up. Aren't you lovely?"

"What a crock of shit," Geri said to me as she took my arm. She spoke in a low voice, but not low enough, and I saw the operator twitch. Geri threw her leg over the black cat. "Did anyone famous ride this one?"

"Not yet. But maybe someday you yourself will be a great celebrity! And then for years to come we will be boasting about the day when," the old fellow told her in an exuberant tone. Then he caught my eye and winked and said, "You'll want to drain that beer, son. No drinks on the ride. And alcohol is hardly necessary – the Wild Wheel will provide all the intoxication you could wish for."

I had finished off two cans of the beer in the car on the ride down. My mostly full wax cup was my third. I could've put it down on the planks, but that casual suggestion – *You'll want to drain that beer, son* – seemed like the only sensible thing to do. I swallowed most of a pint in five big swallows, and by the time I crushed the cup and tossed it away into the night, the carousel was already beginning to turn.

I shivered. The beer was so cold I could feel it in my blood. A wave of dizziness rolled over me, and I reached for the closest mount, the big sea serpent with the black teeth. I got a leg over it just as it began to float upward on its rod. Jake hauled himself onto a horse beside Nancy, and Geri laid her head against her cat's neck and purred to it.

We were carried out of sight of the shore and onto the very tip of the pier, where to my left was black sky and blacker sea, roughened with whitecaps. The Wild Wheel accelerated into the bracing, salty air. Waves crashed. I shut my eyes but then had to open them again, right away. For an instant I felt as if I were diving down into the water on my sea serpent. For an instant I felt like I was drowning.

We went round, and I caught a flash of the operator, holding his thermos. When he'd been talking to us, he'd been all smiles. But in that brief glimpse I caught after we started to move, I saw a dead face, expressionless, his eyelids sagging heavily, that swollen mouth compressed into a frown. I thought I saw him digging for something in his pocket – a momentary observation that would end lives before the night was done.

The Wheel went around again and again, faster each time, unspooling its lunatic song into the night as if it were a record on a turntable. By the fourth circuit, I was surprised at how fast we were moving. I could feel the centrifugal force as a sense of weight, right between my eyebrows, and a tugging sensation in my uncomfortably full stomach. I needed to piss. I tried to tell myself I was having a good time, but I'd had too much beer.

The bright flecks of the stars whipped past. The sounds of the pier came at us in bursts and were snatched away. I opened my eyes in time to see Jake and Nancy leaning toward each other, across the space between their horses, for a tender if clumsy kiss. Nan laughed, stroking the muscled neck of her ride. Geri remained pressed flat against her giant cat and looked back at me with sleepy, knowing eyes.

The cat turned its head to look back at me, too, and I shut my eyes and shuddered and looked again, and of course it wasn't staring at me.

Our rides rushed us on into the night, rushed us into the darkness in a kind of mad fury, round and round and round, but in the end none of us went anywhere.

* * *

For the next three hours, the wind blew us up and down the harbor walk, while Nancy completed her shift. I had already had too much beer and knew it and drank more anyway. When a gust got behind me, it felt dangerously close to swooping me off the ground, as if I were as light as newspaper.

Jake and I banged away at pinball in Mordor's Marvelous Machines for a while. Afterward Geri and I had a walk on the beach that started out romantic – teenage lovers holding hands, looking at the stars – and predictably devolved into our usual giddy game of roughhouse. Geri wound up dragging me by both hands into the water. I staggered in up to my knees and came out with my sneakers squishing, the legs of my jeans soaked and caked in sand. Geri, on the other hand, was wearing flip-flops and had thoughtfully rolled up the cuffs of her Levi's and made it out breathless with laughter and largely unscathed. I warmed myself back up with a pair of hot dogs smothered in bacon and cheese.

At ten-thirty the bars were so full the crowds spilled onto the boardwalk. The road along the harbor was jammed bumper to bumper, and the night resounded with happy shouts and honking horns. But almost everything else around the pier was closing down or already shut. The Bouncy House and the SS *Fuck No* had gone dark an hour before.

By then I was staggering with beer and fairground chow and feeling the first nervous clench of nausea. I was beginning to think that by the time I got Geri to bed, I'd be too tired or maybe too sick to report for action.

Funhouse Funnel Cakes was at the foot of the pier, and when we got there, the electric sign over the order window had been shut off. Nancy used a rag to sweep the cinnamon and powdered sugar from the dented counter, said good night to the girl who'd been working the stand with her, and let herself out the side door and into Jake's arms. She stood on her toes for a lingering kiss, her book under one arm: *All the Pretty Horses* by Cormac McCarthy.

"Want to get another six on our way out of town?" Jake asked me over her shoulder.

The thought turned my stomach, so naturally I said, "We better."

"I'll pay," Nancy said, and led the way to the curb, just about skipping to be free and with her guy, to be eighteen and in love, on a night where it was still seventy degrees at nearly 11:00 p.m. The wind crazed her curly hair, blowing it around her face like seagrass.

We were waiting for a break in traffic when it all began to go wrong.

Nancy smacked herself on the butt – a provocative thing to do, a little out of character, but then she was in high spirits – and fumbled in a pocket for her cash. She frowned. She searched her other pockets. Then she searched them again.

"Shhhhhooooot…" she said. "I must've left my money at the stand."

She led us back to Funhouse Funnel Cakes. Her co-worker had shut off the last lights and locked up, but Nancy let herself in and pulled the dangling cord. A fluorescent tube came flickering on with a wasplike buzz. Nancy searched under the counters, checked her pockets again, and looked in her hardcover to see if she'd been using her money as a bookmark. I saw her check the book myself. I'm sure of it.

"What the heck?" Nancy said. "I had a fifty-dollar bill. Fifty dollars! It was so new it looked like no one had ever spent it before. What the frickenfrack did I do with it?" She really did talk that way, like a brainy girl genius in a young-adult novel.

As she spoke, I flashed to a memory of the carousel operator helping her up onto a horse, his hand on her waist and a big smile on those juicy lips of his. Then I remembered catching a glimpse of him as we were spun past on our steeds. He hadn't been smiling then – and he'd been poking some fingers into his front pocket.

"Huh," I said aloud.

"What?" Jake asked.

I looked at Jake's narrow, handsome face, his set chin and mild eyes, and was struck with a sudden premonition of disaster. I shook my head, didn't want to say anything.

"Spill it," Jake said.

I knew better than to reply – but there's something irresistible about lighting a fuse and waiting for it to sizzle down to the charge, just to hear a loud bang. And there was always something exciting about winding up a Renshaw, for much the same reason. It was why I went into the bouncy house with Geri and why I decided to give Jake a straight answer.

"The operator on the carousel. He might've been putting something in his pocket after he helped Nan—"

I didn't get any further.

"That motherfucker," Jake said, and turned on his heel.

"Jake, no," Nancy said.

She grabbed his wrist, but he pulled free and started out along the dark pier.

"Jake!" Nancy called, but he didn't look back.

I trotted to keep up with him.

"Jake," I said, my stomach queer with booze and nerves. "I didn't see anything. Not really. He might've been reaching into his pocket to adjust his balls."

"That motherfucker," Jake repeated. "Had his hands all over her."

The Wild Wheel was dark, its stampeding creatures frozen in midleap. A heavy red velvet rope had been hung across the steps, and the sign that dangled from it said SHH! THE HORSES ARE SLEEPING! DON'T DISTURB THEM!

At the center of the carousel was an inner ring lined with mirrored panels. A glow showed around one of those panels, and from somewhere on the other side you could hear swanky horns and a tinny, crooning voice: Pat Boone, "I Almost Lost My Mind." Someone was at home in the secret cabinet at the heart of the Wild Wheel.

"Hey," Jake said. "Hey, pal!"

"Jake! Forget it!" Nancy said. She was frightened now, scared of what Jake might do. "For all I know, I put my money down for a moment and the wind grabbed it."

None of us believed that.

Geri was the first to step over the red velvet rope. If she was going, I had to follow, although by then I was scared, too. Scared and, if I'm honest, jittery with excitement. I didn't know where this was heading, but I knew the Renshaw twins, and I knew they were getting Nancy's fifty dollars back or getting even – or both.

We wove through the leaping horses. I didn't like their faces in the dark, the way their mouths gaped as if to shriek, the way their eyes seemed to stare blindly at us with terror or rage or madness. Geri reached the mirrored panel with the light leaking out around its edges and rapped her fist against it. "Hey, are you—"

But no sooner had she touched the panel than it swung inward to reveal the little engine room at the center of the Wheel.

It was an octagonal space with walls of cheap plywood. The motor that drove the central pole might've been half a century old, a dull steel block shaped vaguely like a human heart, with a black rubber drive belt at one end. On the far side of the pole was a sorry little camp bed. I didn't see any photographs of Judy Garland, but the wall above the cot was papered in *Playboy* centerfolds.

The operator sat at a folding card table, in a ratty, curiously grand chair. It had curved wooden armrests and horsehair cushions. He was slumped over, using one arm as a pillow, and didn't react as we entered. Pat Boone pitied himself, tunefully, from a little transistor radio on the edge of the table.

I glanced at his face and flinched. His eyelids weren't fully shut, and I could see the slick, gray-tinted whites of his eyes. His fleshy red lips were wet with drool. The thermos was open nearby. The whole room reeked of motor oil and something else, a stink I couldn't quite identify.

Geri shoved his shoulder. "Hey, jack-off, my friend wants her money back."

His head lolled, but otherwise he didn't stir. Jake crowded into the room behind us, while Nancy stood outside among the horses.

Geri picked up his thermos, had a whiff, and poured it out on the floor. It was wine, a rosé, and it smelled like vinegar.

"He's pissed," she said. "Passed out drunk."

"Guys," I said. "Guys, is he—We sure he's even breathing?"

No one seemed to hear me. Jake pushed past Geri and began to dig around in one of the guy's front pockets. Then, abruptly, he recoiled, yanked his hand back as if he'd been stuck by a needle. At that moment I finally identified the rank odor that had only been partially masked by the aroma of WD-40.

"Pissed is right," Jake said. "Holy fucking shit, he's drenched. Christ, I got piss all over me."

Geri laughed. I didn't. The thought took me then that he was dead. Wasn't that what happened when your heart stopped? You lost control of your bladder?

Jake grimaced and went through the guy's pockets. He dug out a battered leather wallet and a knife with a yellowing ivory handle. Three scrimshaw horses charged across the grip.

"No," Nancy said, entering the room at last. She grabbed Jake's wrist. "Jake, you can't."

"What? I can't take back what he stole?" Jake flipped the wallet open and picked out two wrinkly twenties, all that was in there. He dropped the wallet on the floor.

"I had a *fifty*," Nancy told him. "Brand-new."

"Yeah, that fifty is in the cash register at the liquor store now. Ten bucks is just about exactly what it would've cost for another bottle. Anyway, what are you arguing about? Paul saw him pocket the money."

I hadn't, though. I was no longer sure I'd seen anything more than an old man with a weak bladder adjusting his junk. But I didn't say so, didn't want to argue. I wanted to make sure the old bastard was alive, and then I wanted to go, quickly, before he stirred or anyone else wandered by the carousel. Whatever grubby sense of delight there'd been in this expedition had fled when I caught a whiff of the operator and saw his gray face.

"Is he breathing?" I asked again, and again no one replied.

"Put it back. You'll get in trouble," Nancy said.

"You going to report me to the cops, buddy?" Jake asked the operator.

The operator didn't say anything.

"Didn't think so," Jake said. He turned and took Geri's arm and pushed her toward the door.

"We need to turn him on his side," Nancy said. Her voice was unhappy and shaky with nervousness. "If he's passed out drunk and he vomits, he could choke on it."

"Not our problem," Jake said.

Geri said, "Nan, I bet he's passed out this way a thousand times. If he hasn't died yet, he probably won't die tonight."

"Paul!" Nancy cried, sounding almost hysterical. "Please!"

My insides were knotted up, and I felt as jittery as if I had chugged a pot of coffee. I wanted to leave more than anything and can't explain why I reached for the operator's wrist instead, to search for his pulse.

"He's not dead, asshole," Jake said, but he waited nonetheless.

The operator's pulse was there – raggedy and irregular but measurable. Close up he smelled bad, and not just of urine and booze. There was a cloying odor of caked, rotten blood.

242

"Paul," Nancy said. "Put him on his bed. On his side."

"Don't do it," Jake said.

I didn't want to, but I didn't think I could live with myself if I found myself reading his obituary in the weekend paper, not after we jacked him for forty bucks. I put my arms under his legs and behind his back and lifted him out of his chair.

I lumbered unsteadily to the camp cot and set him on it. A dark stain soaked the crotch of his green velvet pants, and the smell aggravated my already twitchy stomach. I rolled him onto his side and put a pillow under his head, the way you're supposed to, so if he threw up, it wouldn't go back down his windpipe. He snorted but didn't look around. I circled the room, pulled the cord hanging from the ceiling to switch off the light. On the radio, the Gypsy was telling Pat Boone's fortune. It wasn't good.

I thought we were done, but when I came out, I found Geri getting her own revenge. She'd helped herself to the operator's pocketknife, and she was carving a message into Judy Garland's horse: FUCK YOU. It wasn't poetry, but it made a point.

On the walk back to the boardwalk, Jake tried to hand the forty dollars to Nancy, but she wouldn't accept it. She was too angry with him. He stuck the bills in her pocket, and she took the twenties out and threw them on the pier. Jake had to chase them down before the wind could snatch them away and cast them to the darkness.

When we reached the road, the traffic was already tapering off, although the bars were still doing brisk business.

Jake told Nancy he was going to get the car and asked if she would please buy the beer, because obviously they weren't going to have sex now and he was going to need more alcohol to drink away his blues.

This time she took the money. She tried not to smile but couldn't quite help herself. Even I could see that Jake was adorable when he made himself pathetic.

* * *

When we took off for my parents' summer cottage, I was in the passenger seat of the Corvette, with Geri on my lap and Nancy squeezed between my hip and the door. They all had bottles of Sam Adams, even Jake, who drove with one nestled between his thighs. I was the only one who wasn't drinking. I could still smell the operator on my hands, an odor that made me think of decay, of cancer. I didn't have the stomach for any more, and when Geri rolled down the window to chuck her bottle out into the night, I was glad for the fresh air. I heard her empty Sam Adams hit with a musical crunch.

We were careless, irresponsible people, but, in our defense, we didn't know it. I'm not at all sure I've made you see the times clearly. In 1994 those Mothers Against Drunk Driving ads were just background noise, and I had never heard of anyone getting a ticket for littering. None of us wore seat belts. It never even crossed my mind.

I'm not sure I have properly shown you Geri or Jake Renshaw either. I've tried to show you they were dangerous

– but they weren't immoral. Maybe they even had a stronger sense of morality than most, were more willing to act if they saw someone wronged. When the universe was out of whack, they felt obliged to put it back to rights, even if that meant defacing an antique horse or robbing a drunk. They were entirely indifferent to the consequences to themselves.

Nor were they thoughtless, unimaginative thugs. Nancy and I wouldn't have been with them if they were. Jake could throw knives and walk a tightrope. No one had taught him how to do those things. He just knew. In his last year of high school, after showing no interest in drama for his entire life up until then, he tried out for the Senior Shakespeare. Mr Cuse cast him as Puck in *A Midsummer Night's Dream*, and damn it, he was *good*. He said his lines as if he'd been speaking in iambic pentameter all his life.

And Geri did voices. She could do Princess Di, and she could do Velma Dinkley. She could do an amazing Steven Tyler from Aerosmith; she could talk like him, sing like him, do his *acka-acka-acka-yow!*, and dance like him, whipping her hair from side to side, hands on her narrow waist.

I thought she was beautiful and gifted enough to be an actress. I said we should go to New York together after I finished college. I'd write plays, and she'd star in them. When I told her this, she laughed it off – and then gave me a look I didn't understand, not then. It was an emotion with which I was not familiar, a feeling no one had ever turned on me before then. I know now it was pity.

There was no moon, and the road grew darker the farther north we traveled. We followed a winding two-lane state highway through marsh and pines. For a while there were streetlights, spaced at quarter-mile intervals. Then there weren't. The wind had been strengthening all evening, and when the gusts blew, they shook the car and sent the cattails in the swamps into furious motion.

We were almost to the mile-and-a-half-long dirt track that led to my parents' cottage and the end of the evening when the Corvette swung around a horseshoe curve and Jake hit the brakes. Hard. The tires shrieked. The back end fishtailed.

"What the fuck is…?" he shouted.

Nancy's face struck the dash and rebounded. Her hardcover, *All the Pretty Horses*, flew out of her hand. Geri went into the dash, but she rolled as she slid forward and caught it with her shoulder.

A dog looked at us – its green eyes flashed in the headlights – and then it slunk out of the road and lumbered into the trees. If it *was* a dog… and not a bear. It certainly looked big enough to be ursine rather than canine. We could hear it crashing through the brush for several seconds after it disappeared.

"Christ," Jake said. "Now *I'm* the one who looks like he pissed himself. I dumped my beer all over my—"

"Shut up," Geri said. "Nan, honey, are you okay?"

Nancy leaned back, her chin lifted, her eyes pointed at the ceiling of the car. She cupped her nose with one hand.

"I smached my node," she said.

Geri twisted around to stretch an arm into the rear of the car. "There's some rags in the back."

I contorted myself to reach past Geri's feet to collect Nancy's book. I grabbed *All the Pretty Horses* – then hesitated, my gaze caught by something else on the carpet. I plucked it off the floor.

Geri settled back into my lap, clutching a ratty Pink Floyd tee.

"Here, use this," she said.

"That's a good shirt," Jake said.

"That's your girlfriend's face, you prick."

"Fair point. Nan, you okay?"

She balled up the T-shirt and held it to her thin, delicate nose, dabbing at blood. With her other hand, she gave a thumbs-up.

I said, "I got your book. Hey... um. This was on the floor with it."

I handed her the novel – and a crisp fifty-dollar bill, so clean and new-looking it might've been minted that morning.

Her eyes widened in horror around the bloodstained wad of shirt.

"Un-uh! No! *No!* I looked for it, and it wadn't there!"

"I know," I said. "I saw you look. You must've missed it."

Water quivered in Nancy's eyes, threatening to spill over.

"Hon," Geri said. "Nan. Come on. We all thought he stole your fifty. Honest mistake."

"We can tell that to the cops," I said. "If they show up asking whether we rolled a drunk on the pier. I bet they'll be very understanding."

Geri flashed a look like murder at me, and Nan began to cry, and I immediately regretted saying anything, regretted finding the money at all. I glanced anxiously at Jake – I was ready for an icy glare and some brotherly malice – but he was ignoring the three of us. He stared out the window, peering into the night.

"Anyone want to tell me what the fuck just walked across the road?" he asked.

"Dog, right?" I said, eager to change the subject.

"I didn't see," Geri said, "'cause I was trying not to eat a faceful of dash at the time."

"I never seen a dog like that," Jake said. "Thing was half the size of the car."

"Maybe it was a brown bear."

"Maybe it wad Sasquadge," Nancy said miserably.

We were all silent for a moment, letting that one land – and then we erupted into laughter. Nessie can hang it up. Cryptozoology never came up with a cuter beast than Sasquadge.

Two poles with reflective disks attached to them marked the one-lane dirt road that led to my parents' summer cottage, which sat on the estuarial pool known as Maggie Pond. Jake turned in and rolled down his window at the same time, letting in a warm slipstream of salty air that blew his hair back from his forehead.

The lane was cratered with potholes, some of them a foot deep and a yard across, and Jake had to slow to about ten miles an hour. Weeds hissed against the undercarriage. Rocks pinged.

We had gone a third of a mile when we saw the branch, a big oak bough across the road. Jake cursed, banged the car into park.

"I god it," Nancy said.

"You stay here," Jake said, but she was already throwing the passenger door open.

"I need to stredge my leds," she said, and tossed the bloody Floyd shirt on the floor of the car as she slammed the door.

We watched her walk into Jake's headlights: a cute, fragile little thing in pink sneakers. She hunched at one end of the broken branch, where the splintered, reddish wood shone bright and clean, and she began to tug.

"She ain't gonna be able to move that alone," Jake said.

"She's got it," Geri told him.

"Go help her, Paul," Jake said to me. "It'll make up for you being such a douche a couple minutes ago."

"Oh, shit, man, I wasn't even thinking… I didn't mean to…" I said, my head sinking between my shoulders under the weight of my shame.

Out in the road, Nancy managed to turn the eight-foot branch most of the way to one side. She went around to grab the other end, perhaps to try rolling it out of the road and into the ditch.

"Couldn't you just've stuck that fifty under the seat? Nan ain't gonna sleep tonight now. You know she's going to cry her head off as soon as we're alone," Jake said. "And I'm going to be the one who has to deal with it—"

"What's that?" Geri said.

"—not you," Jake went on, as if she hadn't spoken. "You pulled your same old Paul Whitestone magic. You took a good evening, and abra-fuckin'-cadabra—"

"Do you *hear* that?" Geri asked again.

I *felt* it before I heard it. The car shook. I became aware of a sound like an approaching storm front, rain drumming heavily on the earth. It was like being parked alongside a railroad track as a freight train thundered past.

The first of the horses thundered past on the left, so close that one shoulder brushed the driver's-side mirror. Nancy looked up and let go of the branch and made a move like she was going to jump out of the road. She only had a moment, maybe a second or two, and she didn't get far. The horse rode her down, hooves flashing, and Nancy fell beneath them. She was prone in the road when the next horse went over her. I heard her spine crack. Or maybe that was the big tree branch, I don't know.

A third horse flashed past, and a fourth. The first three horses kept going, disappearing past the headlights, into the darkness. The fourth slowed close to Nancy's body. She'd been half dragged and half thrown almost thirty feet from the Corvette, right to the far edge of what the headlights could reveal. The tall white horse lowered its head and seemed to gum Nancy's hair, which was bloody and matted and twitching in the breeze.

Jake screamed. I think he was trying to scream Nancy's name but wasn't able to articulate words. Geri was screaming, too. I wasn't. I couldn't get the breath. I felt as if a horse had run over me also, stamped all the air out of me.

The horse that stood over Nancy had a mangled face, one side pink and flayed as the result of a long-ago burn. Both of its eyes were white, but the one on the ruined side of its head bulged sickeningly from its socket. The tongue that slipped out and lapped Nancy's face wasn't a horse tongue at all. It was as thin and black as a serpent's.

Jake's hand clawed blindly for the latch. He was staring at Nancy, so he didn't see another horse standing alongside the car. None of us did. Jake's door sprang open, and he put his foot on the dirt, and I looked over and had just enough time to shout his name.

The horse alongside the car dipped its powerful neck and clamped its big horsey teeth on Jake's shoulder and snapped its head. Jake was lifted out of the car and hurled into the trunk of a red pine at the side of the road. He struck it as if he'd been fired from a cannon and dropped out of sight into the tangled underbrush.

Geri heaved herself from my lap and into the driver's seat. She grabbed for the door as if she were going to go after him. I got her by the shoulder and hauled her back. At the same moment, the big horse beside the car turned in a clumsy half circle. Its big white rump hit the door and banged it shut on her.

The next I saw Jake, he was pulling himself across the road, into the headlights. I think his back was broken, but I couldn't swear to it. His feet dragged in a useless sort of way behind him. He cast a wild look up at us – at me – and his gaze met mine. I wish it hadn't. I never wanted to see so much terror in anyone's face, so much senseless panic.

The white stallion trotted out after him, lifting its hooves high, as if it were on parade. It caught up to Jake and looked down upon him almost speculatively, then stomped on him, right between his shoulder blades. The force flattened Jake into the dirt. He tried to rise, and the stallion kicked him in the face. It crushed in most of his skull – nose, the ridge of bone above his eyes, a cheekbone – put a red gash right in the middle of his movie-star good looks. The destrier wasn't done with him. As Jake fell, it lowered its muzzle and bit the back of his Levi jacket, pulled him off the ground, and flung him effortlessly into the trees, as if he were a scarecrow stuffed with straw.

Geri didn't know what to do, was fixed in place behind the wheel, her face stricken, her eyes wide. The driver's window was still down, and when the black dog hit the side of the Corvette, its shaggy head barreled right through. It put two paws on the inside of the window and sank its teeth into her left shoulder, tore the shirt from collar to sleeve, mauled the taut, tanned flesh beneath. Its hot breath stank.

She screamed. Her hand found the gearshift, and she launched the Corvette into motion.

The horse that had killed Jake was directly in front of us, and she smashed into it doing twenty miles an hour, cut its legs out from under it. The big horse had to weigh close to twelve hundred pounds, and the front end of the Corvette crumpled. I was slammed into the dash. The horse was thrown across the hood, rolled, legs flailing at the night, turned over, and kicked one hoof through the windshield. It struck Geri in the chest and drove her back into her seat. Safety glass erupted in a spray of chunky blue pebbles, rattled all over the cockpit.

Geri threw the car into reverse and accelerated backward. The big white horse rolled off the hood with a great tumbling crash that shook the roadbed. It hit the dirt lane and hauled itself back up onto its front legs. Its shattered rear legs trailed uselessly. Geri jammed the car into drive and went straight at it again.

The horse pulled itself out of the way, and we zipped past it, so close that its tail lashed my window. I think that was right around the time Geri drove over Nancy. I only saw Nan in front of the car for an instant before the Corvette thudded and lurched, passing over the obstruction in the road. An oily steam gushed from under the hood.

For one terrible moment, the black dog ran alongside us, its great red tongue lolling out of the side of its mouth. Then we left it behind.

"Geri!" I cried. "Roll up your window!"

"I can't!" she said.

Her voice was thin with strain. Her shoulder had been clawed deep into the muscle, and the front of her shirt was soaked with blood. She drove one-handed.

I reached across her waist and turned the window crank, rolled the glass up for her. We hit a rut, hard, and the top of my skull banged into her jaw. Black pinwheels erupted and whirled and faded before my eyes.

"Slow down!" I yelled. "You'll run us off the road!"

"Can't slow down," she said. "Behind us."

I looked back through the rear window. They pelted after

us, their hooves raising a low cloud of white chalk, five figures so pale they were like the ghosts of stallions.

Geri shut her eyes and sagged, lowering her chin almost to her breastbone. We nearly went off the road then, as the Corvette blasted into a hairpin turn. I grabbed the wheel myself and hauled on it, and it still didn't look like we were going to make it. I screamed. That got her attention, drew her up out of her pain. She wrenched at the wheel. The Corvette slung around the corner so hard the back end swished out to one side, throwing rocks. Geri drew a ragged, whistling breath.

"What's wrong?" I asked stupidly – like everything wasn't wrong, like she hadn't just seen her brother and her best friend trampled to death, like there wasn't something impossible coming up behind us in a roar of pounding hooves.

"Can't breathe," she said, and I remembered the hoof coming through the windshield and slugging her in the chest. Broken ribs, had to be.

"We'll get into the house. We'll call for help."

"Can't breathe," she repeated. "*Paul.* They're off the merry-go-round. They're after us because of what we did, aren't they? That's why they killed Jake. That's why they killed Nancy."

It was terrible to hear her say it. I knew it was true, had known from the moment I saw the horse with the burned face. The thought made my head go spinny and light. The thought made me feel like a drunk on a carousel, going around too fast, too hard. When I shut my eyes, it seemed to me I was dangerously close to being thrown right off the great turning wheel of the world.

"We're almost to the house."

"Paul," she said, and for the first time in all the years I'd known her, I saw Geri trying not to cry. "I think there's something broken in my chest. I think I'm smashed up good."

"Turn!" I cried.

The front left headlight had been smashed out, and even though I'd traveled the road to Maggie Pond a thousand times, in the darkness we almost missed the turn to my parents' place. She yanked the wheel, and the Corvette slued through its own smoke. We thudded down a steep gravel incline and swung in front of the house.

It was a two-story white cottage with green shutters and a big screened-in front porch. A single stone stoop led up to the screen door. Safety was eight feet away, on the far side of the porch, through the front door. They couldn't get us inside. I was pretty sure.

No sooner had we stopped than the horses surrounded the car, circling us, tails twitching, shoulders bumping the Corvette. Their hooves threw up dust and obscured our view of the porch.

Now that we were stopped, I could hear the thin, whistling wheeze Geri made each time she drew breath. She hunched forward, her brow touching the steering wheel, her hand to her breastbone.

"What do we do?" I asked. One of the horses swiped the car hard enough to send it jouncing up and down on its springs.

"Is it because we stole his money?" Geri asked, and drew another thin sip of air. "Or is it because I cut one of the horses?"

"Don't think about it. Let's think about how to get past them into the house."

She went on as if I hadn't spoken. "Or is it just because we needed killing? Is it because there's something wrong with us, Paul? Oh. Oh, my chest."

"Maybe we could turn around, try to get back to the highway," I said, although already I doubted we were going anywhere. Now that we were stopped, I wasn't sure we could get going again. The front end of the car looked like it had met a tree at high speed. The hood was mashed out of shape, and something under the crumpled lid was hissing steadily.

"I've got another idea," she said, and looked at me from behind tangles of her own hair. Her eyes were rueful and bright. "How about I get out of the car and run for the lake? That'll draw them away, and you can get into the house."

"What? No. Geri, *no*. The house is right here. No one else needs to die. The house is *right here*. There's no fucking way you're going to pull some kind of movie bullshit and try to lead them—"

"Maybe they don't want you, Paul," she said. Her chest heaved slowly and steadily, her T-shirt plastered red and wet to her skin. "*You* didn't do anything. *We* did. Maybe they'd let you go."

"What did Nancy do?" I cried.

"She drank the beer," Geri said, as if it were obvious. "We took the money, she spent it, and we all shared the beer – all except for you. Jake stole. I slashed up a horse. What did *you* do? You took the old guy and put him on his side so he wouldn't choke to death."

"You aren't thinking right. You've lost all kinds of blood, and you saw Jake and Nan get trampled, and you're in shock. They're *horses*. They can't want *revenge*."

"Of course they want revenge," she said. "But maybe not on you. Just listen. I'm too light-headed to argue with you. We have to do it now. I'm going to get out of the car and run to the left, first chance I see. I'll run for the trees and the lake. Maybe I can make it to the float. Horses can swim, but I don't think they could reach me up on the float, and even with my chest fucked up, I think I can paddle out there. When I go, you wait until they've rushed after me, and then you get inside and you call every cop in the state—"

"No," I said. "No."

"Besides," she told me, and one corner of her mouth lifted in a wry smile, "I can still cut a motherfucker."

And she opened her left hand to show me the carousel operator's knife. It rested in the center of her palm, so I could see the scrimshaw, that carving of stampeding horses.

"No," I said. I didn't know any other words. Language had abandoned me.

I reached for the knife, but she closed her fingers around it. I wound up only placing my hand on hers.

"I always thought that stuff about going to New York together was crap," she said. "The stuff about how I was going to be an actress and you were going to be a writer. I always thought it was impossible. But if I don't die, we should give it a shot. It can't be any more impossible than this."

Her hand slipped out of mine. Even now I don't know why I let her go.

A horse wheeled in front of the Corvette and jumped, and his front hooves landed on the hood. The car bounced up and down on its coils. The great white saddle horse glared at us, and his eyes were the color of smoke. A snake's tongue lapped at his wrinkled black gums. He sank onto his haunches, ready to come right through the space where the windshield had been.

"Bye," Geri said, almost softly.

She was out of the car and on her feet and moving before I had time to turn my head.

She ran from the screened-in porch, past the back of the car, heading for the corner of the house and the pines. I could see the lake between the black silhouettes of the tree trunks, faintly luminescent in the night. It wasn't far to the water's edge. Twenty-five yards maybe.

The horse in front of me snapped its head around to watch her flight, then leaped away from the car and followed. Two other horses joined the chase, but Geri was fast, and the brush was close.

She had just made the edge of the woods when the cat vaulted from behind a chest-high screen of bushes. It was the size of a cougar and had paws as big as baseball gloves. One of them batted her hard enough to spin her halfway around. The cat came down on top of her with a strangled yowl that turned into a high-pitched animal scream. I like to think she got the knife into it. I like to think Geri showed it she had claws of her own.

I ran. I don't remember getting out of the car. I was just out, on my feet, booking it around the ruined front end of the Corvette. I hit the screen door and threw it open and launched myself at the front door beyond. It was locked, of course. The key hung off a rusting nail to the right of the door. I grabbed for it and dropped it and snatched it up. I stabbed it at the lock again and again. I have dreams about that, still – that I am thrusting a key, with a shaking hand, at a lock I must open and which I keep impossibly missing, while something terrible rushes up behind me through the darkness: a horse, or a wolf, or Geri, the lower part of her face clawed off, her throat raked into ribbons. *Hey, babe, be honest: Do you really think I'm pretty enough to be in movies?*

In truth I was probably struggling with the lock for less than ten seconds. When the door opened, I went in so fast my feet caught on the jamb, and I hit the floor hard enough to drive the air out of me. I scrambled on all fours, shouting, making incoherent sobbing noises. I kicked the door shut behind me and curled on my side and wept. I shook as if I'd just been plunged through the ice into freezing water.

It was a minute or two before I brought myself under control and was able to stand. I made my way, shakily, to the door and peered through one of the sidelights.

Five horses watched from the driveway, gathered around the smashed wreck of the Corvette. They studied the house with their eyes of pale poison smoke. Farther up the road, I saw the dog pacing back and forth with a restless, muscular fury. I couldn't tell where the cat had gotten to – but I heard it. At some point in the hours that followed, I heard it yowling angrily in the distance.

I stared at the herd, and they stared back. One of them stood in profile to the house, half a ton of horse. The scars scrawled across his side looked like they might be a decade old, not a few hours, but for all that, they were quite distinct, in silver relief against his fine white hair. Hacked there in the horse's flesh were the words FUCK YOU.

They whinnied together, the pack of them. It sounded like laughter.

* * *

I staggered into the kitchen and tried the phone. There was no dial tone, no connection. The line was down. Maybe it was the work of the horses, the creatures that came off the Wild Wheel, but I think it was more likely just the wind. When it gusted like that out along Maggie Pond, the phone and electric quite often cut out, and as it happened, I had neither that night.

I moved from window to window. The horses watched from the road. Other beasts crashed in the brush, circling the house. I screamed at them to go away. I screamed that I'd kill them, I'd kill all of them. I screamed that we didn't mean it, that none of us meant anything. Only that last bit was true, though, it seems to me now. None of us meant anything.

I passed out on the couch in the living room, and when I woke, to a bright morning – blue skies and every drop of dew glinting with sunlight – the creatures of the Wheel were gone. I didn't dare go out, though. I thought they might be hiding.

It was close on late afternoon when I finally risked the dirt road, and even then I walked with a big kitchen knife in one hand. A woman in a Land Rover rolled slowly by, raising a cloud of dust. I ran after her, screaming for help, and she sped away. Can you blame her?

A state police cruiser collected me fifteen minutes later, was waiting for me where the dirt road met the state highway. I spent three days at Central Maine Medical in Lewiston – not because I'd suffered any great physical injury but to remain under observation after suffering what a clinician described to my parents as a "serious paranoid break from reality."

On the third day, with my parents and our family attorney at my bedside, I admitted to a cop named Follett that the four of us had dropped acid shortly before riding the Wild Wheel. Somewhere on the drive to Maggie Pond, we struck an animal, probably a moose, and Geri and Nan, who were riding without seat belts, were killed instantly. Follett asked who was driving, and the lawyer answered for me, said it had been Jake. I added, in a shaking voice, that I couldn't drive a stick, which was true.

The lawyer told the rest... that Jake had dumped the bodies in the lake and fled, probably for Canada, to avoid what almost certainly would've been a life sentence in jail. Our family attorney added that I, too, was a victim – a victim of the drugs Jake had supplied and the wreck he had caused. All I did was nod and agree and sign what they asked me to sign. It was good enough for the cop. He remembered Jake well, had not forgotten the night Jake decked his buddy at Lewiston Lanes.

The Maine State Police and the Warden Service got out on Maggie Pond and dragged for bodies, but nothing was ever recovered. Maggie Pond is, after all, a tidal pool and opens to the sea.

* * *

I never went to Dartmouth. I couldn't even leave the house. To step outdoors was as hard for me as it would be to walk on a ledge ten stories above the ground.

It was a month before I looked out my bedroom window one evening and saw one of the horses watching the house from the road. It stood beneath a streetlamp, staring up at me with milky eyes, the left half of its face mottled and withered from ancient burns. After a moment it lowered its head and clopped slowly away.

Geri had thought maybe they didn't want me. Of course they wanted me. I was the one who fingered the carousel operator. I was the one who lit Jake's fuse.

I developed a terror of the night. I was awake at all hours, watching for them – and sometimes I saw them. A couple of the horses one night, the cat another. They were keeping an eye on me. They were waiting for me.

I was institutionalized for ten weeks in the spring of 1995. I got on lithium, and for a while the horses couldn't find me. For a while I was better. I had months of therapy. I began to take walks outside – at first just from the front door to the mailbox and then down the street. Eventually I could go for blocks without a care, as long as it was bright daylight. Dusk, though, still made me short of breath.

In the spring of 1996, with my parents' blessing and my therapist's endorsement, I flew to California and spent two months living with my aunt, crashing in her guest room. She was a bank teller and a devout, practicing, but not overbearing, Methodist, and I think my parents felt I would be safe enough with her. My mother was so proud of me for daring to travel. My father, I believe, was just relieved to get me out of the house, to have a break from my nervous fits and paranoia.

I got a job in a thrift shop. I went on dates. I felt safe and, sometimes, almost content. It was just like normal life. I began seeing an older woman, a preschool teacher who was going prematurely gray and who had a man's husky, rough laugh. One night we met for tea and coffee cake, and I lost track of time, and when we went out, the sky was glazed red with sunset and the dog was there. It had emerged from a nearby park and stood glaring at me, spit dripping from its open jaws. My date saw the dog, too, and gripped my wrist and said, "What the hell is that!" I wrenched my arm free and plunged back into the café, screaming for someone to call the police, screaming that I was going to die.

I had to go back to the hospital. Three months that time, and a cycle of electroshock therapy. While I was in, someone sent me a postcard of the Cape Maggie Pier and the Wild Wheel. There was no message on it, but then the postcard *was* the message.

I had never imagined that the creatures of the Wheel might follow me all the way across the country. It had taken them two months to catch up to me.

* * *

In the earliest part of this century, I was accepted to the University of London and flew to the United Kingdom to study urban planning. After I graduated, I stayed there.

I never did write a play, or even so much as a poem. My literary output has been limited to a few reports for technical journals about dealing with urban pests: pigeons, rats, raccoons. In the field I am sometimes half-jokingly called Mr Murder. My specialty is developing strategies to wipe out any trace of the animal world from the chrome-and-glass order of the metropolis.

But Mr Murder is not the kind of moniker that invites romantic interest, and my personal issues – panic attacks, a profound fear of the dark – have left me relatively isolated. I never married. I have no children. I have acquaintances, not friends. Friendships are made in the pub, after hours – and after hours I am safely home, behind a bolted door, in a third-floor apartment, with my books.

I have never seen the horses here. Rationally, I am certain

that whatever their powers, they cannot cross three thousand miles of ocean to reach me. I am safe – from them.

Last year, though, I was sent to an urban-planning conference in Brighton. I was to give an afternoon presentation on the Japanese beetle and the dangers it presents to urban forestry. I didn't realize, until the taxi dropped me off, that the hotel was right across from Palace Pier, with its grand carousel turning out on the tip, the wind carrying the hurly-burly song of the Wurlitzer all up and down the beachfront. I delivered my talk in a conference room with a sick sweat prickling on my forehead and my stomach twisting, then all but fled the room the moment I finished. I could still hear the carousel music inside the hotel, its lunatic lullaby wafting through the imposing lobby. I couldn't go back to London – was scheduled for a panel the following morning – but I could get away from the hotel for a while, and I set out down the beach, until the pier was well behind me.

I had a burger and a pint and another pint, in a beachside place, to steady my nerves. I stayed too long, and when I left and began to walk back toward the hotel along the beach, the sun was touching the horizon. I trekked across cold sand, the salty air snatching at my scarf and hair, going as fast as a man can without breaking into a sprint.

The hotel was in sight before I allowed myself to slow and catch my breath. I had a stitch in my side, and the insides of my lungs were full of icy, abrasive fire.

Something slapped and crashed in the water.

I only saw its tail for a moment, eight feet of it, a glistening black rope, thick as a telephone pole. Its head surfaced, gold and green, like painted armor, its eyes as bright and blind as coins, and then it went under again. I had not seen it in more than twenty years, but I knew the sea serpent of the Wild Wheel at first sight, recognized it in an instant.

They will never be done with me.

I made it back to my hotel room and promptly lost my burger and beer in the toilet. I was sick off and on all night with a chilly sweat and the shakes. I didn't sleep. I couldn't. Every time I shut my eyes, the room would begin to spin, circling in slow revolutions, like a record on a turntable, like a carousel beginning its circuit. Round and round and round I went, round and round, and from a long way off I could hear the music of the Golden Gallopers on the Brighton Palace Pier, the Wurlitzer playing its mad fox-trot to the night, while children screamed, whether with laughter or terror, I could not tell you.

These days it is all the same to me.

SHOES AS RED AS BLOOD

BY A. C. WISE

If she puts the shoes on, she will be cursed. Nessa understands, but what choice does she have?

"I want you to have everything I never had." Her mother leans forward, touching one edge of the box, its froth of tissue paper cradling the shoes.

There is hunger in her eyes, but buried deep beneath that hunger, a kind of sorrow as well. Barely visible, but enough to give Nessa hope – her mother is still in there somewhere, it isn't too late.

"That's all I've ever wanted for you." Her mother smiles.

Hunger and sorrow, that's what the shoes are, and they wake echoes of revulsion and desire as Nessa looks at them. Red as crushed berries and good wine, pomegranate hearts and winter-ripe plums. The shoes are the key to everything. If she puts them on, she will dance without pain. She will push herself farther than she ever could otherwise, all the way to an audience with the prince, to a spot in the Royal Company, to fortune and fame.

And once she has all those things, she'll be able to find her mother – her real mother – rescue her from wherever she's lost inside herself, and bring her back home.

Nessa lifts one shoe from its nest of tissue paper. Satin ribbons trail free, aching to wrap around her calves. Its form, rigid but lovely, will arc her foot into an unnatural shape, remake her into a different kind of creature – one without the human flaws of joints that wear out, skin that can blister and bruise, tendons that can snap. They are not shoes for walking or running; they are shoes meant for only one thing. Dancing. And they stink of magic. Nessa takes a breath and slips the first one onto her foot.

* * *

Once upon a time, her mother was a different woman. Nessa remembers watching from the wings of a shabby theater – the gold paint of its proscenium arch flaking, the plaster of its frescoed ceiling crumbling away – as her mother danced. Her dance was a thing of beauty, her movements pure joy. The music was a living thing, a partner tenderly taking her in its arms and swirling her around. And every single step she took upon those boards brought pain.

This is the lesson of fairy tales: if you do not age gracefully in silence and fade away, you will dance in iron shoes. If you seek to change your lot in life and re-make yourself, every step will be like walking on knives. If you dare take up more space than allotted to you by the narrow standards of beauty, you will be condemned to hack off pieces of yourself until the shoe fits. If you dare step too boldly, if you ever even think of running away, the slipper will shatter and you'll find your foot embedded with splinters of glass.

It all comes down to shoes.

Having learned the lessons of fairy tales well, Nessa's mother, humble and poor, chose to dance in what she had instead of selling herself for shoes she couldn't afford. Plain slippers, not toe shoes, with nothing to support her feet when she rose *en pointe*, leaving her feet twisted, bloodied, purpled, bruised.

But no one, not the audience hungering in the front row, and certainly not the prince, wants their dancers to be human and flawed. They want impossible creatures, reckless with gravity, all beauty and grace. They want a dream to believe in, not a broken, human woman capable of feeling pain.

When she limped off the stage that night, Nessa's mother was forced to peel the rags of her shoes away. Even as a child, Nessa knew shoes should not peel, should not come away like strips of bandages pulling skin with them, revealing blisters weeping and raw.

But if she could hide away that messy imperfection and sell the dream, then oh, Nessa's mother would have her reward. A man in a suit with creases pressed so sharp they looked like knives appeared backstage. He held out a card as white as snow, ink curling and black, the color of a raven's wing. The prince had seen her dance; he wanted her to join the Royal Company. He wanted to make her a star.

She had been humble and good for so long, and Nessa's mother agreed, she could sell the dream. She could hide her pain and buy a better life for herself and her daughter. She could have her reward.

There's a reason why stories end at happily ever after, and what comes next is left out. Stars only last so long, especially those that burn bright. Nessa's mother danced for the prince as long as she could, but princes and audiences, like stories themselves, constantly hunger for fresh blood. The next starlet, the next ingenue, the virgin maid who doesn't know her worth until a prince looks her way, while the old crone is left to dry to dust and vanish, or else be labeled wicked, jealous, full of spite. Lest she be made to dance in red-hot iron shoes.

Nessa's mother danced until she couldn't anymore, until her bruised feet betrayed her, until they bent and cracked under the weight. Lucky for the prince, Nessa's mother had a young daughter who also loved to dance.

Nessa watched her mother fade. Watched her dance until pain took over at last, until being human caught her in the well of gravity and dragged her back down. She ignored her body for too long, save for what it could do for her fame. She pushed herself too far, and eventually collapsed onstage.

She was rushed to the Royal Hospital, where she had all the best and most expensive care. The bills added up and all the while, audiences hungered for their next starlet. Nessa did truly love to dance, and so Nessa's mother let herself believe that pushing Nessa into stardom truly was the best path for her little girl. Nessa could burn twice as bright and go twice as far, starting from a foundation her mother never had.

After all, Nessa had pedigree, and while hospital bills ate fast into their cash, fame bought credit and trust. As long as they kept running as fast as they could, as long as Nessa danced just beyond the flash and snap of debt's jaws, she could go to the best schools, and pay for entrance to all the top competitions, climbing ever further up the ladder of success.

But while debt is a hungry monster, chasing ever behind, its dark twin, excess, often lurks ahead on the path, hidden among the trees. The hospital bills were paid, and Nessa's mother wondered if they couldn't have just a little more – a nicer house, a shinier car, the things to which she'd become accustomed. And not just material wealth, but adoration, the invitation to parties, the fawning patrons desperate for a moment of her time.

Nessa's mother wanted to protect her little girl, of course she did. She found what she thought was a compromise, allowing them to have those bright and shiny things without her daughter suffering. Only she didn't think the protection all the way through to the price, or imagine what a curse-disguised-as-blessing might do. She forgot they were in a fairy tale, even as she bought her daughter a pair of bespelled shoes.

* * *

The shoe feels like rose petals at the height of their bloom, like cream and summer strawberries, as Nessa slides it on. And the moment her foot is encased, teeth bury themselves in her toes, her arch, and the meat of her heel. Nessa doesn't even have the breath to scream.

The ribbons tangle in her hands. She longs to let them go, but she can't, winding and winding them around her calves, like her mother unwinding the rags of her own shoes so long ago. The needle-teeth sink deeper, and what little breath remains snags in Nessa's throat in a terrible, choked sob. It is agony and it is ecstasy, red like good wine and thick strawberry jam flowing through her veins. The shoe is on her foot, but she feels it everywhere, branching through her body, carried in her blood.

Tears blur and sting in her eyes, but at the same time, she cannot wait to put on the other shoe. Such is the way of curses. Hungry, hungry, hungry. And all the while, her mother watches her with hope shining in her eyes, the gleam of their fortune once again on the rise, causing her to lose sight of her daughter's pain.

"Only the best for my little girl." She clasps her hands at her chin, and Nessa sees her drifting farther away, dreaming of galas and champagne.

Once Nessa puts on the second shoe, she will be able to dance forever and never tire. She will be able to dance without feeling pain, never ending up like her mother peeling bloody rags from her feet. The shoes will own her, the prince and his hungering audiences will own her, and Nessa will be able to give them everything they want without suffering. She'll dance like no one they've ever seen before.

Nessa puts on the second shoe.

Then she's standing without meaning to, the shoes sweeping her across the floor. The box with its froth of tissue falls to the ground. Blood thumps in her ears, its own kind of music. She dances and it hurts like nothing has ever hurt before – a numb, distant kind of pain that frightens her more than blisters on her feet, or aching bones. The pain is there, but eaten by the shoes, devoured the moment before she truly feels it. All she feels is the teeth, going deeper and deeper in.

But she can't stop. She doesn't want to stop. She wants to dance until her heart bursts.

The walls recede, replaced with ice-laden branches. Something is terribly wrong. The floor is a frozen lake. Nessa is cold; she will never be warm again. She falls and overhead frost-hardened leaves ripple in the wind and clatter together like chips of bone.

"The shoes," Nessa tries to say, but the words slur and she tastes blood. When she fell, did she bite her tongue?

"Leave them on." Tears shine in her mother's eyes, but whether they are from sorrow or joy, Nessa can't tell. "It's the only way to break them in."

When her mother says *them*, Nessa hears *you*.

She dreams of running. All around her stretches an endless forest of branches whose leaves are ice and beaten gold and flame. It is in this forest that she will find her mother, her real mother, before she changed. A mother who knew how to dance for joy and hadn't been hollowed out by the pursuit of fame, by the endless crushing cycle of the audience's never-ending need. Nessa will find a way to fix this, she will endure one curse to break another curse and set them both free.

But the dream slips away too soon, replaced by blackness, the deep sleep of exhaustion.

When she wakes, somehow back in her bed, she is hungry, tired, and thirsty. She throws back the covers and the shoes are still there, their color so shockingly red against the sheets that Nessa is certain her legs end in bloody stumps.

She leans over, just managing to vomit into the trashcan set thoughtfully close by, as if her mother knew. Tears scald her cheeks and panic fully grips her. This was a mistake, but perhaps it isn't too late. She can still rid herself of the shoes.

But remember what happens to little girls who try to rise above their station? No matter how good their intent, no matter how pure their hearts. The story re-writes itself around her, even as Nessa shudders and sweats on the bed. Regardless of the truth, the story becomes this: Nessa saw beautiful shoes and wanted them for her own. What a vain thing. How dare she want something beautiful? How dare she think she could dance without pain? Does it matter that she willingly took on a curse to save her mother? Does it matter that she didn't really want the shoes, she only wanted to dance and make her mother happy? That doesn't fit the narrative, so out it goes. Good girls die poor, burning matches in the snow in a desperate bid to stay alive. They don't seek out curses, they don't take the threads of the narrative into their own hands, and they certainly don't dare pull.

Nessa pulls.

She yanks at the ribbons bound around her legs as hard as she can. For a reward, silk becomes blade, slicing into her flesh, leaving her fingers slick with blood. She can't untie the knots no matter how hard she tries; the shoes have their teeth in and they will not let go. And the shoes only want one thing. To dance and dance and dance, take a thing of joy and turn it into a horrid lesson.

Exhausted, Nessa gives up, at least for now, and lets herself sink back among her bloodied sheets and pillows. This time, she doesn't dream. And she doesn't even wake when the shoes on her feet twitch her legs and trace the steps of a dance all of their own accord.

* * *

The prince is predictably enthralled. No one in the kingdom has ever danced like her. When she rises *en pointe* it seems as though Nessa will leave the ground. She wears a white tutu sewn with dozens upon dozens of red crystal beads across the bodice and skirt, a gift from her mother, a spray of arterial blood against snow. Her skirt flares when she pirouettes, her head whipping around to spot and keep her upright, her arms tucked close, spinning impossibly faster until it seems she will never stop. When she leaps, it's an age before she comes down, and she lands with grace where a fall from that height seems as though it should shatter her bones.

All the while, she never even breaks a sweat. Her chest doesn't heave; she is incapable of tiring. Oh yes, she can sell perfection even better than her mother did.

The prince throws velvet-petaled roses the same color as Nessa's shoes at her feet. He sits in the front row, leading a standing ovation every time. He will take her on tour, introduce her to just everyone. Patrons will commission her to dance, master composers will write new orchestral scores just for her. She will rise and rise, her star burning ever brighter until no one even remembers her mother's name.

The prince throws a gala in her honor, inviting barons and duchesses and dignitaries from across the land. Teeth and tiaras gleam bright as diamonds honed to glass-cutting points. Everyone wants to meet Nessa, everyone wants to shake her hand. The red shoes carry her through it all.

So nice to meet you. I really can't stay. I would love to talk, but…

She flits like a butterfly, in constant restless motion. The shoes never let her land, never pause for long. She twirls across marble floors, under glittering chandeliers. Past towers of sparkling champagne and plates of hors d'oeuvres she would love to taste. From outside, it looks like grace, like she is dancing with every dignitary, kissing each hand. Feathers shiver, jewels glint, fox-fur stoles flash their smiles. Top hats and tails in every color, billows of satin and lace, all flare awake in the wind of her passing and settle like fallen leaves when she's gone. Everyone feels seen, feels loved, basking in her glow.

From the outside, it looks like a magic trick. Inside, Nessa screams.

What she sees: teeth bared on dead animals wrapped around throats, glassy eyes and frozen smiles mocking her. Ears and fingers dripping with jewels, a single one of which could have made her mother's medical bills disappear. Extravagant piles of food she cannot stop to touch, even though she is starving, food that if she could put it in her mouth would taste of ash. Everything good is devoured by the shoes, leaving her nothing, leaving her hollow, leaving her cold.

Laughter chimes like brittle shards of falling ice as Nessa swirls into yet another room. The stems of champagne glasses, slender and chilled, tug free a memory. A forest full of trees. She was looking for someone, wasn't she? Another room, this one paneled all in mirrored glass. She sees herself dancing among dozens of reflections, a forest of dancing girls, and her breath catches. She remembers what the shoes tried to make her forget.

Her mother. She needs to find her mother. She needs to find her in the forest of her dreams and lead her back out.

* * *

The shoes try to leave her no time for anything but dancing. They try to keep her numb, exhausted, luring her to bed if she even thinks of running. But sleep is exactly where Nessa wants to be. She reads books on directed dreaming, even if her feet insist on tap-tap-tapping while she does, even if she has to hold the book and fight off motion-sickness, reading as the shoes spin her around the room.

Her mother is, of course, thrilled with Nessa's success. She orders her bouquets of flowers and tiny, delicate, pink-iced cakes. She suggests vacations and fancy restaurants, parties they might throw. Things Nessa doesn't have time for, because she's always dancing. Her mother paints a picture of success antithetical to what success actually looks like – wake, perform, live life in the public eye, sleep, repeat.

Nessa's mother is lost deeper in the forest than ever before. If Nessa isn't quick, she'll disappear.

Nessa reads book after book in every spare minute she does not have. She practices looking at her hands the moment she slips into sleep and suspects she might be dreaming. Because fuck this noise. She learns how to take control.

* * *

Nessa runs between silver trunks, beneath interlaced branches laden with ice. Leaves fall in her wake and make a sound like shattering glass. There's a path, footprints, leading the way ahead. Someone else was here before her, if she can just…

The shoes drag her awake.

Dance. Red carpet. Cameras flash, flash, flash. Another party, a blur of faces and wealth and food Nessa can't eat. Dance. Laugh. Smile. Repeat.

A little further this time. Snow churns to slush as Nessa pushes herself to run faster. Her feet soak and freeze and the drifts rise to meet her, holding her back like a rising tide. She makes it just to the edge of the frozen woods where the trees are instead crowned in flames. The heat rolls over her, battering her and pushing her back, but she's determined to go on. If she can just…

The shoes twitch her awake.

Perform. Tour. Another party. Repeat. Smile. Dance. Repeat, repeat, repeat.

Nessa's skin crisps, flames crackle overhead weighting the branches down. The path is the faintest suggestion of footprints sketched in the dust, obscured by smoke. Nessa coughs. Her hair curls and burns. The forest will turn her to ash, but if she could just...

Her legs kick out violently, kicking off the sheets, a motion that looks like cramping or spasming, but is actually a dance. A puppet on tangled strings. The shoes haul her up, make their demands.

Repeat, repeat, repeat.

The forest of gold is quiet, somehow worse than the ice and flames. No breeze stirs through the leaves hammered thin as gilt, but they stir nonetheless, sighing, rippling with laughter. They are a veneer over something ugly; something truly terrible and rotten lies underneath. Nessa pushes herself to run as fast as she can, but the whispers pursue.

You can't do this. You don't belong. A phony. A fraud. We see your seams. Poor girl. Trash. You'll never rise as high as this without crashing down. We all know how your story ends.

Nessa blocks them out with the pounding of her blood, the heaving sound of her breath. If she could just...

Awake. The shoes fling her from her bed with a violence that crashes Nessa into the wall. She is sure for a moment her rib is snapped, but the shoes won't let her take stock, don't give her a moment to recover before they're dancing her out the door.

Repeat.

The iron forest beyond the forest of ice, the forest of fire, and the forest of gold, is full of girls. Once she sees them, Nessa is amazed that she missed them before. They are everywhere, all around her, and they are dancing.

They hang from the iron branches of the trees, their feet tracing steps on the empty air. They're fighting for their lives, but of course the forest makes it look beautiful, because that's how dying girls in fairy tales go. Frost laces their hair and shimmers like diamond-dust on their lips and cheeks. It blooms across their eyes and makes them glimmer. Wreaths of flame light them from above and their fingers are dipped in gold. They are lovely, and they suffer so.

This one dances in shoes of red-hot iron. This one's feet are studded with splinters of glass. This one wears knives against her skin in place of shoes.

"I can help you." Nessa stretches out her hands.

The iron-shod woman with black hair hanging almost to her waist snaps open her eyes. They burn like flame.

"If you help us, you'll suffer," she says, twisting at the end of her branch, her dance carrying her away so Nessa has to wait through her slow rotation to see the woman's face again. "Will you bear the pain?"

"Yes." Nessa answers without hesitation.

She put on the shoes to help her mother; she willingly accepted the curse. And now she will break these curses as well, leading them all into a better story.

"It will hurt like fuck," says the girl with knives strapped to her feet, eyes gleaming like blades to match. "You'll be cut, you will burn, and if you persevere, you'll be left with scars.

Everyone will forget your name. They'll rewrite your story and that will be your reward."

Being forgotten sounds like bliss to Nessa right about now. Outside the forest, outside the dreams, the shoes tug at her. They chew and chew, trying to wake her up again, but she holds on, refuses to let go.

"That's what happens to girls in fairy tales," says the girl whose feet are studded with glass, whose eyes crackle just the same. "It's a shitty story, but it's the one we have."

"Then I'll find us a better one," Nessa says.

She lunges forward and seizes hold of the iron shoes. They sear her palms, her skin blistering and bubbling. She screams, but once again, she refuses to let go. The woman above her twists and screams right back, spitting and cursing Nessa's name. She looks like a witch now, like what has become of her in her tales. She fights, but Nessa finally pulls her shoes free, falling back and panting, but not giving herself time to rest – as her own shoes taught her well how to bear – and she jams the iron shoes onto her feet.

The silk of her red shoes sizzles and crackles and burns away to ash.

Nessa lunges forward again, pulling free knives and splinters of glass. The girls they belong to hiss and wail.

Her hands are cut, they freely bleed, but they're full of sharp things now. Nessa uses the knives to hack at the ribbons binding her calves. She uses the splinters of glass to dig out the embedded teeth. She clenches her jaw hard enough she swears it'll crack and once the last tooth is dug free, she lets out a raw-throated scream.

On the iron branches, three women sway. Nessa can't tell if they're smiling beatifically down at her, peaceful and serene, or if they're only finally dead. The dream lets her go, spits her out, but the pain doesn't end.

Nessa flings the covers back to stare at her feet. The shoes are gone, but her feet remain red – covered in blisters, covered in burns. There are scars, gouges in her flesh and when she swings her feet over the side of the bed to place them on the floor, the first step is like fire shooting through her veins. It hurts like a motherfucker, but for the first time in what feels like years, it isn't her shoes waking her. Nessa wakes of her own accord.

* * *

Nessa takes her mother's hand and leads her through the camera flashes dazzling from either side of the velvet rope. The carpet beneath their feet is a red, red tongue, lolled out through the hungry doors, leading into the theater's maw. Her mother's expression is glazed, remembering when the flashbulbs were all for her, and she doesn't notice when Nessa winces with every step.

Her mother is still in there somewhere, Nessa is certain. All Nessa has to do is remind her what it's like to own her pain, to dance for herself, not waiting on a man with a knife-crease suit to save her with a too-crisp business card and drag her away to see a prince. Tonight, Nessa will remind her. Tonight, she will show the prince what fuels his burning-bright stars, what dancing costs.

Nessa leaves her mother seated in the front row and makes her way backstage. She changes into the snow-white tutu, sprayed with arterial blood, then slips on a pair of white satin slippers with simple elastic bands. No ribbons, no reinforced toes for when she rises *en pointe*. Ready, she limps her way to the center of the stage.

The curtain rises and the spotlight pins her in place. All through the theater, breath is held, anticipation stretched taut until the first note sounds. Nessa dances as she's never danced before.

She leaps and gravity tugs her back down. She lands and allows it to sound painful, a human body made of flesh and bone striking hard against the boards. She spins and her pirouette wobbles. And when she rises *en pointe*, oh, when she rises *en pointe*, everybody knows the flashing of her teeth isn't a smile and they hear her scream even when she doesn't make a sound.

The music ends. There is no applause. An uneasy hush grips the crowd and in the front row, Nessa's mother looks lost and confused. It breaks Nessa's heart, but it's a good sign. Lost means she's ready to be found.

The lights sweep downward as Nessa bows, highlighting her shoes which gleam a terrible red. When Nessa steps forward, right up to the edge of the stage, the spotlight follows. Behind her, the boards are patterned with what looks like rose petals – red, like the crystal droplets on Nessa's bodice and skirt – even though the prince has yet to throw a single flower from the bouquet crushed in his hands.

Nessa bends at the waist, as gracefully as she can with her ribs aching around her racing heart and her lungs feeling like they'll explode. She slips off one shoe and then the other, holds them up red and dripping for the crowd to see.

In the front row, Nessa's mother's eyes well with tears and she puts a hand to her mouth, remembering rags peeled away from her feet and another time. A time on the other side of the woods when she danced for herself and owned her pain, but it brought her joy. A time when no one owned her and she made her choice and her story still tried to punish her for it.

"It's okay," Nessa says. Her voice is soft in the theater's hush, trembling from exhaustion. But she's learned things about bearing up under pain, about directing her own dreams, and holding on even when it hurts.

Nessa turns her attention to the prince and tosses him her bloody shoes. They land like rose petals in his lap, staining his fine clothes with Nessa's blood.

"This is what perfection costs." In the shock that follows her words, Nessa climbs barefoot from the stage, limps to her mother, and holds out her hand.

Her mother's fingers tangle in hers, warm and calloused, feeling hollow and weighing nothing at all. Nessa squeezes them as gently as she can and leads her mother away. The prince is stunned, and no one tries to stop them.

Nessa's bare feet leave a trail of red behind. Branches rustle, a sound only Nessa hears. She hopes they are lighter now, less burdened, the dancing girls free from their iron trees following the red path of her footsteps out of the woods.

"It's okay," she tells her mother. "I know it hurts, but we'll find our way into a better story somehow."

JUST YOUR STANDARD HAUNTED DOLL DRAMA

BY KELLEY ARMSTRONG

My sister's birthday is coming, and I need to get her a cursed doll. I'll settle for one that just looks evil. I can handle the cursing part.

Don't get me wrong. I love my sister, and I'm actually getting her exactly what she wants. She runs a side business buying and selling creepy dolls, and since she stocks them in my antique shop, it is in my best interests to support her side gig. I'm also kind of obligated to, since I'm the one who got her started. When she was little, I'd tried to freak her out with stories about creepy dolls, and – contrary brat that she is – she fell in love.

As for the cursing part, she's *not* going to want that. But as her sister, it is my duty to be as much of a pain in her ass as she is in mine. It won't be a nasty curse. Just annoying and hilarious – annoying to her and hilarious to everyone else, as most practical jokes are. Like her – and our older sister – I'm a curse weaver. My specialty is the joker's jinx. This year I'm going to outdo myself with a secret weapon: a hot billionaire with black-market connections.

Okay, Aiden Connolly isn't a billionaire. He's the son of one. Also, his black-market connections are more gray market. He is hot, though, and I say that with only a smidgen of adoring-girlfriend bias.

Today, he's perched on a stool, working in my shop, which is not something I'd have imagined physically possible for the guy I met six months ago. He's trying to relax more and to accept that his insurance business will not fall apart if he leaves Boston… even if it's only to work in the corner of my shop. Baby steps.

"I have found the doll," he says.

I stop polishing a teapot and glance over. "I thought we weren't doing that until tonight."

"I have a call at one-thirty, and my inbox is empty. There was a window that needed filling."

He turns around his laptop as I walk over. I stop short and pull back.

"That's…" I rub the back of my neck as the hairs rise on it.

"Creepy?"

"Beyond creepy."

He pulls me in for a quick kiss. "I'll find another one."

"No, I'm just…"

I peer at the image as I try to figure out why it's particularly disturbing. It's a bisque doll in amazing shape for its age. The head – unglazed porcelain – gives the skin a matte, realistic look, almost too realistic, which must be the issue.

"Kennedy?" Connolly says. "It's really bothering you. Could it be cursed?" He knows my powers, being from a magic-wielding family himself, their specialty being luck working.

"I've never picked that up through a photo before." I glance at him. "What do you see? Is it just the uncanny valley effect?"

He frowns at the photo. "I'm not certain. I know you wanted the creepiest doll you could find, preferably one with a history, and when this popped up, it certainly fit the bill. But there's something else about it, isn't there?"

He hits the Back button. "Either way, that is not a properly fun gift for Hope's twenty-first birthday."

"Look at you, calling creepy-ass dolls 'fun.'" I rest my head on his shoulder as I fake sniffle. "Let us cherish this relationship moment, one of us coming to see the joy in the other's unique interests."

"And now we'll discuss risk management and modeling?"

I clap him on the shoulder. "Nope. But about that doll, you said she has a history? What—"

His phone rings with his meeting call.

"You take that," I say. "I'll wait for story time."

* * *

I run an antique shop in a Massachusetts tourist town that specializes in the supernatural. No, not Salem. That's a whole different vibe. Unstable – pronounced Un-sta-bull – is a haven for a mix of real magic users, those who think they're magic users and those who know they aren't but put on a suitably entertaining show.

My shop sells uncursed objects. Were they *all* actually cursed? No, but their former owners thought they were, and I can confirm that they aren't now.

It's midweek in early November, that slow time between fall-colors tourism and holiday shoppers. While he's on the phone, I get a customer who buys a lovely and not-at-all cursed necklace. Then I put up the "Back in 20 Minutes" sign so we can retreat to the storage room for Connolly's mid-afternoon caffeine fix.

He hands me his laptop as he heads to brew the coffee.

"Uh-uh," I say. "You have to tell it."

He picks up his phone and begins reading.

"Nope," I say. "In your own words. As if we're sitting around a bonfire, and you're telling me a spooky tale."

"Storytelling is your forte."

"Consider it a training exercise."

He lifts a finger while the roar of the coffee grinder fills the room. When it stops, he starts the story.

"The doll is for sale within the magical gray market," he says. "Whoever buys it must sign a waiver, releasing the seller from any liability."

"Nice touch."

"I thought so. The doll is being sold in a glass case. The buyer is strongly advised to leave her in it."

"Naturally."

"The story is that the doll is possessed by the spirit of an evil child, as the result of a curse."

"Mmm, that's a little mundane. Also, not actually possible for a curse, but go on."

"The 'child' was actually a twelve-year-old girl who poisoned her entire family in the early nineteenth century. The neighbor – a curse weaver – knew of the child's guilt. The girl had bragged about it, but no one would believe such a thing of a pretty little girl."

"Slightly better. Go on."

"The authorities refused to even question the girl, so the neighbor took matters into her own hands. It is believed she intended only to cast a curse that would compel the girl to tell the truth, but it went awry, and the girl accused the neighbor of her parents' deaths. When the neighbor was arrested and sentenced to hang, the girl came, clutching a doll that belonged to the neighbor, a rare porcelain doll that the girl had always coveted. As the crowd gathered around the gibbet, the girl made sure the woman saw her with the doll. When asked whether she had any final words, the neighbor spoke in a foreign tongue, and the girl dropped dead just as the hatch opened below the poor woman's feet."

"Nice. Still not actually possible, but you're doing an excellent job of telling it."

"I could do better with fewer interruptions."

I make a show of zipping my lips.

He continues, "The town mourned the loss of the poor girl. They laid her to rest, and the mayor's wife took the doll for her own daughter, it apparently not being as creepy to them as it is to us. Or, perhaps, that is because the curse had not yet truly begun to warp the toy into its present, chilling form."

"Good, very good."

He sips his coffee.

"And then what?" I say.

Connolly shrugs. "Just your standard haunted doll drama. Eyes that seem to follow you. A penchant for not staying where you put it. Also, at the hour the girl died, if you put your ear very close to the doll's lips and concentrate, you may hear her soft voice, singing 'Bohemian Rhapsody'. That's the worst part. It's a terrible earworm."

I smack his arm. "You were doing so well there for a while."

"It was running long. And the stories really are what one might expect from a haunted doll."

"Fine, but we should get it for Hope. Worst case, it's actually cursed and I can fix it."

He opens his laptop. I walk behind him and look down at the screen.

"Is that… Is that the price? *Connolly*. Seriously? How do I buy that? Sell my car?"

"I believe it's in pesos."

"The seller lives in Rhode Island."

"Are you questioning their right to sell their products in the currency of their choice? We'll make it a joint gift."

"You buy the doll, and I buy the birthday card?"

"Sounds reasonable." He lifts his phone and starts dialing.

"*Aiden.*"

"Shh, I'm on a call." He covers the speaker. "If you will not allow me to buy gifts for you, at least allow me to buy them for your family."

"You bought me something last week."

"An ice cream cone?"

"At four times the price—"

"Hello," he says. "This is Aiden Connolly. I'm calling about the bisque doll."

As much as Connolly dislikes trading on his family name, he's not above doing it when it proves useful, like when he wants a gray market seller to pay attention. This one obviously does, judging by his pained expression and the woman's voice gushing on the line.

"Yes, well, I would like to purchase the doll. May I do so?"

The voice goes lower, and Connolly frowns. His gaze flicks my way. Then he says, "I understand."

The seller says something.

"No, that is perfectly understandable, and I appreciate you taking the time to speak to me. May I leave my contact information in case the sale falls through?"

When he hangs up, I say, "Already sold?"

"Yesterday. The buyer is picking it up in an hour. I'm sorry."

"Nothing to be sorry about. We'll keep looking. But can we find something in my budget? Please?"

"I will."

* * *

It's almost four. We're both still in the shop, hard at work, Connolly typing away on his laptop while I sit across from him, texting with a potential customer. Connolly's phone rings. I glance down to see his brother's name. Connolly's gaze shunts that way, but he keeps typing.

My sigh is enough to have Connolly tapping the answer button. Rian and Connolly are in remedial sibling therapy, hosted by their girlfriends: Hope and me. Yep, two sisters dating two brothers. It's a classic setup.

Rian is the black sheep of the family, and Connolly is the golden boy. That's particularly difficult when it's just the two of them, cast into these antagonistic roles by their parents. Rian is the wild child, the rich playboy, the fun one… and the screwup who can't do anything right. Connolly is the responsible adult, the respectable scion, the boring one… and the good son who can do no wrong.

They're slowly recognizing what this has done to their relationship and trying to recapture more of what they had as children, where, yes, Connolly might have been constantly getting Rian out of trouble, but Rian wasn't exactly pulling him *into* trouble against his will, either.

"Rian," he says as he answers.

"Fair warning you're on speaker," I call. "Don't say anything you don't want me hearing."

I expect a laugh and some joking reply. Instead, there's silence.

"Rian?" Connolly says. "Would you like me to take you off speaker?"

292

When the reply comes, it fades in and out. "Aid—need—"

"You're cutting out, Rian. Where are you?"

"Eighty—Unstable."

"You're on Route 80?" I say. "Eighty isn't around Unstable. Do you mean eighty-two or—"

"Turned off eighty-two—Past service—Car—stopped—"

"Are you having car trouble again, Rian?" Connolly says. "I told you not to buy the Cayman. It's very pretty but far too temperamental."

"Doll—wrong—something—" There's a gasp. Then a bang. And the line goes dead.

* * *

Connolly is on the phone while I'm frantically calling Rian back, only to have the call go to his voicemail, as it has the last five times I've tried. He'd said something about his car stopping just off Route 82, which runs outside Unstable. Rian lives in Boston, which means he wouldn't be coming to see Hope from that direction... but he might if he was driving back from Rhode Island. From where there was a supposedly haunted doll for sale on the magical gray market, when his girlfriend – who adores creepy dolls – has a birthday next week.

"Hello," Connolly says when the seller picks up. "It's Aiden Connolly calling back about the doll. I believe the buyer picked it up about an hour ago?"

He switches to speaker as the seller says, "Your brother, yes. Rian."

"The buyer was my brother?"

The woman laughs, a little nervously, as if thinking she's stumbled into the middle of a family drama... a place she really doesn't want to be with the Connollys. "I had no idea until he arrived and paid for it. He'd only given his first name."

"That's fine," Connolly says. "But you are certain it was my brother, yes?"

"Rian Connolly. He said he was buying it for his girlfriend. I, uh, told him you'd contacted me. He laughed about it. Said he was glad he beat you to the punch for once. I honestly had no idea when you called."

"It really is fine. Thank you."

Connolly signs off. Then he looks over, but I'm already heading for the front door. I flip the sign to "Closed".

"Let's go," I say.

* * *

There's no question of calling the police to help Rian. Not when what happened involves a curse. Rian said he'd pulled off Route 82 just past a service station. He'd driven onto a gravel road – in a hurry, it seems, because we find the car after I notice burnt rubber on the asphalt and then erratic tire treads on gravel. The Cayman is another quarter mile along that side road, pulled over and hidden under a massive willow tree.

The driver's door hangs open.

I run to the car while Connolly scouts and calls for his brother.

Route 82 had been quiet, but this side road is absolutely empty. When I reach the car, I find soda spilling from a fountain drink on the leather seat. I run around the vehicle, and there's Rian's cell phone in the grass.

"Here!" I say as I point to an erratic trampled path leading into the forest. "He went this way."

I scoop up the phone, and we set off at a jog. We follow the signs as best we can. Or I should say that I do. I'm the one who grew up camping and hiking. The fact that Connolly is running straight through mud without even wincing shows just how freaked out he is.

I follow footprints and trampled grass until we're in the forest on hard ground, and the signs disappear.

"Rian!" Connolly shouts.

A scuffling comes from our right. We break into a run, only to hit a thick patch of brambles. Connolly takes the lead, shoving through even as thorns rip his trousers.

When he stops, panting slightly, I call, "Rian!"

Silence.

"I know I heard something."

Connolly closes his eyes and makes a quick gesture. The air seems to crackle with the sudden burst of luck he unleashes.

"There," he says, pointing at an almost-hidden footprint.

Connolly starts forward and seems to push effortlessly through the thorny bushes. He takes three more steps, and I move in behind him.

A figure swings from behind a tree, and I wheel, stumbling back into Connolly, who catches me. The figure materializes into a guy my age, with dark hair and a killer smile.

"Boo," Rian says.

We both stare at him.

"Happy birthday, bro," Rian says. "Belated birthday anyway. Don't say I never get you anything."

"You…" Connolly begins and then seems to run out of words.

I finish for him. "You aren't actually in grave danger, run off the road by a cursed doll."

Rian rocks back, hands in his pockets. "Just the other day, Aiden was saying how quiet it's been for you two. No adventures, no mysteries, no fun. Oh, he pretended it was a relief, but I could tell he missed the adrenaline rush. When the doll seller told me he'd called about it, I saw an opportunity to inject a little excitement in your afternoon."

"You are such an asshole," I say.

"Oh, come on. Don't tell me it wasn't fun."

Connolly glares at him. Then he takes my hand to lead me back through the bushes, but as he turns, he stumbles and falls straight into them. That's not clumsiness – it's magical rebalancing. After summoning a spurt of good luck, he'll endure a bout of bad.

I help him back to clearer ground, where he proceeds to trip over a twig.

When Rian snickers, I cast a little magic of my own, and Rian's shoe lands on a muddy bit of ground. His foot flies out from under him, as if he stepped on a banana peel. When he prat-falls flat on his ass, I say, "Jinx."

"Okay, I deserved that," he says as he rises, brushing himself off. "Not for the doll prank though, that was awesome."

He offers his arm to his brother, who ignores it and keeps walking. I jog along to help him.

"Fine," Rian says as he catches up. "I am also slightly sorry for the prank, but only because I didn't expect you to be quite so worried about me. I was aiming for an adrenaline rush, not heart failure." He offers his arm again. "Forgive me?"

Connolly still glowers, but he does take his brother's arm. I keep an eye on them, just in case Rian decides to try something else. The guy has a good heart – otherwise, I wouldn't want him near my sister – but he doesn't always know where to draw the line between funny prank and cruel one. Once he'd thought it'd be hilarious to mess with Connolly's calendar while borrowing his phone... and Connolly nearly lost a client by missing a meeting. As a curse weaver who specializes in the joker's jinx, I have figured out exactly where the line lies between funny and mean, and I will teach him, even if it kills us both.

By the time we reach the car, Connolly's balancing has passed, and he can walk on his own, but I still keep the excuse to stay under his arm, my head resting on his shoulder when we pause at the roadside.

"Make you a deal," Rian says as I hand back his phone. "Forgive me for a questionable prank, and I'll let Aiden buy the doll for Hope. I presume that's what you wanted it for?"

"It was," I say. "But it was out of my price range, and I would rather someone" – I bump Connolly's hip with my own – "not buy expensive gifts for my sister. You keep it."

Connolly clears his throat. "While the attack-of-the-haunted-doll was clearly a prank, Kennedy was concerned that it might actually be cursed. She should examine it before we go any farther. She has her uncursing kit in my car."

I make a face. "I'm sure it's not actually cursed. It just gave me the creeps. You can bring it by the shop, and I'll take a look."

We take two steps toward Connolly's car before I glance back at the Cayman. Yes, this was a prank, but what if something actually was wrong with it and Rian went off the road for real. "Actually, I should take a quick peek, now that you've mentioned it."

"Sure," Rian says. "It's definitely creepy, but I didn't get any magical vibes. Still, I wouldn't want to give Hope an actual cursed doll."

He pops open the trunk. Then he stares inside. "It's gone."

"Ha-ha," I say as I walk behind the car.

"No, I'm serious."

Rian waves at the trunk. I glance in to see a pile of torn plastic.

"The woman taped up the doll box with that bubble packing," Rian says.

Connolly walks over, looks in and slowly lifts his gaze to his brother.

Rian backs up, hands lifted. "I swear I didn't do this. It's disappeared."

Connolly shakes his head as we start toward his car. "Bring it to Kennedy's shop. Tonight, please."

Rian jogs over in front of us. "Seriously, this isn't part of the prank. If it was, I'd have been the one suggesting you take a look." Rian stops, eyes narrowing. "Wait. Kennedy, you figured it out, didn't you? This is a reverse practical joke… on me."

"Look at your brother's trousers and shoes. If we knew you were pranking us, he wouldn't have been tearing through mud and thorns looking for you." I meet his gaze. "You're serious that you didn't do this?"

"I absolutely did not do it."

I glance at Connolly. "The story behind the doll *is* that it disappears."

"Which the box is supposed to prevent. It was in the box, wasn't it?"

"Uh…" Rian says.

"Tell me you didn't take it without the box," I say.

"She wanted extra for the box, which was cheap and butt ugly. I thought the bubble packing would be enough. I figured I'd buy a nicer box before I gave it to Hope, but honestly…" He throws up his arms. "I didn't see the point because dolls can't actually be haunted."

"Haunted, no. Cursed, yes."

"Well, then, it's gone, and I'll need to find Hope a new gift."

He heads to the driver's door of the Cayman.

Connolly clears his throat. "If the doll has vanished, that suggests it is actually cursed, so we cannot simply leave it here."

Rian glances at the forest. "Seems pretty safe to me."

I walk over and poke him in the back. "You bought a cursed object. The cursed object remains your responsibility until it is uncursed. That's how this works."

"How about I give you the doll? You find it, and it's yours to gift—"

I poke him harder. "Move. We're finding her."

* * *

We've been in the forest for ten minutes, and I'm already tempted to agree with Rian's plan to just abandon the doll. This is empty land, with no sign of use. It's not as if it'll hurt anyone out here. Not as if it can hurt anyone at all. It's probably nothing more than, as Connolly said, "Just your standard haunted doll drama." Disappearing. Watching. Whispering.

No, it's more than that, because my gut begs me to abandon this hunt. I've been in this forest only a few minutes, and dread already creeps up my spine. When I catch a glimpse of something moving in the trees, I wheel.

"Did you see something?" Rian asks.

"I… don't know." I roll my shoulders. "I don't like this."

To Rian, Connolly says, "The photograph made Kennedy particularly uneasy because she doesn't usually pick up curse vibes from a mere image."

"And you did?" Rian asks.

"I… picked up something." I glance around.

"Which you are picking up now, as well," Connolly says.

"But the doll can't be haunted by a human spirit," I say. "That doesn't happen."

"So whatever it is—"

A giggle sounds behind us, and we all spin around.

"Everyone heard the creepy laugh, right?" Rian says.

"We did," Connolly says. "It came from—"

I tap his arm and point. There, at the foot of a tree, is an antique bisque doll with flaxen hair, slumped sideways, as if dropped by a careless child.

"I think someone's screwing with us," Rian murmurs. "The woman who sold it seemed a little too interested in who I was."

"You think she followed you," I say. "And now she's playing tricks. If she's in the gray market, she's part of the magical community. Any idea what her power is?"

He shakes his head.

"Illusion," Connolly murmurs. "That's my guess. She's setting us up for extortion."

"Pay her for the doll and then pay her even more to take it back?"

"Perhaps."

We continue moving toward the doll. It's about fifty feet away, and the clearest path veers around a stand of trees. We lose sight of the doll for less than three seconds, but when we see the spot again, the doll is gone.

I slow.

"It was right there," Connolly says.

"Illusion magic," Rian says as he strides forward.

Connolly glances at me. His arm goes around my shoulders, and I realize I'm shivering.

"I'm not certain it's illusion—" Connolly begins.

He stops as the doll appears on the grass to our right. It's sprawled there, as if some unseen force flung it from where it had been moments ago. I want to say that's illusion magic or even telepathy, but I can't stop shaking as that cold dread solidifies like a blanket of ice.

Curse.

I hear the music of it whispering, the words of the curse woven in. They're in ancient Greek.

I yank from the curse's spell to see Rian striding forward. He picks up the doll by the arm as I shout, "No!"

"It's illusion magic," Rian says, "and if that lady thinks she can trick me—"

His head jerks back. He rises onto his tiptoes, free hand clawing at his throat as his eyes bulge.

The words of the curse slide around me, tugging with them images. A woman standing on a scaffold. People ringed around her. The woman's face a mask of cold rage as her lips move, her gaze fixed on a little girl clutching a doll, the girl staring in horror at the sight before her.

This wasn't an evil child's soul plunged into a doll. It was a curse weaver hanged for practicing her craft, lashing out at the crowd that came to watch her swing. Cursing the first object she saw, a doll held by an innocent child.

Rian gasps as Connolly tries to pull him down from that

invisible noose. The doll still hangs from his hand, as if he can't release it. I dart forward, wrench the doll from him, and throw back my arm to pitch it away.

Terror fills me. A sudden blast of terror as the crowd shouts for my death, as the noose tightens—

I fling the doll. Fling it as hard as I can. The vision breaks, and I fall into Connolly's arms. Rian leans against a tree, coughing and sputtering.

"Go!" I say.

I push Rian along as we run from the doll. When I glance back, it lies there, just like before. A heap of fabric with one arm outstretched toward us.

"Stay away from it," I say as we pause to catch our breath. "Stay far away."

"And get your uncursing kit?" Connolly asks.

"Please."

* * *

I've uncursed the doll, and now I'm sitting on the ground, recovering as I lean against Connolly. A few feet away, Rian has started a fire with dry twigs and leaves. In it, the doll burns. We sit in silence and watch the thing catch fire with a *whoosh*.

"Everyone's okay?" Rian asks as he comes over to us.

We nod, and we watch until the doll burns to ashes, only the head remaining, which Rian happily smashes.

"So now we all need a new gift for Hope," Rian says as he sits beside us. "I have an idea."

I slowly glance his way.

"How do you think she'd feel about a shopping trip?" he says. "Milan? Or Paris? No antique shops. No quirky little boutiques. Just a really boring, high-fashion shopping trip."

I lean my head onto Rian's shoulder. "I think she'd love it."

ST DIABOLO'S
TRAVELLING MUSIC HALL

BY A. K. BENEDICT

Madame Angela St Diabolo strode on stage wearing the pelt of the moon as a headscarf. That's what she told the audience, anyway. "I'm also sporting a corset fashioned from Venusian rock and knickerbockers made from Uranus." The audience laughed, sending snorts and guffaws into the music hall's rafters. They packed the auditorium like teeth in a ventriloquist's dummy's mouth.

Madame Angela held up a hand and the laughter stopped dead. Attention fixed on her like a dove flying to her palm on command. "But enough about me, I am merely your host, here to present the finest performers in the world. Each night we appear in a different town with the intention of capturing your imagination and ensnaring your heart, and tonight we are here, in the beautiful town of—" She stopped in a theatrical pause, "wait, where are we again?" She winked to indicate she didn't mean it. But she did. All towns looked the same to her now.

"Bournemouth!" someone shouted from the audience.

"Ah yes, glorious Bournemouth. Famous for hands in your knickers and giving big rounds of applause for the first act tonight of the St Diabolo Travelling Music Hall!"

The crowd pealed into laughter again, heads thrown back in rapture.

From the side of the stage, Angela felt the gaze of Itsabelle, absorbing her every word, every gesture. From the other side of the stage, Itsabelle's husband, Carron, was watching her, too. Angela felt his eyes sweep up and down, left to right over her body. His mouth worked backwards and forwards as if wanting to chew on her. She could hear his heart beating under smooth, hairless skin and his cock rise like the wooden hand of a puppet.

"Your first act tonight," Madame Angela said, as she walked towards the wings, "is a stunning opera singer. You'll embrace her arias and cheer her top and bottom notes." She paused, and looked back with a lewd wink. "So give her top and bottom a round of applause, it's the one and only Itsabelle Fintaira, singing 'Voi Che Sapete'." Angela took Itsabelle's hand and drew her onto the stage. "Or 'You Know What Love is' for those of us not schooled in Italian, from Mozart's *The Marriage of Figaro*."

Angela ducked behind the curtain as Itsabelle walked with stiff legs to centre stage. She blinked in lights that glared up from the foot of the stage. Her hand went to the white lace choker around her neck. Even back there, Angela could hear poor Itsabelle's heart beating too fast. Itsabelle's mouth opened as if to let the song out, then closed again.

The audience began to shift in their seats. Angela willed them to sit still and for Itsabelle to relax.

And then Itsabelle began to sing. Her voice soared, gilding the peeling ceiling. Angela could hear the audience breathe more deeply. Two hundred lungs filled with tobacco smoke and sweetened notes.

"That was so embarrassing," Carron said, close behind Angela. His breath caressed her earlobe.

Madame Angela twisted round. "What do you mean?"

"That's the third time she's choked on stage this week." Carron's eyes were fixed on Itsabelle. They were the colour of walnut wood and seemed to get darker the longer he stared at his wife.

"She'll shake it off," Angela said. "I've seen this before, many times. She needs love and support, not criticism."

"That's one way to run a show I suppose." Carron rolled his eyes. "But if the crowd isn't warmed up by the time I come on, then there'll be trouble."

"Trouble for whom? Me or your wife?" Madame Angela stretched herself up to nearly her full height. She was now able to look down on Carron's head. In places, his hair looked painted on. "Because if you upset Itsabelle in any way, you will be the one who is in trouble."

Carron looked up at her in surprise then down to her feet, as if wondering how she could suddenly have grown. "Nice trick," he said, smirking. "If Itsabelle had even a third of your skills, I'd be a proud man."

"You should be proud anyway," Maliana, the show's snake charmer, said, slinking out from the shadows. Her eyes blinked sideways and her snake coiled round and round her neck. "Itsa is astounding. You don't give her a chance."

Carron moved towards Maliana, shoulders tensed, fist raised. Her snake hissed. Carron backed away, teeth bared.

When Itsabelle came off stage to warm applause, Carron grabbed her arm. She flinched, hid her face with her other hand. "What do you think you're doing?" He was whispering but was still loud enough for stagehands to turn and place their fingers over their lips. Maliana's snake lifted its head and stuck out its tongue.

Itsabelle flushed and, as her hand went to her throat, she moved the choker slightly, exposing small purple marks. "I'm sorry, darling." Her voice was pianississimo and snake-belly low.

Angela felt her own throat tighten and rage rising inside her. "Can I talk to you, please, Itsabelle? In private?"

"Please don't tell me to leave." Itsabelle's eyes pleaded with Angela. "I'll be better, I promise."

Carron laughed. "I've heard that before."

Angela could feel the shame that rose like flood water in Itsabelle. "In private, please." She then turned and marched towards the stage door, knowing Itsabelle would follow.

Outside, seagulls creaked and cawed across a dull sky. Rain was on its way. Rain was always on its way. "Does he hurt you?" Angela asked.

Itsabelle's eyes became fright-wide. She glanced round as if expecting Carron to appear from every shadow. Her nod was barely perceptible.

"But you're not going to talk?"

"I can't."

Angela tried another cue. "When you joined the show, before you met Carron, you wanted to do comedy songs, make people laugh. Is that still how you feel?"

Itsabelle lowered her head. "I'm not funny. I couldn't entertain people. I've got a nice voice, when it comes out, but that's where my talent stops."

"Who told you that?"

Itsabelle didn't answer.

"How about you give it a try? Come up with a new act and I'll help you get it ready for the show."

Itsabelle's eyes ignited. "Thank you," she said.

"And tell me if he hurts you again. That is an order from your employer."

Back in the wings, Itsabelle watched Carron get ready for his act – preparing the chains, checking the padlock and key, tying the right knots on the ropes. His heartbeat was slow, calm, assured. She had never heard it go faster.

On stage, Carron twisted and coiled in a ballet of domination. He pirouetted with the chains and wrapped the rope around him with such care it was as if he loved it. The sack was placed over him and, after a sand-timered minute of contortion, he slipped out of the rope casing and left it on the boards as if it were a snake's skin.

* * *

Next morning, Angela asked a very pale Itsabelle to join her in the main stagecoach. "What did you come up with, then, for your new act?"

Itsabelle went even paler. The wheels turned and the seagulls cried as if to fill the silence. "I've decided to stay as I am."

"But you were so enthused yesterday. It's him, isn't it?"

"Carron thinks it best, that I'm best, when I'm singing opera. And he's right. He said that wanting to make people laugh meant I was a whore."

Angela held onto Itsabelle's arm, but Itsabelle pulled it away, wincing. "Show me your arm," she said, and she was not asking this time.

Itsabelle peeled back her sleeve slowly. Most of her forearm was the colour of the sea in a storm. Blues mixed with greys and purples, a flash of green and yellow. "Please don't say anything. This is what happens if I say things."

"This is not the time for silence," Angela said. "You've had your voice taken away enough. It's time to get it back."

* * *

After the show that night, Angela approached Carron and asked him to go for a drink with her. He was so busy preening, he didn't see Maliana nod to Angela and escort Itsabelle out the other door.

They found a public house in one of the back streets, with green tiles and sticky floors and gin that tasted of watered-down sin. It didn't take many drinks or much flattery to get Carron where she wanted.

He leant forward in his too-tight suit and stroked her inner arm. "What's your real name?"

"Real?" Angela asked, taking hold of his hand. She gently pulled back the fingers to expose the palm. Barely touching his skin, she traced his broken life-line with the tip of her little finger. "Do you think there is such a thing?"

He grinned, showing charcoal embedded in his gums from trying to whiten his teeth. "I know you're real." With his other hand, he pinched her arm.

She didn't react, not on the skin side. Didn't even blink. "Then you'll know your name at birth is for your parents," she said. "It's the one you give yourself that matters. Shows the world who you truly are." Very slowly, she bent his hand over till the back of it rested against his watch.

He looked, eyes goggling as his hand did something it shouldn't, but this time it was not in his control. "I can't feel my hand." He looked at it as if it were made of rubber, not part of him.

"You should be glad, grateful," Angela whispered. "It'd hurt."

At the bar, the man serving seemed stuck in a loop, wiping the same surface again and again.

"Who are you?" Carron asked. His eyes went from right to left as if searching the wings for help. None of the other drinkers could look their way.

"You don't ask if I'm a Madame," she said. "And yet you call Itsabelle, the woman you married and claim to love, a whore."

"She does not deserve to be mentioned in the same breath as you," he said. He recoiled as if the very mention of her was like opening a parcel of weeks-old fish. "You are majestic. Ethereal. Itsabelle can sing, of course she can, although I fear even that gift is fading. But she is no match for you."

"You really think you've got a chance with me, don't you?" Madame Angela said, marvelling at him. People really were such oddities. She placed her hands either side of his head and said words that had been passed down from mother to daughter, from aunt to niece, from woman to anyone who needed them and could hold the words in their head without breaking.

Carron's face froze. His arms went stiff against his sides. His teeth crowded together like a packed music hall. His eyes creaked to one side and when he opened his mouth, only silence spilled out.

* * *

The next day, the St Diabolo's Travelling Music Hall arrived in yet another grey and rainy town by the sea. When it was showtime, Madame Angela strode out carrying a small chest in her arms. She placed it at the front of the stage and said, "Good evening! I am Madame Angela St Diabolo, your host for tonight's show. And this evening I am wearing a new ensemble just for you."

An audience member whistled and someone else said, "Ooooh."

"You are right, my garb is worthy of both 'ooh'ing and wooing. My petticoat is sewn from the skin of an unrighteous man, my wooden wig made from the shavings that came off his grave."

The audience murmured, shifting uncomfortably in their seats.

"But don't worry, you're all safe. Probably. Now, sit back in your seats and let us take your minds off the mundanity and horror of everyday life. You are going to love our first act. She'll make you laugh, she'll make you cry, she'll make you gasp. Please welcome, Itsabelle Fin!"

The ventriloquist's dummy sat on Itsabelle's lap, its eyes shifting from side to side as if seeking escape in the wings. "Help," it said, but the voice that came out of the pine mouth was Itsabelle's.

The audience clapped and laughed.

"Help! I'm trapped in here," the dummy said.

The people in the front row, visible under the lights, were laughing so hard that two of them were crying. Real tears fell down their flesh faces.

"I'm the great Carron. The escapologist. But I can't get out. I was in placed in here, by her." The dummy tried to move its stick arms and point at Madame Angela standing at the back of the auditorium but was stuck.

The crowd rocked backwards and forwards in helpless laughter.

"Are you saying you're trapped?" Itsabelle asked, looking down at the dummy. "I took you out of your suitcase, didn't I?"

"Someone help me, please. Get me out of here!"

"How dare you be so rude about," Itsabelle looked puzzled and turned to the audience. "Which hellhole are we in again?"

"Bognor Regis!" the crowd shouted back.

"That's the one. How dare you be rude about Bognor Regis? I'd say it was the second nicest place we've visited in the last two days!"

Madame Angela directed the laughter, lifting her hands high in the air.

"Why won't anyone listen to me?" the dummy screamed. Its mouth was wide open, plaster teeth gleaming.

Laughter danced round the music hall, ricocheting off rococo mirrors, slamming into shell-like lights.

"Did someone say something?" Itsabelle asked, cupping her hand behind her ear.

"Me! It's me! Your husband!" The dummy's head creaked as it turned from side to side. "She did it. Angela. Made me into wood."

"Yes, you are my husband. And what a terrible husband you are." Itsabelle shook her head as if in despair. "And as for being made out of wood, well, I think we know *that's* not entirely true." Her eyebrows wiggled an innuendo of an insinuation. "But as for you being an escapologist, well, how likely is that?"

Holding the dummy in the crook of her arm, she walked across the stage with confidence and freedom, as if wearing trousers and not full costume and stays. "I mean, really. What do you expect us to believe? That you could be covered in ropes and get yourself out?"

"Yes!" the dummy shouted. But the more frustrated the dummy became, the harder the audience laughed.

"Looks like the fella is getting frustrated," she said to the audience. "Should I let him try?"

"Yes!" the audience roared.

"So you think I should give him head?" She paused, eyebrows wiggling. "I mean, give him his head? Let him show off his skills?"

"Do it, do it, do it!" The chants soared to the ceiling.

"Very well, then," Itsabelle said. She looked directly at the dummy. "If you manage to escape then I'll release you."

"Really?" The dummy's bottom lip wobbled. A woman in the front row was laughing so hard she'd gone bright pink.

"And then you'll let me go?"

"I promise." Itsabelle stroked the dummy's painted head and horse-hair toupee.

The dummy nodded, slowly. "Then I'll do it."

"Luckily I prepared for this very situation." Itsabelle bent down and opened the chest that Angela had placed on the stage. She took out six ropes, a padlock, a sand timer and a canvas pouch. She showed each item to the audience, holding them aloft. "Now these could make for a very interesting evening to invigorate an ailing marriage." She pointed at a couple in the front row. "Just so you know, you two, I rent the whole kit out at a very reasonable rate."

The husband blushed and the wife smiled. Her eyebrow kinked.

"But these are also the tools of the escapology trade. I'm going to tie my dummy of a husband up and he's going to get out. To show there are no hard feelings—" Itsabelle threw a pointed glance down to the dummy's crotch and someone in the audience cheered, "—I'll even give him a head start." Itsabelle took the key from the pouch, yanked open the dummy's crowded mouth and placed the key between its teeth. "Here you go, darling. Here's the key."

"What do I do now?" the dummy said, but all the audience could hear was mumbling.

"I'm sorry, did you say something, love of my life?" Itsabelle said. "Speak more clearly next time." Placing the dummy on top of the chest, she wound the ropes round its chest and neck, then padlocked several together.

"It's too tight!" the dummy shouted.

"Sorry, dear. Didn't catch a word. You'll have to enunciate."

The audience were rocking in their seats, holding their sides and each other.

"Now, you'll have one minute to get out of the ropes, which will be no problem at all for an escapologist of your calibre." Itsabelle turned over the sand timer. "Your time starts now."

Angela could hear the dummy's heart beating, its wooden arms straining to move. The dummy's eyes swivelled to look at Angela at the side of the stage, pleading with her to help. Angela just smiled.

The sand timer ran out of sand and time. "No escaping for

you," Itsabelle said. She plucked the key from its mouth then dumped the ventriloquist's dummy into the suitcase and did up all the straps. "Now say you're sorry for what you did to me."

"What do you mean?" The vent's voice, dressed up as hers, came from inside the suitcase.

Several people in the audience gasped. "How did she do that?" one asked.

"We can do better than that, can't we dummy?" Itsabelle said, and handed the suitcase to a woman in the front row. "Please pass it to the row behind you, and if that row could pass it back again and so on until it's at right at the far end of the auditorium."

"Ow, you're hurting me," the dummy said from inside the suitcase as it was passed over heads.

The crowd got to their feet, amazed.

"How are you feeling in there?" Itsabelle asked the dummy.

"You are going to pay for this, Itsabelle," it replied.

"I heard it come from right inside," the person holding the suitcase said, their ear against the leather. "How do you do it?"

"Like all talent, it's a blessing and a curse," Itsabelle said. "And I can't reveal my secrets."

When the case had got to the back of the room, Itsabelle said, "To complete my act, I'd like one of you to ask my dummy a question, and he'll answer, while I'm eating my supper."

Maliana then brought out a round silver tray with a plate of cheese and bread. She placed her hand on Itsabelle's shoulder and whispered in her ear.

Itsabelle smiled. "So, who is going to ask my vent a question?"

Almost everyone put up their hands.

"You, madame." Itsabelle pointed with a hunk of bread to a woman in the middle of the second row. She then started chewing, taking big bites of bread, slathered with butter and topped with chunks of cheese.

The woman, who was wearing a hat full of purple feathers that almost tickled the nose of the man behind, said, "What is your greatest secret?"

"Good question!" Itsabelle said, cheese and cracker fragments falling from her mouth.

The audience laughed and leaned forward to hear what the dummy would reveal.

The dummy was silent, and Angela wondered whether the dummy would be clever enough to thwart them by not speaking. Then it said, "That I'm worth nothing. I'm an empty husk of a man who doesn't know how to love. Or be loved."

The audience was quiet for a moment, then erupted into laughter so loud the dummy tried to cover its ears with its wooden hands. Which only made them laugh more.

"Why are you laughing?" the dummy asked. "This is me, broken. Asking for help, and all you can do is laugh."

As the dummy spoke, the guffawing audience looked from Itsabelle, mouth closed and chewing, to the case containing her voice, a hundred yards away or more.

"Don't look at her, look at me!" the dummy screamed to the roaring crowd.

Itsabelle raised her hands, lips still pressed together. As one, the audience then stood and banged their feet on the floor, cheering and clapping.

Itsabelle stood and bowed, then ran into Madame Angela's outstretched arms. "Thank you," she said, her voice loud and strong.

One of the stagehands had gone to retrieve the suitcase, and presented it to Itsabelle. She shook her head. "I don't want it. Would you take this to props, please? Maliana has asked me to go to dinner with her."

"No!" the dummy tried to shout from inside its suitcase.

"Did you say something, Itsabelle?" Angela asked.

"Nothing at all," Itsabelle replied.

Maliana, snake wrapped round her neck in a scaley scarf, held out her hand. Itsabelle took it, her face flushed. Angela waved as they headed out through the stage door, a kiss waiting between them.

Madame Angela St Diabolo went to the props cupboard and placed the suitcase in a corner. Next to it were a penny-farthing built from one man's bones and an accordion made from another's lungs. The wheels turned and the bellows wheezed. Inside the suitcase, the dummy screamed. Its shrunken heart beat loud and fast in its smooth wooden chest. Every one of the props in the cupboard joined in, a symphony of made-use-of abusers.

"Keep your voices down," Angela said to them. "Nobody wants to hear from you." She closed the door on the props and, with a wave of her forefinger, strengthened the spell that ensured no one else heard them. Let them scream.

Madame Angela St Diabolo then entered her dressing room and poured herself a drink. Sitting down in her velvet chair, she felt every one of her centuries. Her flesh ached and she longed for someone to share this with. She had once been like Itsabelle, and the other women she watched over. Men had tried to skin her, too. Some succeeded. She had tried for years to swallow those memories, but bad ones digested slowly, like a snake with an egg in its middle.

That was when she started helping others. It was the only thing that stoppered the nightmares. In the next seaside town, and the next, more women would come. That was their, and her, curse. She raised her glass to the flensed moon that shone in the bloodshot sky. Whisky burned her throat, and her voice would scorch the world.

THE MUSIC BOX

BY L. L. MCKINNEY

"Mother Barbot is nice, but creepy." I slide my stack of books off the table and into my waiting backpack. The sudden weight nearly yanks my arm out of socket. "*Christ.*"

"Language." Mom spins from where she's stirring something savory and sizzling on the stove. "And what've I told you 'bout dumpin' books in your bag like that. You gon' rip your arm clean off." Frown lines etch her brown face.

"I think I did." The burn in my shoulder subsides as my fingers work the abused muscle.

Mom shakes her head before sliding over – her house shoes *scritching* across the tile – to kiss my forehead. "Dinner'll be ready soon. Sure you don't wanna wait so I can pack you some?"

"Naaa." I grab a bottled water from the fridge, my stomach giving an angry twist at my refusal. Not like I didn't eat a whole No. 3 from In'n'Out on the way home, hungry thing. "Running late as it is. Wanna reach Castle Barbotula before dark."

"Drama queen." Mom lops at something green and crunchy, the knife clacking against the cutting board. "It's just a house."

"A creepy house. Owned by a creepy, old, white lady."

"Ain't nothing wrong with creepy. You say your cousin Byron is creepy."

My shoulders hunch at the mention of my second least favorite relative. Byron was always trying to follow the other kids around, trying to find out what folks was up to so he could snitch and win brownie points with the adults. They let him sit in the living room and watch whatever was on TV instead of being banished to the basement or the back yard like the rest of them.

We found out when me and my cousins Jasmine and Lexi asked him why he was always just standing and watching, never doing nothing with us; he tried to act like it was because he had asthma. Which, true, he did. When we were all toddlers. Now he done clearly outgrew it but still like to use it as an excuse.

So, we faked a conversation about asking to walk to the QuikTrip down the street and instead meet some boys at Price Chopper on over the hill. Sure enough, ten minutes later here come our mommas asking where we was planning on going. Our plans were "ruined," but we caught Byron red-handed, ol'snitchin ass.

"Byron is I-wear-the-same-outfit-all-three-days-during-a-con-even-though-I-have-access-to-a-shower creepy. Mother Barbot is double-double-toil-and-trouble creepy. There's a difference."

Mom sputters, her shoulders shaking with silent laughter. "Regardless, that woman ain't been nothing but nice to us, for years. She always spoke, always wore a smile, and never missed an opportunity to tell me my baby is such a purty theeng."

Mom coated those last few words with her imitation of Mother Barbot's French accent. "I was like, I know, mm-mhm, she get it from her momma, okay?"

"She always touchin' my hair and pinchin' my cheeks." I rub at my face as my lips twist. "One of these days she's gonna pull 'em right off. Talkin' bout how she wishes she had my good skin, whatever the he—whatever that's supposed to mean."

Mom cuts me a look but keeps on chopping.

"Now she talkin' 'bout how I remind her of her dead granddaughter, Belle or whatever."

"Her granddaughter is a missing person, not a corpse. Such a shame, too, after the girl's momma passed last year." Mom dumps the green stuff into a pot. Setting the board aside, she brushes her hands together then folds her arms over her chest. One of her eyebrows shoots up. "You know how these old ladies be. And if you have a problem with her, why you say yes whenever she asks you over for tea?"

I make a face. "Her tea tastes like hotdog water."

"Or watch her place while she does…" Mom trailed off and gestured at nothing. "Whatever it is she does out in the world?"

I shrug, playing at nonchalant. "Y'all told me to respect my elders."

"That doesn't mean doing things that make you uncomfortable."

"I know. And I'm not. Not really. Besides, fifty bucks for sitting and watching TV for a couple hours is worth a pinched cheek or two. Oh! I ever tell you why she has me 'house-sit' for so little? So the plants don't get lonely." I set a hand on my hip. "The *plants*."

"Plants need conversation. Your Nana used to say that." Mom nods and *scritch-scritches* over to the fridge. "Text me when you get in, then when you're on your way home."

"Yes ma'am." I grab my bag, minding my shoulder, and head for the door.

The screen bounces closed behind me, and the humidity sucks my clothes against my body. Florida in May is like midsummer everywhere else, but twice as hot and thrice as miserable when the rains are burning off. Thankfully Mother Barbot only lives a few blocks over.

Ten minutes later, I'm close to drowning in my own sweat as I approach the oldest house in the neighborhood. It's two stories tall, resembles a brownstone, and looms over a shadowy lot darkened by weeping willows that are more shaggy, green clouds than trees. Weeds sprout along the cracked driveway, the latest in a long line of shrubbery rebellion. The rest of the yard is just as scraggly and unkempt. I'm surprised the HOA hasn't made her do something about the mess, but at the same time not really. Everyone tends to steer clear of her, including various embodiments of authority.

The front door swings open as I approach the stairs and Mother Barbot steps out. "If it isn't my favorite house sitter." The porch wood creaks under her feet, or maybe that's her bones because she's more wisp than person. Her frame has shrunk in on itself, her pale skin wrinkled and spotted. Her bony hands reach to grasp mine as I top the steps.

"Hey Mother Barbot." I smile and squeeze her fingers gently. At least it's not a hug. I hate hugs. But then those fingers go for my face and I hold my breath as she pinches and pulls.

"Oooooh you're such a purty theeng!" She bites at some of the words a little, her long years in America fighting with her native tongue. Sometimes she rambles about how different living here is from growing up in some place in France I can barely pronounce. "If I could I would just box you up and put you on my mantel like a leetle doll."

I force a smile, a half-hearted laugh escaping between my teeth. My nose wrinkles when I catch a whiff of what smells like mold and old cinnamon.

Mother Barbot pats one of my stinging cheeks and takes my hand again. Her knuckles bulge, the skin of her fingers stretched over them. "Come in, come in."

The inside of the house is as creepy as the outside. Old furniture covered in old blankets and pillows, surrounded by old tables with old lamps, and old pictures on every wall. The only thing that doesn't look 100 is the television, a 52-inch smart TV that takes up nearly the whole wall.

Mother Barbot bustles around inside the door, getting ready to go… wherever. I never ask.

"Make yourself at home, dear." She ties a scarf around her head, white curls poking out around her ears. "Eat what you want, drink what you want. Like always, there's a spare room upstairs if you get tired."

"I think I'll just settle in down here." I run my hands over my shorts then shove my fingers in my pockets. "Do some homework, watch a movie."

"Such a good girl, looking after your grades." Mother Barbot brushes my cheek with her fingers and it's like ice exploding along my skin. I clamp down on the urge to recoil, and I'm smiling so hard my teeth hurt. That was new.

"Order any movie you like. I'll be back in a tick or two." She smiles, all dentures, dark eyes peering out from her sunken face. They lock with mine and my chest tightens.

I look away and wave a hand over the room to play it off. *What the hell?* "I'll be here."

"That you will." Mother Barbot waves, her wrist bending oddly. "Au revoir!"

I'm still "smiling" as I lock the door behind her. Shivers crawl through my limbs and I shake them out with a low groan. "Soooooooo creepy."

After making the rounds to water the plants and make sure the place is locked down, I flop across the couch and start channel surfing. Even after nearly killing myself to haul my books over here, I don't feel like bothering with homework.

Half an hour into a rerun of *House Hunters International*, the music starts, real faint. Bobby, a Korean boy I know from school – gorgeous – practices with his band in the garage next door. He might be the main reason I don't mind coming over here. I hit mute, hoping I can hear him sing, but… that isn't his guitar. No, the sound is gentle. Fluid. Beautiful.

And it isn't coming from outside.

The remote clatters against the floor. I jump, freed from staring at the ceiling like some sort of zombie. The music is coming from inside, somewhere upstairs. At least I think it is. My heart pistons in my chest so loud it pushes everything else aside.

"Calm down," I whisper, shutting my eyes. "Stop acting so scary." After a few deep breaths my nerves settle, and I can hear more than blood rushing through my ears. I push to my feet and cock my head to the side, listening, straining. Silence fills my ears with so much nothing it gives me a headache. I hadn't imagined it, had I?

Naw, I know I'm not trippin'. There was music coming from upstairs. Maybe she left the radio on, or another TV going. And it would be rude to just leave it running. *Two seconds*, I tell myself. I'll peek around, turn whatever it is off, and be back down in no time.

A strip of carpet down the center of the stairs mutes my steps, but the wood still creaks under my tennis shoes. Light from the street sweeps in through a small window overlooking the landing. There's enough for me to make out three doors along the hall. My fingers slide along the wall, searching for a switch and dodging photos of a girl in flowing gowns and pointed slippers, her auburn hair bound at the back of her head. Each picture is a different dress, but it's the same girl I think, a ballerina. Her face is always turned away or smudged or something. Mom has some pictures of me that're like that, from years of being touched. It's usually the edges, though, not the face.

I stop at the first door to listen. Nothing.

It's unlocked, and swings inward. There's a switch just inside. Yellow light bathes a dusty bathroom full of ceramic turtles. Big turtles, little turtles, Teenage Mutant Ninja Turtles.

I stifle a snicker and turn the light out again, shutting the door.

The next door reveals a simple bedroom. Dresser, bed, closet. Ballet slippers dot the cream-colored paper on each wall. Similar shoes cover the pillows, the bedspread, the carpet. Pictures and posters of dancers in poses line the far wall. There's one poster that stands out, black with the white silhouette of a dancer and the words:

Beauty is grace. Beauty is pain. Heavy is Beauty's crown, long may she reign.

"I'm starting to sense a theme, here." I search the room for signs of a radio. There isn't one, but something on the dresser catches my eye. It's one of those wood cutouts that spells your name or LOVE or something.

Belle.

This must be the granddaughter's room. I'm convinced when I spy another picture, this one with Mother Barbot and the ballerina from the pictures in the hall hugging each other, though the girl's face is blurry again.

Feeling a pang of sympathy for the old lady, and saying a quick prayer that her granddaughter is found safely, I back out of the room and close the door behind me.

I'm heading for the stairs when I hear it again. The music. Louder this time, light and clear, like the twinkling of chimes. I'd forgotten that's why I was up here in the first place.

The notes string together in a familiar melody. I'm not big on ballet, but I know this song. It's from *Swan Lake*.

There's one more door at the end of the hall. That's where the music's got to be coming from. I set my hands against it and press my ear to the wood. The tinkling builds into a chorus of strings and horns so crisp and clear it's like there's a symphony on the other side. Before I realize what I'm doing, my hand grips the knob and twists.

This room is smaller than the other two. Plain walls and floorboards stare back at me. Shelves corkscrew around the room, set with dozens of small boxes spaced meticulously. They're different sizes and colors, some made of metal, some of wood knotted and worn. Paint chips and fades on several of them. A couple even look like they're carved from stone.

"Okaaaaaaay." I start to back out when I notice the stool at the center of it all and the small box placed on the seat. Bright gold with rounded corners capped in copper hinges. Color and light dance in the metallic surface. A single, red rose is etched into the center of the lid. There's one on all the lids, now that I look closer.

Suddenly the air is charged with music, bright and loud. I clap my hand over my ears, but then it starts to fade. Crest then fade, crest then fade, in and out, the notes drift through the air. One second they're loud enough to hurt, the next they teeter on the edge of being heard at all. I search the corners of the room for hidden speakers or something, but I don't see any. There's just these shelves of boxes and the stool.

The music shifts, shrinking in on itself, leaving my ears ringing with the abrupt absence of its fullness. The tinkling tones are quiet, muffled. The gold box shivers with a beat I hadn't noticed before.

Maybe…

I cross to the stool. The music swells just a little and I'm certain this is the source. I press the latch on the front and jump when the top pops.

A little ballerina in a red dress pirouettes on a spring, the notes of *Swan Lake* rising around her. Her skirts glitter. Her arms twist. Her painted face is smeared. A music box. It's beautiful.

I trace the little black notes etched into the inside the of lid, watching as the ballerina spins, and spins. And spins. And… spins…

The music swells as she twirls. I'm not sure if it's my mind playing tricks, but she begins to wave her arms and lift her legs to the melody. The twist in her limbs is slow and elegant, in and out, around and through.

Beauty is grace.

My eyelids grow heavy. My body refuses to listen when I try and move.

The music intensifies. Chords invade my senses, burrowing into my limbs and coaxing them into motion. I mirror the ballerina's movements without trying. Our arms lift, arching through the air. We sway together and twirl. I'm so light on my feet, but every inch of me feels like lead. I push up onto my toes, and draw one leg up higher than I ever thought possible. A white-hot stab jolts through my hip and clear to the sole of my foot.

Ouch! I'm not supposed to bend this way, but when I try to lower my leg it won't give. The rest of my mutinous body continues the dance, snaking around and around. Faster and faster.

Beauty is pain.

Stop! I leap into the air. Bone snaps when I land. I scream, or try to, but my mouth won't open. Fire erupts from my ankle and boils over, spreading up my leg as I rotate on the same foot. My stomach lurches.

Something tickles my face. It takes me a moment to realize it's my hair, stuck to my cheeks with tears. They blur my vision, run down my neck, but I can't wipe them away.

Stop...

Darkness dances on the edges of my vision. The heavy feeling in my body deepens. I can't fight it. Can't keep my eyes open.

Everything fades.

Heavy is Beauty's crown.

* * *

Every evening Mother Barbot opens the music box to peer down at me. I know it's her, even though she doesn't look like herself, anymore. The change was gradual, but not subtle. Her face filled out, her skin tightened, her hair brightened. All the while my body bent, contorted, and broke just a little more each day. I don't know how much longer I'm going to last.

"Are you ready to perform, my Flower?" Mother Barbot asks. She looks younger now, but she's still creepy as hell. "I need you to give me one last dance."

My name is Trisha, and I'm not hers, but I've stopped correcting her. She can't hear me. Neither can the neighbors talking outside about another missing girl from the block. Not the police officers who came to question Mother Barbot about being the last one to see me two months ago, though they wound up speaking with her "granddaughter" who – surprise, surprise – turned up shortly after I went missing with some story about running away with a boy.

"A shame," "Belle" had drawled, her words iced in that familiar French accent. "Gramma was so fond of that purty theeng."

No one can hear me. I don't even remember the sound of my own voice.

Mother Barbot twists the knob with her young, fleshy fingers, winding the clockwork as words spill over her lips. "Beauty is grace. Beauty is pain."

My body moves outside of my control, like always. I've stopped fighting it. The burn of joints popping and muscle stretching has long thinned into a memory.

"Heavy is Beauty's crown."

There's just the tinkling of music and the echo of words as my mind starts to darken and my thoughts harden on the edge of unconsciousness. Finally. I'm so tired.

Long may she reign…

ABOUT THE AUTHORS

Joanne Harris (OBE) was born in Barnsley in 1964, of a French mother and an English father. She studied Modern and Mediaeval Languages at Cambridge and was a teacher for fifteen years, during which time she published three novels, including *Chocolat* (1999), which was made into an Oscar-nominated film starring Juliette Binoche.

Since then, she has written over 20 more novels, plus novellas, short stories, game scripts, the libretti for two short operas, several screenplays, a stage musical (with Howard Goodall) and three cookbooks. Her books are now published in over 50 countries and have won a number of British and international awards. She is an Honorary Fellow of St Catharine's College, Cambridge, has honorary doctorates in literature from the universities of Sheffield and Huddersfield, and has been a judge for the Whitbread Prize, the Orange Prize, the Desmond Elliott Prize, the Betty Trask Award, the Prima Donna Prize and the Royal Society Winton Prize for Science, as well as for the Fragrance

Foundation awards for perfume and perfume journalism (for which she also received an award in 2017).

She is a passionate advocate for authors' rights, and is currently the Chair of the Society of Authors (SOA), and member of the Board of the Authors' Licensing and Collecting Society (ALCS).

Her hobbies are listed in *Who's Who* as: "mooching, lounging, strutting, strumming, priest-baiting and quiet subversion of the system", although she also enjoys obfuscation, sleaze, rebellion, witchcraft, armed robbery, tea and biscuits. She is not above bribery and would not necessarily refuse an offer involving perfume, diamonds, or pink champagne. She works from a shed in her garden, plays in the band she first joined when she was 16, and lives with her husband in a little wood in Yorkshire. Joanne can be found on the internet at joanne-harris.co.uk, @Joannechocolat (Twitter) and joannechocolat (Instagram).

Neil Gaiman is the award-winning and #1 *New York Times* bestselling author and creator of books, graphic novels, short stories, film and television for all ages, including *Norse Mythology*, *Neverwhere*, *Coraline*, *The Graveyard Book*, *The Ocean at the End of the Lane*, *The View from the Cheap Seats*, and the *Sandman* comic series. His fiction has received Newbery, Carnegie, Hugo, Nebula, World Fantasy, and Will Eisner Awards. *American Gods*, based on the 2001 novel, is a critically acclaimed, Emmy-nominated TV series, and he was the writer and showrunner for the mini-series adaptation of *Good*

Omens, based on the book he co-authored with Sir Terry Pratchett. Since 2017, he has been a Goodwill Ambassador for UNHCR, the UN Refugee Agency. Originally from England, he lives in the United States, where he is a professor at Bard College. Neil's website is neilgaiman.com, and he can also be found at @neilhimself (Twitter) and neilhimself (Instagram).

Angela Slatter is the author of five novels, including *All the Murmuring Bones* and *The Path of Thorns*, and eleven short story collections, including *The Bitterwood Bible* and *The Tallow-Wife and Other Tales*. She's won a World Fantasy Award, a British Fantasy Award, a Ditmar, two Australian Shadows Awards and seven Aurealis Awards. Her work has been translated into multiple languages. She has an MA and a PhD in Creative Writing, teaches for the Australian Writers' Centre, and occasionally mentors new authors. Dark Horse Comics has recently announced her Hellboy Universe collaboration with Mike Mignola, *Castle Full of Blackbirds*. She can be located on the internet at angelaslatter.com, @AngelaSlatter (Twitter) and angelaslatter (Instagram).

M. R. Carey is a BAFTA-nominated screenwriter, novelist and comic book writer. Born in Liverpool, he worked as a teacher for fifteen years before resigning to write full-time.

He wrote the movie adaptation for his 2014 novel *The Girl With All the Gifts*. Distributed in the UK by Warner Bros Pictures, the movie opened the Locarno Festival in 2016 and subsequently went on international release. Mike received a British Screenwriters Award for his screenplay (as best newcomer, ironically – he was 59 at the time).

Mike has worked extensively in the field of comic books, completing long and critically acclaimed runs on *Lucifer*, *Hellblazer* and *X-Men*. His comic book series *The Unwritten* has featured repeatedly in the *New York Times*' graphic novel bestseller list. His latest comics work was *The Dollhouse Family*, for Joe Hill's Hill House Comics imprint.

He is also the writer of the Felix Castor novels, and (along with his wife Linda and their daughter Louise) of two fantasy novels, *The Steel Seraglio* (published in the UK as *The City Of Silk and Steel*) and *The House Of War* and *Witness*. His most recent novels are *The Book of Koli*, *The Trials of Koli* and *The Fall of Koli*, collectively known as the Rampart trilogy and published by Orbit Books. Mike can be found at @michaelcarey191 on Twitter.

Sarah Pinborough is a *New York Times* bestselling and *Sunday Times* Number one and internationally bestselling author who is published in over 30 territories worldwide. Having published more than 25 novels across various genres, her recent books include *Behind Her Eyes*, now a smash hit Netflix limited series, *Dead to Her*, now in development with Amazon Studios, and *13 Minutes* and *The Death House* in development with Compelling Pictures. Sarah lives in the historic town of Stony Stratford, the home of the Cock and Bull story, with her dog Ted. Her most recent novel, *Insomnia*, is out now and is in development with Left Bank Pictures. She can be found online at sarahpinborough.com, @SarahPinborough on Twitter, and sarahpinboroughbooks on Instagram.

Mark Chadbourn is a two-time British Fantasy Award winner and a *Times* bestseller for his collaboration with the adventure writer Wilbur Smith, and for his historical fiction under his pseudonym James Wilde. His urban fantasy series *Age of Misrule* has sold all over the world and been translated into many languages. A former UK national media journalist, Mark is also a screenwriter with many hours of produced work on BBC1. Mark's website is markchadbourn.co.uk, and he can be found at @Chadbourn on Twitter, and chadbourn on Instagram.

Laura Purcell is the author of six novels, including *The Silent Companions*, which won the WH Smith Thumping Good Read Award. Her short story "The Chillingham Chair" featured in the *Sunday Times* Bestseller *The Haunting Season*. Recently, Laura wrote *Roanoke Falls*, an original podcast for Realm executive produced by John Carpenter and Sandy King Carpenter. She can be found online at laurapurcell.com, @spookypurcell on Twitter and spookypurcell on Instagram.

Christina Henry is a horror and dark fantasy author whose works include *Horseman*, *Near the Bone*, *The Ghost Tree*, *Looking Glass*, *The Girl in Red*, *The Mermaid*, *Lost Boy*, *Alice*, *Red Queen*, and the seven-book urban fantasy *Black Wings* series.

She enjoys running long distances, reading anything she can get her hands on, and watching movies with samurai, zombies and/or subtitles in her spare time. She lives in Chicago with her husband and son. Her website is christinahenry.net, and she can be found @C_Henry_Author on Twitter and authorchristinahenry on Instagram.

Katherine Arden is the *New York Times* bestselling author of the Winternight Trilogy and the Small Spaces Quartet. She lives in Vermont. Katherine can be found online at katherinearden.com, @arden_katherine on Twitter, and arden_katherine on Instagram.

Adam L. G. Nevill was born in Birmingham, England, in 1969 and grew up in England and New Zealand. He is an author of horror fiction. Of his novels, *The Ritual, Last Days, No One Gets Out Alive* and *The Reddening* were all winners of The August Derleth Award for Best Horror Novel. He has also published three collections of short stories, with *Some Will Not Sleep* winning the British Fantasy Award for Best Collection, 2017.

Imaginarium adapted *The Ritual* and *No One Gets Out Alive* into feature films and more of his work is currently in development for the screen.

The author lives in Devon, England. More information about the author and his books is available at: adamlgnevill. com. He can also be found @AdamLGNevill on Twitter, and adamlgnevill on Instagram.

Helen Grant has a passion for the Gothic and for ghost stories. Joyce Carol Oates has described her as "a brilliant chronicler of the uncanny as only those who dwell in places of dripping, graylit beauty can be". A lifelong fan of the ghost story writer M. R. James, Grant has spoken at two M. R. James conferences and appeared at the Dublin Ghost Story Festival. She lives in Perthshire with her family, and when not writing, she likes to explore abandoned country houses and swim in freezing lochs. Her novels include *Ghost* (2018) and *Too Near the Dead* (2021). Helen's website is helengrantbooks.com, and she can also be found @helengrantsays on Twitter, and helengrantsays on Instagram.

Joe Hill is the #1 *New York Times* bestselling author of *Heart-Shaped Box*, *The Fireman*, and others. Much of his work has been adapted for film, including the Blumhouse smash *The Black Phone*, adapted from his short story, and *Locke & Key*, a hit Netflix series based on the comic he co-created with artist Gabriel Rodriguez. He lives in New England. His website can be found at joehillfiction.com, and he's @joe_hill on Twitter and joe_hill on Instagram.

A. C. Wise is the author of the novels *Wendy, Darling* and *Hooked*, and the recent short story collection, *The Ghost Sequences*. Her work has won the Sunburst Award for Excellence in Canadian Literature of the Fantastic, and has been a finalist for the Nebula, Stoker, Locus, Sunburst, Aurora, Ignyte, and Lambda Awards. In addition to her fiction, she contributes a regular short fiction review column to *Apex Magazine*. Find her online at acwise.net and on Twitter as @ac_wise.

Kelley Armstrong believes experience is the best teacher, though she's been told this shouldn't apply to writing her murder scenes. To craft her books, she has studied aikido, archery, and fencing. She sucks at all of them. She has also crawled through very shallow cave systems and climbed half a mountain before chickening out. She is however an expert coffee drinker and a true connoisseur of chocolate-chip cookies. Kelley is also the author of the *Rip Through Time* and *Rockton* mystery series. Past works include the *Otherworld* urban fantasy series, the *Cainsville* gothic mystery series, the Nadia Stafford thriller trilogy, the *Darkest Powers* & *Darkness Rising* teen paranormal series, the *Age of Legends* teen fantasy series and the *Royal Guide to Monster Slaying* middle-grade fantasy series. Kelley's website can be found at kelleyarmstrong.com, and she's also @KelleyArmstrong on Twitter, and kelleyarmstrongauthor on Instagram.

Once an actor, a singer and a composer, **A. K. Benedict** is now a bestselling, award-winning writer of novels, short stories and scripts. Her stories have featured in many journals and anthologies including *Best British Short Stories*, *Best British Horror*, *Great British Horror*, *Phantoms*, *New Fears*, *Exit Wounds* and *Invisible Blood*. She won the Scribe Award for one of her many *Doctor Who* universe audio dramas and was shortlisted for the BBC Audio Drama Award for BBC Sounds' *Children of the Stones*. Her novels, including The *Beauty of Murder* and *The Evidence of Ghosts* (both Orion), have received critical acclaim. Her most recent, under the name Alexandra Benedict, is the bestselling *The Christmas Murder Game* (Bonnier Zaffre) which was longlisted for the CWA Gold Dagger Award.

A. K. is currently writing scripts, another Christmas-based murder mystery and a high concept thriller for Simon & Schuster. She lives in Eastbourne, UK, with writer Guy Adams, their daughter, Verity, and their dog, Dame Margaret Rutherford. More information on A. K. can be found at akbenedict.com, as well as @ak_benedict on Twitter and a.k.benedict on Instagram.

Named one of The Root's and BET's 100 most influential African Americans, **L. L. McKinney** is an advocate for equality and inclusion in publishing, and the creator of the hashtags #PublishingPaidMe and #WhatWoCWritersHear. Her works include the Nightmare-Verse books, *Nubia: Real One* through DC, *Marvel's Black Widow: Bad Blood*, and more. L. L. McKinney's website can be found at llmckinney.com, and she can also be found online @ElleOnWords on Twitter.

ABOUT THE EDITORS

Marie O'Regan is an Australian Shadow Award and Shirley Jackson Award-nominated author and editor, based in Derbyshire. She won the British Fantasy Society's Legends of FantasyCon Award in 2022, and has been nominated for several other BFS awards both as a writer and editor. Her first collection, *Mirror Mere*, was published in 2006 by Rainfall Books; her second, *In Times of Want*, came out in September 2016 from Hersham Horror Books. Her third, *The Last Ghost and Other Stories*, was published by Luna Press early in 2019. Her short fiction has appeared in a number of genre magazines and anthologies in the UK, US, Canada, Italy and Germany, including *Best British Horror 2014*, *Great British Horror: Dark Satanic Mills* (2017), and *The Mammoth Book of Halloween Stories*. Her novella, *Bury Them Deep*, was published by Hersham Horror Books in September 2017. She was shortlisted for the British Fantasy Society Award for Best Short Story in 2006, and Best Anthology in 2010 (*Hellbound Hearts*) and 2012 (*The Mammoth Book of Ghost Stories by Women*). She was also shortlisted for the Australian Shadow Award for "Edited

By" in 2019 (*Trickster's Treats #3*), and the Shirley Jackson Award for Best Anthology in 2020 (*Wonderland*). Her genre journalism has appeared in magazines like *The Dark Side*, *Rue Morgue* and *Fortean Times*, and her interview book with prominent figures from the horror genre, *Voices in the Dark*, was released in 2011. An essay on "The Changeling" was published in PS Publishing's *Cinema Macabre*, edited by Mark Morris. She is co-editor of the bestselling *Hellbound Hearts*, *The Mammoth Book of Body Horror*, *A Carnivàle of Horror – Dark Tales from the Fairground*, *Exit Wounds*, *Wonderland*, and *Cursed*, as well as the charity anthology *Trickster's Treats #3*, plus editor of the bestselling anthologies *The Mammoth Book of Ghost Stories by Women* and *Phantoms*. Her first novel, the internationally bestselling *Celeste*, was published in February 2022. She is co-chair of the UK Chapter of the Horror Writers' Association, and was co-chair of ChillerCon UK in 2022. Visit her website at marieoregan.net. She can also be found at @Marie_O_Regan on Twitter and marieoregan8191 on Instagram.

Paul Kane is the award-winning (including the British Fantasy Society's Legends of FantasyCon Award 2022), bestselling author and editor of over a hundred books – such as the *Arrowhead* trilogy (gathered together in the sellout *Hooded Man* omnibus, revolving around a post-apocalyptic version of Robin Hood), *The Butterfly Man and Other Stories*, *Hellbound Hearts*, *Wonderland* (a Shirley Jackson Award finalist) and *Pain Cages* (an Amazon #1 bestseller). His non-fiction books include

The Hellraiser Films and Their Legacy and *Voices in the Dark*, and his genre journalism has appeared in the likes of *SFX, Rue Morgue* and *DeathRay*. He has been a Guest at Alt.Fiction five times, was a Guest at the first SFX Weekender, at Thought Bubble in 2011, Derbyshire Literary Festival and Off the Shelf in 2012, Monster Mash and Event Horizon in 2013, Edge-Lit in 2014 and 2018, HorrorCon, HorrorFest and Grimm Up North in 2015, The Dublin Ghost Story Festival and Sledge-Lit in 2016, IMATS Olympia and Celluloid Screams in 2017, Black Library Live and the UK Ghost Story Festival in 2019, plus the WordCrafter virtual event 2021 – where he delivered the keynote speech – as well as being a panellist at FantasyCon and the World Fantasy Convention, and a fiction judge at the Sci-Fi London festival. A former British Fantasy Society Special Publications Editor, he is currently serving as co-chair for the UK chapter of The Horror Writers Association and co-chaired ChillerCon UK in 2022.

His work has been optioned and adapted for the big and small screen, including for US network primetime television, and his novelette "Men of the Cloth" has just been turned into a feature by Loose Canon/Hydra Films, starring Barbara Crampton (*Re-Animator, You're Next*): *Sacrifice*, released by Epic Pictures/101 Films. His audio work includes the full cast drama adaptation of *The Hellbound Heart* for Bafflegab, starring Tom Meeten (*The Ghoul*), Neve McIntosh (*Doctor Who*) and Alice Lowe (*Prevenge*), and the *Robin of Sherwood* adventure *The Red Lord* for Spiteful Puppet/ITV narrated by Ian Ogilvy (*Return of the*

Saint). He has also contributed to the Warhammer 40k universe for Games Workshop. Paul's latest novels are *Lunar* (set to be turned into a feature film), the YA story *The Rainbow Man* (as P.B. Kane), the sequels to *RED* – *Blood RED* & *Deep RED* – the award-winning hit *Sherlock Holmes & the Servants of Hell*, *Before* (an Amazon Top 5 dark fantasy bestseller), *Arcana* and *The Storm*. In addition he writes thrillers for HQ/HarperCollins as P. L. Kane, the first of which, *Her Last Secret* and *Her Husband's Grave* (a sellout on both Amazon and Waterstones.com), came out in 2020, with *The Family Lie* released the following year. Paul lives in Derbyshire, UK, with his wife **Marie O'Regan.** Find out more at his site shadow-writer.co.uk which has featured Guest Writers such as Stephen King, Neil Gaiman, Charlaine Harris, Robert Kirkman, Dean Koontz and Guillermo del Toro. He can also be found @PaulKaneShadow on Twitter, and paul. kane.376 on Instagram.

ACKNOWLEDGEMENTS

And now for the important bit – our opportunity to say thank you. Firstly to all the authors for their contributions, to George Sandison, Daniel Carpenter and all of the team at Titan Books for their support and tireless efforts on our behalf, as always. Finally, thanks to our respective families, without whom etc.

ISOLATION
EDITED BY DAN COXON

"Each well-written tale hits home with how scary it can be to be alone."
San Francisco Book Review

Lost in the wilderness, or alone in the dark, isolation remains one of our deepest held fears. This horror anthology from Shirley Jackson and British Fantasy Award finalist Dan Coxon calls on leading horror writers to confront the dark moments, the challenges that we must face alone: survivors in a world gone silent; the outcast shunned by society; the quiet voice trapped in the crowd; the lonely and forgotten, screaming into the abyss.

Experience the chilling terrors of Isolation.

Featuring stories by:

Nina Allan	Alison Littlewood
Laird Barron	Ken Liu
Ramsey Campbell	Jonathan Maberry
M. R. Carey	Michael Marshall Smith
Chikọdịlị Emelumadu	Mark Morris
Brian Evenson	Lynda E. Rucker
Owl Goingback	A. G. Slatter
Gwendolyn Kiste	Paul Tremblay
Joe R. Lansdale	Lisa Tuttle
Tim Lebbon	Marian Womack

TITANBOOKS.COM

CURSED

EDITED BY MARIE O'REGAN AND PAUL KANE

ALL THE BETTER TO READ YOU WITH

It's a prick of blood, the bite of an apple, the evil eye, a wedding ring or a pair of red shoes. Curses come in all shapes and sizes, and they can happen to anyone, not just those of us with unpopular stepparents…

Here you'll find unique twists on curses, from fairy tale classics to brand-new hexes of the modern world – expect new monsters and mythologies as well as twists on well-loved fables. Stories to shock and stories of warning, stories of monsters and stories of magic.

TWENTY TIMELESS FOLKTALES, NEW AND OLD

Neil Gaiman	Jen Williams
Jane Yolen	Catriona Ward
Karen Joy Fowler	James Brogden
M. R. Carey	Maura Mchugh
Christina Henry	Angela Slatter
Christopher Golden	Lillith Saintcrow
Tim Lebbon	Christopher Fowler
Michael Marshall Smith	Alison Littlewood
Charlie Jane Anders	Margo Lanagan

THE OTHER SIDE OF NEVER: DARK TALES FROM THE WORLD OF PETER & WENDY
EDITED BY MARIE O'REGAN AND PAUL KANE

"Like a fistful of fairy dust, these stories transform *Peter Pan* into something thrillingly contemporary."
British Fantasy Award winner Dan Coxon

The award-winning Marie O'Regan and Paul Kane bring together the masters of fantasy, science-fiction and horror, to spin stories inspired by J. M. Barrie's classic tale.

A murder investigation leads a detective to a strange place called Neverland, pupils attend a school for Peters, a young boy loses his shadow and goes to desperate lengths to retrieve it.

These stories take the original tales of Peter & Wendy, the Lost Boys and Tinkerbell, twisting and turning them. From dystopias to the gritty streets of London, these stories will keep you reading all night and straight on 'til morning.

Featuring stories from:

Alison Littlewood	Anna Smith Spark	Laura Mauro
Muriel Gray	Paul Finch	Kirsty Logan
Rio Youers	Robert Shearman	Claire North
Cavan Scott	A.K. Benedict	A.C. Wise
Guy Adams	Premee Mohamed	Gama Ray Martinez
Edward Cox	Lavie Tidhar	

TITANBOOKS.COM

For more fantastic fiction, author events,
exclusive excerpts, competitions, limited editions and more

VISIT OUR WEBSITE
titanbooks.com

LIKE US ON FACEBOOK
facebook.com/titanbooks

FOLLOW US ON TWITTER AND INSTAGRAM
@TitanBooks

EMAIL US
readerfeedback@titanemail.com